Acknowledgment

I would like to thank Mrs. Judy Garguilo for reviewing my book for punctuation and grammatical errata.

TABLE OF CONTENTS

VENGEANCE

By
Alfred V. Cafiero

First Edition

Biographical Publishing Company
Prospect, Connecticut

VENGEANCE

First Edition

Published by:

Biographical Publishing Company
95 Sycamore Drive
Prospect, CT 06712-1493

Phone: 203-758-3661   Fax: 253-793-2618
e-mail: biopub@aol.com

Copyright © 2012 Alfred V. Cafiero
First Printing
PRINTED IN THE UNITED STATES OF AMERICA

Publisher's Cataloging-in-Publication Data

Cafiero, Alfred V.
Vengeance/ by Alfred V. Cafiero.
1st ed.
p. cm.
ISBN 1929882769 (Paperback)
13-Digit ISBN 9781929882762
1. Title. 2. 3.
BISAC   FIC002000 -- FICTION / Action & Adventure
         FIC014000 – FICTION / Historical
Dewey Decimal Classification: 813 Fiction, American
Library of Congress Control Number: 2012915364

THE OVERTURE

 My name is Harry Dillon and I am a reporter for the Republic newspaper located in Dallas, Texas. For over two decades I've traveled the Southwest from Texas to California and from Oklahoma to the Mexican border and beyond. My assignment was to uncover interesting stories, tales, and legends of historical events concerning the post Civil War era that would titillate the imagination of our readers. Some tales were folklore passed down from generation to generation, others appeared in pamphlets and newspapers of the period and still others were nuncupative. During the course of my travels the names of three individuals Simon Ganz, Billy Reed and Joe Young – surfaced repeatedly. Whether I was traveling through Texas or the New Mexico territory their names would be evoked during conversation. At times the tales of these individuals would be revealed in lengthy stories by old timers, encouraged by a few glasses of whiskey; but more often than not, I would obtain this information by bits and drabs whenever the names of these individuals were mentioned.

Finally after decades of traversing the Southwest, witnessing the departure of most of my hair and growing gray at the temples in the pursuit of history and entertainment, I decided to retire to the solitude of my office in Dallas to review and analyze the many tales and stories I've heard together with the fragmentary reports tucked away in my files and try to piece together a cogent story which could breathe life into one of the great sagas of the American West.

The action took place in the latter half of the nineteenth century. The war between the states had ended and slowly receded onto the pages of history. People in the North and South were beginning to think of themselves as Americans, rather than New Yorkers, Virginians, or Texans. Antebellum America witnessed the westward migration of Easterners in search of adventure and to lay claim to land and settle new territories. The influx of new pioneers continued well after the end of the Civil War, which brings the reader to the beginning of this Western saga. It would be impossible to separate the stories of these individuals since their lives were interwoven with destiny.

At times you may question the veracity of my knowledge of that which had transpired between two individuals when I was not privileged to be present during their discourse. I can justify this interpolation by many years of research, resulting in an intimate knowledge of their character and disposition as it relates to their meetings. Now I will put my pen to paper and begin the saga of Simon Ganz, Billy Reed, and Joe Young.

CHAPTER ONE
THE ESCAPE

It was high noon on a dry and sunny Saturday morning in Astec, New Mexico, when the weekly stagecoach left town. The stagecoach kicked up a cloud of dust as it left the outskirts of town, when a frail 12 year old boy jumped on to the rear portion of the stagecoach and held on for dear life.

Inside the coach were a woman and two gentlemen. The woman was middle aged and well dressed and judging by her appearance she was well to do. She wore a beautiful full length royal blue dress with white lacing around the collar and wrists and on top of her head was an attractive blue bonnet with three yellow feathers protruding from the rim. What was conspicuously absent from her integuments was the lack of jewelry; she wore no earrings, no necklace, no bracelets, nor rings. It was a bit unusual to see a well dressed woman completely void of jewelry, looking so out of place; similar to a person putting on clean clothes on an unwashed body. However, occasionally a faint metallic sound could be heard emanating from beneath her garments. She did indeed have jewelry, lots of it, all of which was neatly tucked away in a leather pouch and sewed to her undergarments. She was prudent enough to realize that stagecoaches sometimes get robbed by bandits and she was taking no chances traveling through open country with little or no protection.

One of the other passengers riding the stagecoach was an elderly man in his early sixties wearing a black suit, white shirt, a black ribbon tie dangling from his neck and wearing a black derby hat. He would occasionally look over his glasses to scrutinize the other passengers. His occupation was bank inspector and he was traveling to El Paso for his next assignment. The only indication of his opulence was a gold chain stretched across his chest, with an elegant time piece attached to one end and tucked in his vest pocket.

The third passenger was an unemployed cowboy, traveling to El Paso in search of employment. He was an attractive young man in his late twenties, a typical cowboy in blue jeans, plaid shirt, and of course a six shooter hanging from his side. He was clean shaven and sat with his hat pulled over his eyes, pretending to be asleep.

As the stagecoach rambled on, the trail to El Paso was dusty and bumpy, unfit for four wheel travel which made it uncomfortable for the passengers within; especially for Billy hanging on to the rear of the stagecoach. Finally, about five miles out of town Billy thought now was an opportune time to make his presence known. Billy was getting tired and didn't think he had the strength to hang on much longer. He therefore began to bang on the wooden portion of the coach to attract the attention of the occupants within. They were all quite puzzled as to what could be causing such a racket. The stagecoach driver also became aware of the extraneous noise and decided to stop the coach to investigate. Just as the coach slowed down preparing to stop, Billy dropped to the ground completely exhausted. The coachman realized it was the boy making the noise, and rushed over to Billy. Standing over the boy the coachman shouted,

"What the hell are you doing hitching a ride on this coach?"

Billy was too exhausted to reply. He looked at Billy for a few seconds and said,

"Well, I can't leave you here in the desert, so climb aboard and I'll deal with you later."

As Billy climbed aboard the coach, all eyes began to scrutinize him, probably wondering what possible reason could this boy have for taking such drastic action as to hitch a ride to El Paso. Up till now the passengers in the coach were extremely reticent and hardly spoke two words to each other. But Billy's presence seemed to loosen up their tongues, commencing in conversation.

"What's your name son? And where are your parents?" Asked the matronly woman.

"My name is Billy Reed," replied the boy.

That exchange prompted the woman to reply,

"And my name is Rose Engle."

The cowboy didn't wait to be asked his name and chimed in.

"They call me Tim Thompson and what might your name be Sir?"

"Al Forkenbush, but everyone in the banking business calls me Al Fingers because of my profession," retorted the bank examiner.

Now that everyone was formally introduced all eyes were now focused on Billy, who continued his explanation, saying,

"My parents are both dead; they died during the last fever that hit Astec some time back and I'm on my way to El Paso to try and locate an elderly aunt of mine."

Everyone found Billy's explanation a little strange, but accepted it without question.

Now the conversation focused on the passengers in the coach. Curiosity was mounting as to why each was going to El Paso. The reasons why Tim Thompson and "Al Fingers" were simple enough - employment and bank inspection; but why was Rose Engle leaving Astec, New Mexico? She was relatively well to do coming from a small poor town like Astec, this was most unusual. When asked why she was leaving Astec, Rose would equivocate in explaining her reasons for leaving Astec. Rose would only say that she was going to El Paso for business reasons and that Astec was too small a town for expanding her business, and that was as far as her explanation went. The occupants of the coach continued their amiable conversation with each other, and became quite friendly and sociable by the time the stagecoach reached its first watering hole and rest area. This was an opportune time for the coachman to pull Billy aside and interrogate him further. He walked over to Billy, put his arm around Billy's shoulder, and said.

"Now Billy, why was it necessary for you to hitch a ride in such a dangerous manner like that? Why didn't you just ask for a ride to El Paso?"

"For one thing, I didn't have the fare and I wasn't sure I could ride free."

"If you had explained your circumstances in town, you might have gotten a ride."

"If I had explained my reasons a whole lot more questions would have been asked and I still might not have gotten a ride. I really couldn't take that chance," said Billy.

"Well, why was it so important for you to leave town in such a hurry Billy?"

"I would rather not answer that question Sir, if you don't mind?"

"Why don't you tell me the real reason you had to leave town in such a hurry. Did you kill somebody or rob a bank?" asked the coachman jokingly.

Billy smiled and said,

"No, nothing like that. It's really a personal matter and I would be much obliged if I didn't have to explain further."

"O.K.,Billy, that's good enough for me; you look and speak like a well mannered boy and a pretty smart one at that, so I'll respect your request and give you a free ride."

Billy couldn't tell the coachman the real reason he was leaving town since it was a matter of life and death - Billy's life and Billy's death.

After passing a pleasant forty five minutes at the rest area, everyone was in a jovial mood having had something to eat and quenched their thirst. They were now ready for the final leg of their journey and proceeded to file into the coach, led by Rose.

As the stagecoach rolled on through terrain that was becoming conspicuously more mountainous they were consoled by the fact that they were within sixty miles of their final destination. They were comfortably relaxed when suddenly out of nowhere two bandits emerged from the sparsely wooded area, firing their pistols at will and forcing the stagecoach to a halt. Charlie, riding shotgun attempted to defend the integrity of the coach but was quickly dislodged with a bullet through his right shoulder. As the coachman and passengers observed the two bandits, they were immediately recognized as the Romero brothers; their calling card was their physical appearance. The brothers were in abeyance for some time and this was their first sighting in eighteen months, resurrecting their nefarious activities. The brothers were not only bandits but sometimes hired guns from south of the border, wanted by the law dead or alive with a price tag of $7,500 for each of them. They would be hired by questionable characters to do that which they themselves would not do. When not employed by others, they would periodically conduct raids across the border on unsuspecting parties, and strip them of anything of value, then flee back across the border into Mexico and safety. This was the action which was about to take place.

There the two Romero brothers stood, sloven in appearance and as big as life. Pedro, the older brother was in his mid twenties standing about six feet tall, donning a two inch long beard and mustache and an unruly crop of black hair sprouting from beneath his sombrero, partially covering his forehead and ears. A greasy band surrounded the base of his sombrero and blended in nicely with his dirty red and gray plaid shirt; with two bandoliers crisscrossing his chest.

Jose was the younger brother by two years and a bit shorter. He didn't have a beard but was badly in need of a shave at all times. If there were anyone more offensive to the human eye or dirtier in appearance than Pedro, it was his brother Jose. Jose had the same greasy band around his tan sombrero; and instead of a shirt he wore a long sleeve cotton undershirt stained red and blue from remnants of his last meal. To partially cover his dinner napkin he wore a black leather sleeveless vest and a red bandanna around his neck. Both brothers had six shooters strapped to their legs. Together with their blue jeans and black leather boots they made an indelible impression.

Pedro's six shooters were pointed at the occupants of the coach, while Jose had his rifle pointed at the coachman. Their shibboleth of dress was so unsightly that if a disguise was required, all they would have to do is scrub themselves clean, get a haircut, and shave down to the skin, don clean conventional clothes and they would be unrecognizable. They would be able to walk through any border town and never be noticed.

As of now the two brothers stood in front of the stagecoach demanding that everyone climb down from the coach to be scrutinized. As the passengers lined up in front of the stagecoach, Pedro ordered the coachman to throw down the strong box from the top of the coach, which he did. Jose aimed his rifle at the lock on the strong box and fired twice. When Pedro opened the strong box he discovered $10,000 in gold bullion together with some land deeds and legal documents. After Pedro sighted the gold bullion his eyes widened and a smile danced on his face, as he yelled out,

"Jose, we got gold!"

Both brothers were now smiling from ear to ear which put them in a very good mood. With all that booty in their possession they were in a hurry to leave, but still had to inspect the occupants of the coach. As Pedro walked toward the passengers he immediately caught sight of the gold chain stretched across the chest of "Al Fingers" and walked over to him. Al knew what was on Pedro's mind and became very nervous with beads of sweet forming on his forehead. Pedro looked at Al with a broad smile on his face and said,

"That's a very nice chain you have amigo; you give it to Pedro?"

Al began to stutter a bit, then replied,

"Er, er, well it's been in my family for two generations and I would hate to part with it."

"Oh, that's nice amigo, I will take very good care of it."

And he lifted the chain from Al's chest discovering a gold watch attached to the other end.

"Look, Jose, we got a gold watch too," he proclaimed, laughing as he walked toward the next victim. As Pedro stood before Rose and Billy he showed no interest in Billy but Rose was of some concern. Rose was holding on tightly to the leather pouch beneath her undergarments to prevent any sounds that would give away the location of her valuables; she pretended that she was lifting her dress slightly to prevent it from getting dirty and it worked. Pedro looked her over a few times, didn't see anything of value, and moved on to the cowboy. He too appeared to have nothing of value. The brothers were quite satisfied with their take for the day and were eager to abscond with their loot into the wooded terrain and back across the border, to the safety of Mexico; and off they went.

As the passengers started to climb back on to the stagecoach they noticed that "Al Fingers" was wet between his legs and was terribly embarrassed because of it. All had a smirk or grin on their faces as they boarded the coach in silence. The cowboy thought to himself, "well, it could have been worse; we might have had to ride the next sixty miles to El Paso with a terrible stench in the coach."

After their encounter with the Romero brothers the remainder of their journey was anticlimactic and uneventful. "Al Fingers" sat there dejected and mourning the loss of his prize possession, plus trying to live down the humiliation of wetting his pants. Rose on the other hand, sat there with half a smile on her face while gazing out the window of the coach, cognizant that she had outwitted the Romero brothers by her foresight and sagacity. Then there were Billy and the cowboy sitting quietly in thought, contemplating their future in El Paso.

Arriving in El Paso at dusk, the coachman pulled up in front of the sheriff's office and yelled out,

"We've been attacked and robbed by the Romero brothers, and Charlie was shot; get a doctor!"

A crowd was starting to gather around the stagecoach and an audible buzz could be heard emanating from the crowd. The passengers slowly started to disembark from the coach while being bombarded with questions from the citizenry. Billy, sensing the excitement and confusion, used the opportunity to slip away from the crowd in search of something to eat and a place to sleep for the night.

The sheriff invited the passengers into his office for questioning as to the circumstances and events pertaining to the robbery; and their reasons for coming to El Paso. One by one, they gave their account of the robbery and their reasons for coming to El Paso. However, Rose's explanation left many questions unanswered. After Sheriff Rooney's interrogation of the passengers they were told that they could leave, and did so except for Tim Thompson, the cowboy.

"Is there anything else you would like to tell me Mr. Thompson?" asked the sheriff.

"Yes there is sheriff, as I stated during your interrogation I'm unemployed and would like to apply for the position of deputy that you have posted on your bulletin board."

"Sure thing Mr. Thompson, just fill out this application with a brief history of your comings and goings for the past ten years, and you'll be considered for the job."

"Thanks sheriff, I'm much obliged," and the cowboy walked out.

The reappearance of the Romero brothers made it imperative that they be brought to justice. An increased bounty of $15,000 a piece was placed on their heads. New posters were printed proclaiming the increased reward and disseminated not only in El Paso but in every town along the border and beyond.

CHAPTER TWO
THE NEW ORDER

 After several days had elapsed, Tim Thompson entered the sheriff's office to deliver his application and resume, for employment as sheriff's deputy. Unfortunately, the sheriff was not in his office and away on official business, so Tim left his application and resume on the sheriff's desk with a note attached stating that he would return the next day. This would give Sheriff Rooney time to evaluate his qualifications and make a decision.

When the sheriff returned late that day he noticed Tim's application and resume on his desk. He picked them up and began to read. The application asked some basic questions and revealed no surprises. However, the resume was a different story, as it was most interesting and quite revealing and greatly impressed Sheriff Rooney. He learned that this young man had enlisted in the Union army at the tender age of seventeen and fought in the last battle of the Civil War under the command of Gen. William Tecumsch Sherman. For all intents and purposes the Civil War ended when Gen. Robert E. Lee surrendered his army of Northern Virginia to Gen. Ulysses S. Grant at Appomattox Court House, Virginia, on April 9th 1865. However, Confederate Gen. Joseph E. Johnston was still at lodge with an army in the Carolinas and Gen. Sherman was in hot pursuit. Gen. Johnston realizing the futility of further resistance, wanting to avoid senseless bloodshed, surrendered his army to Gen. Sherman on April 21st 1865, officially ending the Civil War.

The next day when Tim Thompson returned to the sheriff's office, the sheriff greeted him with a big smile and a hardy hand shake, saying,

"Your application for Sheriff's deputy has been accepted and as soon as I swear you in, you'll be my deputy."

Tim thanked Sheriff Rooney and both chatted awhile, discussing the various problems unique to El Paso before departing

The sheriff himself was a veteran of the Civil War; he had enlisted in the Confederate army at the outbreak of hostilities when logic and reason gave way to unrestrained emotions and sectionalism. At the time he was overwhelmed and swept away by empathy, more for his fellow Southerner than for the Southern course. Now he was in the army and had already fought in a few minor skirmishes during the course of several months. His emotions were quenched by the realities of war, so Pvt. Rooney began to think a great deal concerning the meaning and consequences of this conflict and how the war would change his life and that of his fellow Southerners. Pvt. Rooney was a self educated man well read who thought a great deal, especially now when so much was at stake. He would question everything and never again be influenced by emotions or sophistry. As a white Southerner from Texas he had to work for a living before the war and would have to work for a living after the war regardless of which side prevailed in this struggle. He reasoned, if the South was successful in seceding from the Union the only real beneficiaries would be the slave owners, the same folks who instigated this war. They still would occupy their multi-room mansions, ingratiated with all the luxuries that slave labor could provide. He was disenchanted with the idea of institutionalizing Southern royalty or aristocracy and saw no reason for the effusion of blood to maintain a lavish life style for the slave owners. Rooney was never really enthusiastic about secession to start with and still harbored warm feelings for the old Union. These reasons were the determining factor for Pvt. Rooney's decision to quit the army and the war after his enlistment expired in one year's time. True to his word, Pvt. Rooney left the army when his enlistment was up and headed for El Paso, Texas, to start a new life.

When Mr. Rooney arrived in El Paso he found a town that was overrun with renegades, army deserters, miscreants, and individuals with little or no respect for law and order. The lawless and deplorable condition that existed in El Paso were perpetuated and tolerated by an inept mayor, who cared only for his own aggrandizement and the enrichment of his coffers and a sheriff who would rather ignore the law than enforce it. The city governance and management had a chilling effect on the good people of El Paso who chose not to venture out of doors after sunset for fear of their personal safety. It didn't take Mr. Rooney long to become aware of the physical violence and shootings that occurred nightly. The lack of law enforcement and the excessive consumption of whisky were the twin demons driving the violence. When whiskey is factored into the human equation, all physical and emotional restraints are abandoned and the bestial nature of man rears its ugly head. These killings were needlessly inflicted on innocent victims, not because of hatred, grudges, or vendettas, but simply because they dare criticize people in power or law enforcement.

However, Rooney would not allow the shadow of darkness to deter or prohibit his freedom of movement in town. He was mighty handy with a six shooter but his real expertise was with his rifle, which he could handle as well as anyone with a six shooter, twirling it around his middle finger as if it were a six shooter then firing from his hip with dead accuracy. And when he brought the rifle sight up to his eye ball there was no escape for man or beast. This was the man who sooner or later would have a confrontation with one of the most notorious of miscreants; and Rooney's character was such that he would not tolerate any abusive language or conduct directed at him.

It was a hot summer's night when Rooney decided to quench his thirst with a cool beer at the Gladstone saloon. While drinking his beer at the bar and engaging a patron in friendly conversation he made a casual remark, suggesting that the sheriff should take his job more seriously and take a more active roll in cleaning up this town of its criminal element. Giggs, a notorious and feared character having had several deaths attributed to his violent disposition was standing at the bar a few paces from Rooney and overheard his critical remarks. Giggs took offense and walked over to Rooney and said,

"What did you mean by that remark stranger?"

"I think it's self explanatory and needs no further explanation," replied Rooney.

"You know stranger, boot hill is overflowing with do-gooders like you and if you don't watch your tongue, you'll be joining them."

Rooney was now hot under the collar and looked Giggs straight in the eyes and said,

"Mister, let me make myself clear, I have no intention of relinquishing my freedom of movement nor my freedom of speech for you or anyone else; now go back and finish your beer."

With that remark the patrons stepped back from the bar and receded into the background sensing an impending shootout. Giggs' face turned red with anger: no one dared talk to him like that before and he went for his gun. Rooney expected him to draw and when he did, Rooney slammed him in the jaw with the butt of his rifle. Giggs fell to the floor like a lead weight, unconscious. He was out like a light for fifteen minutes until the bartender doused him with a pail of cold water to revive consciousness. After coming to and although still dazed he discovered three of his teeth were missing. Rooney picked him up off the floor and grabbed him with both hands around the collar of his neck and gave him fair warning.

"You're lucky you didn't wind up on Boot Hill yourself Mr., and I can guarantee that you won't be that lucky if you ever try something like that again."

Giggs left realizing he was outmatched. He took Rooney's warning seriously and in the future he tried to stay clear of Rooney whenever possible. The town's desperados knew that if he could handle Giggs he would be more than a match for anyone else in town. Henceforth, Rooney went wherever he pleased and said whatever he thought and no one was foolish enough to challenge him or interfere with his freedom of movement or question his motives.

Everyone in town was now aware of the encounter between Rooney and Giggs; and while Rooney was free to roam through town at will, day or night, without fear of being harassed or annoyed that did not translate into a trouble free or law abiding town. The criminal element was ever present and very much in evident. Rooney's presence quenched some of the violence in town especially when he was around. The improved atmosphere in town, little as it was did not go unnoticed by the local inhabitants many of whom thought maybe the town could be brought under the rule of law with the proper governance and law enforcement. The town's people, therefore decided to call a town-hall meeting to discuss such a possibility. The conversation and discourse that pursued kept bouncing back and forth from person to person for a considerable length of time and in the end they all agreed that Mr. Rooney was the only person qualified and capable of bringing civility to El Paso. They decided that Mr. Rooney should replace Sheriff Eagan and subsequently selected a committee of four to approach Rooney with the proposition of running against Sheriff Eagan in the next election three months hence.

When the committee went to see Mr. Rooney to present him with their proposal to run for the office of sheriff, Rooney was a bit surprised, but receptive to the idea of being sheriff and was willing to listen to what they had to say. After discussing the sheriff's job with the committee for the better part of the afternoon, Rooney decided to accept their endorsement and run for the office of sheriff. The office of sheriff had a special significance for Rooney because he would be in a position to establish the rule of law in a town that was in desperate need of reform. He was living in El Paso and was now part of its social fabric and the job of sheriff would provide him with the opportunity to suppress the activities of the disruptive elements in town and make the town safe for people to live, work and raise a family. Up till now Rooney had been working at odd jobs around town and the job of sheriff would provide him with full time employment and a steady income. Mr. Rooney had found his calling. As the committee was about to leave one member of the committee asked,

"By the way Mr. Rooney, do you have a first name? I have never heard anyone refer to you other than Mr. Rooney."

"I do indeed, it's Erasmus but my friends call me Ray."

With that they all smiled and left with a good felling and a good omen for the future.

The campaign for the election of sheriff got under way immediately after the meeting between Ray Rooney and the citizen's committee had consummated their business. The enthusiasm and interest in the campaign was at a fever pitch amongst the average citizens, circulating posters and flyers all over town. The drifters, hoodlums, and miscreants didn't like it one bit, to see Rooney's picture plastered on every sideboard in town, and the persons who disliked it most were Sheriff Eagan and his cronies. Sheriff Eagan realized his job was in jeopardy and that he was being seriously challenged. He therefore decided to round up all the undesirables and derelicts in town and put them behind bars to demonstrate that he was conscientious in the performance of his duties. He put on a good show but fooled no one; everyone knew that the real criminal elements were still at large and doing business as usual and his round up of those pathetic individuals was inconsequential. His present actions could not camouflage his past indifference to law enforcement.

As much as Sheriff Eagan and his cronies tried they could not prevent a fair election. Mr. Rooney, together with the citizens of El Paso organized a large contingent of poll watches and placed three sentinels at each of the two polling locations in town to insure that no one stuff the ballot boxes with more than one vote per person, or deposit names of the deceased. The polling committee knew the number of eligible voters in town and made sure that the total number of votes cast did not exceed the number of registered voters. The presence of Mr. Rooney in and around town insured an honest election. Without his visible presence a fair and honest election would not have been possible and the town would remain the same as it was before the election. When the committee counted the votes that were cast, they declared Mr. Rooney the winner and the new sheriff in town, having received 95% of the votes cast. When the crowd heard the election result they expressed themselves with a resounding cheer; they were overjoyed and jubilant and some danced in the street as the committee chairman pinned the sheriff's badge on Rooney's chest.

Sheriff Rooney wasted little time in organizing his department of law enforcement. He realized that sheriffs do not make laws but are required only to enforce them. He was also keenly aware that as long as Mayor Doolittle remained as the chief executive officer of El Paso he could not depend on his cooperation to propose new legislation that would curtail the criminal and disruptive elements in town. Determined to control most of the event in town Sheriff Rooney decided to augment the parameters of the existing laws to achieve a greater degree of freedom in the execution of his duties. Mayor Doolittle and his cronies were infuriated with Sheriff Rooney's interpretation of the law and its enforcement. Those individuals who were operating under the protective umbrella of Sheriff Eagan were now stymied and frustrated, and were constantly being investigated by Sheriff Rooney. They were recidivist, constantly in and out of jail for lone sharking, selling bogus deeds, factitious mining rights as well as a host of other offenses. When Sheriff Rooney reached his limit of tolerance, some of the criminal elements could no longer brook his harassment and decided to leave town for more fertile pastures with less oppressive law enforcement. Those who decided to stay in town became more devious and cautious in their deceptive business transactions. Sheriff Rooney realized it would be a daunting task to rid the town of corruption without the full cooperation and support of Mayor Doolittle; and since his cooperation was not possible he set in motion a citizens committee to find someone with unquestionable integrity and intelligence to run against Mayor Doolittle in the upcoming election. After the committee was organized and in place, the time consuming process of finding a suitable candidate had begun. Several names were mentioned and after a thorough background check to determine the most qualified person for the job of mayor, they reached a consensus. The person chosen was Karl Schmidt the town lawyer, an honest man with impeccable credentials and a crusader for women's rights. He would be a guaranteed winner especially with the women folks. So when election day rolled around the prognosticators proved correct, Mr. Schmidt won in a landslide and became the next mayor of El Paso.

The stage was now set for the wheels of government to move into action. It was not an easy task; officials are always reluctant to relinquish their power and influence without a kick down, dragged out fight. Sheriff Rooney was slowly winning his fight and after 5 years of law enforcement, with the cooperation of Mayor Schmidt, Sheriff Rooney was successful in ridding the town of its most egregious offenders and establishing El paso as a law abiding town although there were still some bad apples living on the edge of the law. This was the social climate in El Paso when the stagecoach rolled into town after being robbed by the Romero brothers.

Chapter Three
A Friend and Brother

 While many of the town's people were crowded around the stage coach curious about the robbery, others were going about their daily business. Billy was roaming through town observing all that came before him including a dry goods store located in the center of town. He thought he might try to find employment there; it seemed like a nice store and a good place to start looking for a job. The early hours of the afternoon had waned and it was dusk when Billy walked into the dry goods store and asked to speak to the proprietor of the store.

"I'm the owner young man, what can I do for you?"

"Well sir, I'm looking for a job and would very much like to work here," replied Billy.

"Well son, I certainly could use the help since my wife and I are the only two running this store, but frankly I can't afford to hire anyone right now."

Billy bowed his head in obvious disappointment, thought for a while, then looked up at the owner of the store, and said.

"Well Sir, you need help and I need a job and a place to stay, so I'll tell you what I'm willing to do; I'll work for just room and board and at the end of the month if you could afford to pay me something fine, if not, that's O.K. too. You can't ask for a better deal than that."

The owner looked a bit puzzled and bewildered, then replied,

"Well, that is certainly a strange business arrangement and I'm almost inclined to take you up on it, but I don't think it would be fair to you young man."

"I repeat Sir, if you provide me with room and board I would be more than satisfied with the arrangement,"the owner then asked,

"What is your name son? And where are your parents?"

"My name is Billy Reed and my parents both died of the sickness that hit Astec, New Mexico, last year."

Whenever questions concerning his parents were asked, Billy was deliberately evasive and prevaricated in his reply, since the subject was just too painful for him to recall.

"O.K. Billy, you have a job and a place to stay. My name is John Adam; let's go upstairs and meet my wife Molly; she's preparing dinner so we'll be just in time to enjoy her delicious beef stew. I'll lock up the store then we'll go upstairs and I'll introduce you to the her."

As they both walked upstairs Billy began to salivate from the aroma of a home cooked meal. John introduced Billy to Molly, saying,

"Molly meet Billy Reed, our new employee."

Molly's eyes widened in a state of shock, and said,

"Now John, you know we can't afford help!"

"But Molly, it's not costing us anything but room and board for this young man."

"No John, I can't allow you to take advantage of this boy like that."

The conversation between John and Molly ensued for a while until Molly understood and approved of Billy's employment status. With that settled they sat down to enjoy their evening meal. The expression on the faces of Molly and John indicated they were pleased to have this young man around the house. They had no children of their own, and Billy would be a pleasant addition to their household. After dinner Mr. Adam showed Billy to his room, telling him that breakfast is at 6:30, after which he showed Billy around the store to familiarize him with the merchandise. That evening Billy sat there admiring his room: a large bed, desk and a window facing Main Street. As Billy sat there gazing out the window he felt content, satisfied and free of worry for the immediate future. He wondered what was in store for him down the road and how he would accomplish his intended vendetta.

In the meantime, Rose took up temporary residence in the local hotel while exploring a suitable location to establish her new business. Rose was engaged in the oldest profession in the world, providing female companionship for those willing to pay for the service. In Astec, she was the madam of a small bordello and had a thriving business, but the town was too small for Rose to exercise her entrepreneurial skill. So she decided to move to a larger town where she would not be restricted by a small and limited clientele. After several days of exploration she finally located a large house on the outskirts of town that she deemed most suitable for her type of business.

She made arrangements to purchase the house then began to renovate it in a style commensurate with her clients needs. When all was ready she contacted the girls she left behind in Astec, asking them if they would like to join her in El Paso. After hearing from Rose they were most willing and eager to resume their relationship with Rose and all the amenities that went with it. The four girls who Rose imported from Astec, would not be nearly enough to satisfy the demand that she anticipated; so Rose corralled the women in town who were free-lancing and asked them if they would like to join her in a secure environment and a steady income. After a short discussion as to the arrangements and conditions, they accepted her offer and were brought under Rose's protective wing. In some respects she improved the social atmosphere in town by removing these strumpets from the streets of El Paso and out of public view. Rose now required only one more week of preparations before opening the doors of her establishment to the general public. The most sophisticated citizen in town referred to Rose's place as "the brothel," while most of the patrons called it "the cat house," but Rose preferred a more euphemistic name calling it "the fun house." Whatever the name it went by, it served a useful purpose in El Paso: releasing pent up energy that otherwise would be channeled for violence or mischief.

The next morning, Billy was up bright and early and eager to start work at the dry goods store. After finishing breakfast, Billy excused himself and went downstairs to familiarize himself with the merchandise in the store. Mr. Adam's dry goods store was rather unique in its size and variety of items in stock. It was considered a large store by the standards of the 19th century. Out front was a hitching rail for horses; plus additional room at the side of the store for those traveling by wagon or different types of four wheel vehicles to accommodate his customers. The store made a very favorable impression with a six foot platform at the entrance and a large glass pane window bearing a sign reading, "John Adam's Dry Goods Establishment." On the platform stood two rocking chairs, one on each side of the entrance door to accommodate those folks who would like to rest awhile before entering or leaving his store. As you entered the store, immediately to your right is a display of farm tools, shovels, picks, saws, hoes, etc. Walking further down the isle is a collection of blankets, shirts, dungarees and other types of garments meant for work or Sunday wear. A large section was reserved for the display of fire arms, including a variety of six shooters, rifles and a goodly supply of ammunition to compliment all types of shooting apparatus. The next to last section, included the most popular brands of smoking and chewing tobacco; but the section that attracts most of Mr.

Adam's customers is the section of staples: sugar, salt, flour, rice, barley, and oats, sold by the pound or by the sack. And the most striking feature of the store was at the far end. An area a few feet wider than the isle and about ten feet in depth, the source of attraction in this room was a pot-belly stove with two small circular tables on each side and three or four chairs at each table.

In winter, the patrons would congregate around the pot-belly stove for warmth, and tell stories or simply engage in local gossip. Whenever a small group gathered in this area, it was destined to be filled with smoke, emanating from their corncob or clay pipes and when cigar smoke was added to the mix, it guaranteed the absence of flies and mosquitoes. There was also a spittoon close by to accommodate the tobacco chewers. When the women folk were not around or the absence of children in the vicinity, the silence in the room would be broken by hearty laughter, caused by someone telling a raunchy joke that he had heard circulating around town. In the summer months when the pot-belly stove was retired, they still gathered there to socialize and talk about their favorite subject, Rose's cat house. Billy would observe all that went on and occasionally would enter the conversation by asking the men at the table a question,

"Who do you think was the best gun fighter in the West?"

The answers had a special meaning for Billy, and provoked a cascade of comments and stories in reply. It was a revelation for Billy, for each and every person invariably evoked the name of Simon Ganz, in short commentaries or lengthy stories. There was a consensus within the group that Simon Ganz was the best shooter in the Southwest. Billy was always enthralled when hearing tales of Simon Ganz, from individual cowboys and gunslingers from all over the Southwest who would drop into Adam's dry goods store, to replenish their supplies. Billy heard these legendary tales of heroics day after day and year after year.

While working at the dry goods store Billy met a variety of different people, but only two individuals did Billy befriend and become especially fond of. One was a young girl named Rachel, about Billy's age, the daughter of Janette Richardson, a middle aged widow who would shop at the dry goods store twice a week accompanied by her daughter. Rachel was a beautiful young girl with blue eyes and light brown hair and an engaging smile. It was obvious from her pulchritudinous stature that she would develop into an attractive young lady. Billy was instantly attracted to her and would use any excuse to engage her in conversation while her mother was shopping. Five years into the future, Rachel's body parts did indeed develop to the point where she was the envy of most women and desired by all men. But for now, she was the focus of Bill's attention.

The other person Billy took a liking to was Joe Young eight years Billy's senior, and his 6'2" frame towered over Billy. Joe Young was a handsome young man; an impressive figure with brown eyes and black wavy hair and a face with finely chiseled features. He walked with an air of self confidence, dressed in a black shirt and navy blue dungarees with six shooters hanging from both sides of his hip. Joe would come into the store about twice a week mainly to buy bullets for his six shooters and rifle. When Joe wasn't working he would ride out of town to his favorite location, to practice his marksmanship with his six shooters. Everyone in town knew that Joe Young was a shooter to be reckoned with since he had proven his ability with his six shooters time and time again. Part of his income was derived from tracking down wanted outlaws with attractive bounties on their heads. When he wasn't tracking down outlaws he would work for ranchers, driving cattle from one location to another, for slaughter or for sale. He would also be hired by horse dealers to break wild horses at $10 a head. These various jobs kept Joe quite busy and provided him with a steady and substantial income. Everyone in town knew Joe and everyone liked him, as he was good natured and would help any person in need. As good as Joe was, you would never want to cross him or do him ill, for then you would see a part of his nature that would be most unpleasant to witness.

Joe was sitting at home resting one evening when he received a message from Hank the rancher that a new lot of wild horses arrived and needed breaking. He decided to walked over to Hank's ranch to view the new arrivals and while observing the horses circling around the enclosure, he noticed one horse in particular that stood out from the rest. This horse was a magnificent black stallion, standing about two inches taller than the other horses, but what really caught Joe's attention was the manner in which this horse trotted around the enclosure. He was snorting and kicking up his heels in a defiant and belligerent manner, suggesting he resented being confined to the enclosed area. For the next couple of days Joe couldn't think of anything else but that magnificent animal. At present, Joe had no horse of his own. His last horse died of pneumonia nine months ago and he became so distraught over the loss of his horse that he avoid getting another. He preferred to rent or borrow different horses from Hank, which he found more convenient and less emotional than owning a horse of his own. But the black stallion changed all that. The emotional attachment Joe had for his last horse had diminished with time and the black stallion severed the final emotional link. Joe decided he wanted that horse and went to see Hank about buying the black stallion. He asked Hank to name his price for the black stallion, Hank replied,

"Joe, I've known you a long time and consider you a good friend; I just wouldn't feel right taking your money. I would feel that I had cheated you. That horse has a bad temper and a mean streak in him and can't be broken; others have tried with little success, even Stubby who's known to be the best horse buster in these parts; even better that you Joe, has tried and failed. Stubby has tried to break him several times but gave up on him, in his last attempt to break the stallion he wound up with three broken fingers and a badly bruised rib cage. No Joe, I could not in good conscience sell him to you."

But Joe would not be dissuaded.

"Well Hank, thanks for being honest with me but I still want to buy the black stallion."

"O.K. Joe, don't say I didn't warn you; but if you insist on buying the stallion I'll tell you what I'll do: if you can break the stallion I'll let you have him for just $20."

Joe smiled shook hands with Hank, and said,

"It's a deal."

Now Joe had to find an appropriate name for his horse; till then he simply referred to him as Blacky and was presently confronted with the awesome task of breaking him. He knew that the standard methods of breaking wild horses would not apply or be effective with Blacky; so Joe first separated Blacky from the rest of the wild horses, then corralled him into a separate area where only he and Blacky would be present. Joe would then talk to Blacky for a while whispering sweet nothings in his ear in an attempt to familiarize Blacky with the sound of Joe's voice as well as his presence. The following day he did the same, trying to gain Blacky's confidence; while offering him an apple or carrot which Blacky rejected out of hand. But Joe was persistent in his efforts throwing the apple on the ground about ten feet from where Joe was standing. At first, Blacky ignored the apple but after a while he walked over to the apple and sniffed it; he must have liked the smell and ate the apple. Joe threw another apple and carrot to the ground this time a little closer to himself. Blacky was less reluctant to eat this time since he must have relished the sweet taste of the apple and carrot. Joe kept cajoling Blacky with apples and carrots for the next couple of days. By now Blacky recognized Joe and would look for his offerings whenever he appeared. They were no longer strangers. Blacky would allow Joe to pat him on the head, neck and back. Constant persistence on Joe's part eventually paid off. Early one morning after Joe had been making nice to Blacky for eight days, he still hadn't attempted to put a blanket on his back and now was the time to try the impossible. Joe was friendly enough with Blacky to stand beside him and try to throw a blanket over his back but Blacky wasn't accommodating and threw the blanket off. Joe tried several more times with the same results. This procedure continued till Joe or Blacky prevailed, and it wasn't going to be Blacky; Joe had invested too much time and effort to concede defeat. Eventually, it was Blacky who conceded and accepted the blanket. Every step in breaking Blacky was difficult, with each step more difficult than the one that preceded it. Now came the penultimate step, putting a saddle on Blacky. Joe brought him into a narrow and confined area, severely restricting his ability to move then placed the saddle on his back and turned him loose. Joe watched, as Blacky displayed his defiance by bucking, snorting, and kicking his hind quarters high in the air trying to extricate himself from the saddle. Joe watched for fifteen minutes while Blacky went from a violent display of anger, to a subdued acceptance of the saddle. Then Joe walked away leaving the saddle on Blacky all day for him to get accustomed to having the saddle on his back; returning in the evening to remove the saddle. Come morning, the saddle went back on and eventually Blacky accepted having a saddle on his back and henceforth put up no further resistance. Joe's job was not yet complete, since the final and most difficult stage was to ride Blacky. Joe had at least some advantage over Stubby in that the horse knew Joe and had some liking for him; so hopefully that would work in Joe's favor. The next morning Joe approached Blacky and greeted him with two apples, then looked him straight in the eyes while patting him on the head and whispering in his ear. After socializing for ten minutes Joe thought it time to mount him. When Blacky felt the additional weight on his back he began to buck, gallop, and snort for a couple of minutes but never showed the same fierce intensity toward Joe that he displayed toward Stubby. After another minute or two Joe sensed that Blacky's intensity of behavior was waning and soon Blacky would be broken. It was a climatic moment when Joe calmly rode Blacky around the enclosure and felt a sense of pride and satisfaction in his accomplishment. He then rode to see Hank and pay him the $20 for Blacky and boast of his achievement. When Hank saw Joe on top of Blacky he scratched his head in disbelief, saying,

"Well, well, well, congratulations Joe, I never would believe it possible for you to break that horse, but you did it and he's all yours."

Joe then rode off with Blacky to introduce him to his new home.

That evening while Joe was at home reposing on a couch trying to come up with a suitable name for his horse, a typical Texas thunder storm was in the making. It began with a heavy downpour accompanied by an unusual amount of thunder and lighting. Every time the thunder broke loose from heaven and crackled across the night sky, Blacky could be heard in his stall pounding his hooves on the ground, snorting and making a ruckus. Joe took notice of Blacky's reaction every time he heard thunder and associated the thunder with Blacky's nervous behavior. It then struck Joe that "Thunder" would be an appropriate name for Blacky and decided that Blacky's new name would be Thunder. Having chosen a suitable name for Blacky Joe lay on his bed in silence, shut his eyes and listened to the thunder roar across the night sky and the raindrops dancing on his roof.

The next morning, the skies cleared and Joe decided to ride Thunder through town. When Joe and Thunder sauntered through the streets of El Paso all eyes were fixed on the statue like figure of Joe and Thunder. It was an image of magnificent beauty and while Joe might have looked like a mythical god he was no saint. Joe had his weaknesses and foibles; for one thing, he was a frequent visitor at Rose's entertainment parlor. After a little flirtation with the girls of the night he would indulge himself with a few glasses of whiskey or play some poker with the boys before returning home. After all, there wasn't much more a single man could do in El Paso.

The existence of Rose's establishment was well known to Sheriff Rooney but because of its popularity he chose to ignore it, since most of the male residents in town used its services and would not want to have it closed down. Sheriff Rooney himself would occasionally visit Rose's place and rarely would there be a problem or a disturbance there. Sheriff Rooney had more trouble in the local saloons than he did at Rose's place. However, there were some folks in town who were opposed to having a brothel on the outskirts of town. The major antagonist of Rose's place was the Reverend

Vengeance

Michel Bigelow.

Parson Bigelow was a tall thin framed man, in his late forties and looked more like an undertaker than a preacher, with his brown deep set eyes separated by a large thin nose and a crop of gray hair sprouting from his head which wasn't always well groomed. He was usually dressed in black with a white shirt and a black ribbon tie. He wore a black round doomed hat with a four inch rim, that added five inches more to his 6'2" height. His wife Matilda was ten years his junior and the antithesis of her husband. She was short, 5'3" in stature and a bit on the chubby side, displaying a beautiful pair of blue eyes. In the middle of her face was a small nose that complimented the rest of her features; her hair was brownish in color and parted down the middle coming to a bun at the back of her head. On her forehead the onset of lines could be seen. Whenever her emotional state of displeasure, nervousness, or embarrassment, would occur, it was evident by the sudden appearance of a red nose. All things considered she was on the attractive side. She did not always dress in black like her husband, but wore a variety of colored garments with a white laced collar around her neck. They were an odd looking couple, but they earned the respect of the town's people and that's all that mattered to them. Parson Bigelow preached every Sunday with his two daughters sitting in the front pew; they were twelve and eight years of age and not very attractive looking. There was nothing in their facial features that was unattractive or needed improvement, they were just frumpy looking.

However, their father, Parson Bigelow had a natural gift for rhetoric. He could give a sermon that would convince the devil to change his ways. And every Sunday he would dedicate a portion of his sermon in condemnation of that "House of Inequity." He preached to his parishioners that those young men who visit "That House" were marching straight into the jaws of hell. God's condemnation of such behavior will elicit His wrath and manifest itself in a form of retribution too terrible to contemplate. The women in his congregation loved his diatribe the men were much less enthusiastic.

One Sunday, Parson Bigelow's sermon was so extraordinarily bombastic and ad hominem in his unrelenting denunciation of Rose's place causing his women parishioners emotional anguish to demand action; after services they marched in mass to Sheriff Rooney's office to demand that he do something about this stain on their community. Sheriff Rooney listened patiently to the women's complaints, while nodding his head in agreement to placate their heightened emotions and distemper. He was reluctant to disagree with the ladies since they were instrumental in voting him in office.

"Alright, alright ladies, I'll take care of this matter."

The ladies were satisfied that they evoked a positive commitment from Sheriff Rooney and left quietly. However, he was reluctant to clamp down on Rose's place since he knew most of the men who frequented her establishment. After giving this problem some serious thought, he decided to ride out to the cat house and talk to Rose. After the usual greetings and salutations he sat down with Rose to explain the situation. Sheriff Rooney told Rose what had transpired in his office with the women of Reverend Bigelow's congregation, then said,

"Rose, I don't have any positive or negative feelings about this place but if I shut you down I'll have to contend with the displeasure of the men folks in town including some of the married ones; if I do nothing, the women will be all over me, so here's what I propose. Me and my deputy will raid your place sometime this week and take into custody those men present along with the women and incarcerate them just long enough for a lecture and a small fine, then release them. This will make the women of the town happy and no real harm will be done."

"Well, I guess that's the best I could hope for under these circumstances." Said Rose.

"So what day would you suggest we make our raid, Rose."

"Well, the slowest night of the week is always Monday, I barely have more than two or three patrons on that day and most of my girls are off on Mondays."

"O.K. then it's settled, we'll raid your place this coming Monday."

Rooney then engaged Rose in small talk while drinking his whiskey before departing for town.

The following Monday evening was hot and sultry when he and his deputy Tim Thompson rode out to Rose's place to fulfil his promise to the women of the town. There was a good breeze in the air that felt refreshing as they rode along. Deputy Thompson asked his boss,

"Why are we doing this?"

"It was a request by the good women of the town to shut down the cat house."

"You're not going to do that, are you?" Asked Tim

Vengeance

"No of cause not, I'm just going to put on a good show; you know who's behind all this ruckus don't you, Tim?"

"Of course." replied Tim, "It's that do good fire and brimstone preacher Parson Bigelow. I wish he would take his preaching to another town, every Sunday when my wife returns from church I have to listen to her regurgitate his sermon. She sure gives me a headache."

This chit-chat continued all the way to the bordello. Upon their arrival Rooney and his deputy walked in and declared everyone under arrest. There was only one pathetic sole sitting at a table having a drink of whiskey; Sheriff Rooney felt a little embarrassed and awkward having to arrest this old man. While the sheriff was dealing with Rose and this individual, deputy Thompson was upstairs opening all the doors. Upon opening the third door he found a guy in the saddle and said,

"O.K. finish up what you're doing, then come downstairs you're both under arrest."

Tim knew all the patrons and none would try to escape. Tim continued walking down the hall, opening door after door and after finding the forth room empty he opened the fifth and last door. As Tim walked in nonchalantly he glanced at a man struggling to put his pants on. Tim was shocked and frozen in place for a few seconds before regaining his composure, and shouted,

"Well, if it isn't the most Reverend Bigelow."

He was standing there with one leg in his trousers and struggling to get the other leg in; in the background, lying in bed was a nude woman trying to conceal her nudity with a bed sheet. Tim was standing there with a grin on his face from ear to ear, while Parson Bigelow's face was somber and turning beet red from embarrassment and beads of perspiration forming on his forehead. Tim walked slowly to the door never taking his eyes off the parson and yelled out to Sheriff Rooney,

"Hay sheriff, come up here; I have a surprise for you!"

Sheriff Rooney couldn't imagine what kind of a surprise awaited him as he walked slowly upstairs and into the room to find Parson Bigelow half dressed with a naked woman in the background, lying seductively in bed. Rooney shouted in amazement,

"Well, I'll be GOD DAMMED, if it isn't the good Reverent Bigelow. You know I'm going to; no, I have to, lock you up with the rest of the men and women in this cat house."

Vengeance

Suddenly the parson looked like he was about to faint as the color in his face turned from red to white, and with a trembling hand he asked to speak to Sheriff Rooney in private.

"Sure, let's go in the next room," replied Rooney.

The reverend had to deliver the most important sermon of his life now to try an extricate himself from this mess he was in. He said to Sheriff Rooney,

"Sheriff, you just can't take me in, I'm pleading with you, think of the ramifications of your action. You'll destroy my family, my wife will lose her respect for me, my poor innocent daughters will be humiliated and embarrassed and wouldn't be able to show their faces in town. To say nothing of what my parishioners would think, or do, as a result of this calamity. You would not only destroy my life, but the lives of three other innocent individuals. And there are a dozen more reasons why you shouldn't go through with my arrest."

Then grabbing Sheriff Rooney's chest garment with both hands and tears rolling down his face he pleaded,

"Please, please, Sheriff, have mercy."

He almost brought tears to Sheriff Rooney's eyes, although Rooney had no intention of taking Parson Bigelow into custody especially not after such an eloquent speech. The sheriff was thinking of working out some kind of deal with Parson Bigelow but as for now he was keeping his cards close to his chest then replied,

"How can I not take you in and then take into custody that poor creature down stairs, along with Rose and her girls; That's just not fair."

The reverend replied with wide open eyes,

"Well, why not pretend that this raid never happened."

"No, no, no, that would make me and my deputy part of a coverup."

Sheriff Rooney wasn't all that concerned about ethics he was more concerned with squeezing concessions out of the good Parson. So he continued with his charade, and replied,

"After all this raid was initiated because of the insistence by the women in your congregation."

The reverend stood motionless for a few seconds as did the sheriff. Then the Sheriff started to speak again.

"Well, maybe we can solve this problem together."

The parson's eyes widened again and he gave Sheriff Rooney his undivided attention and was eager to hear what he had in mind.

"Parson, I have to tell you, I don't consider it a crime for a person to visit a place like this, it provides a necessary service for those men who need it; but what I do consider a crime, not in the legal sense of course but in the moral sense, is hypocrisy. Hypocrisy is a greater injustice and danger to society than this place could ever be. Now I'll tell you what I propose: I'll let you off the hook and forget all about this incident if you will promise to ascend you pulpit every Sunday and preach to your congregation about tolerance, understanding, redemption and forgiveness for those who do not conform to your standard of morality. No more bombastic indictments of individuals or groups, especially Rose's place. Now do you understand what I'm saying? And do you agree to those terms?"

The parson realized he had no other alternative, sadly bobbing his head up and down in compliance without saying a word. Then Rooney continued,

"Parson, the only fucking your going to do from now on is with your wife."

The few occupants that were there filed out and went their separate ways. Before Sheriff Rooney left he pulled Rose aside and asked her,

"Rose, did you know that the parson was going to be here this evening?"

"Yeah, that hypocrite wouldn't come on any other night but a Monday, he enters through the back door in a pseudo disguise and scuts upstairs to await his inamorata."

Sheriff Rooney then asked,

"If you knew that he was going to be here this evening why didn't you let me know? And how could he not be recognized?"

Rose's answer was honest and straight forward,

"Sheriff, I never reveal the names of the gentlemen who come and go in my establishment; it's bad for business and it would be unethical for me to do so; and as far as the parson not being recognized you have to understand that most of the men who visit my place travel in different circles than the parson's parishioners. And if anyone did recognize him, he would say that he was preaching to the girls, which he actually does on occasions. His routine worked to his advantage until you ruined it for him with your raid."

"I didn't ruin his deceptive routine; he did!, with his zealous preaching."

Rooney chattered a while longer with Rose, had a couple of whiskeys, then left with his deputy.

The Sheriff was not a church going man. After a week or two had passed he heard through the grape vine that the parson was true to his word, preaching tolerance, understanding and forgiveness, saying in part,

"Let us not condemn those who do not share the same moral conviction that we do; we are all God's children, let us all pray for their salvation."

And soon the female contingent of his congregation became more understanding, tolerant and pacified, and settled down to normalcy.

CHAPTER FOUR
SHOOT EM UP

Back at the dry goods store Billy was sweeping up around the counter when Joe Young walked in. Billy greeted him with a big smile. "How are you today Mr. Young."

"Fine Billy, are you busy this morning?"

"No, it usually gets a little busy around 11 o'clock. So until then you have my undivided attention," replied Billy,

"Fine Billy, let's start off by getting me six boxes of bullets for my six shooters."

"Boy you sure use a lot of ammo Mr. Young."

"Yeah Billy, I practice every chance I get when I'm not gainfully employed."

"The word around town is that you're already the fastest and best shot in the West, since Simon Ganz is now retired."

"Well, I appreciate the compliment and comparison, but the truth is there is no one in the past or living today who is as good as Simon Ganz." "Why do you spend so much time practicing if you can't improve your shooting skill much more?" "Billy, I never look for trouble but sometimes trouble has a way of finding you and if it does, or when it does, I want to make sure that I come out on top."

"Mr Young, I bought myself a six shooter from my savings and I would very much appreciate it if you would take me shooting with you sometime."

"Sure thing Billy, why don't we give it a try on your day off or after work."

"Great!" Billy shouted. "How about tomorrow morning since I'm off on Wednesdays Mr. Young."

"Fine Billy, I'll pick you up at eight tomorrow morning in front of the dry goods store."

"O.K. Mr. Young, I'll be waiting for you."

Sure enough, Billy was out in front of the dry goods store twenty minutes before eight, eager to get started. Around about eight Joe rode up on top of Thunder wearing a black decorative shirt, and looking like a mythical god riding from cloud to cloud. As Joe approached he yelled out to Billy,

"O.K. Billy, jump on the back of Thunder and hold on tight,"

and off they went. About two miles out of town they stopped and dismounted.

"Billy this is my favorite shooting area where there are plenty of target to punch holes in, but before you start shooting up the place let me give you a little advice. I want you to understand from the start that it is just as important to be fast on the draw, as it is to be a crack shot. You'll have to spend as much time practicing the art of the draw as you spend on target practice. Being a crack shot is of little value if you're slow, both go hand in hand. Do you understand what I'm telling you Billy?"

"I sure do Mr. Young," Billy replied.

"One other thing Billy, let's drop that Mr. Young moniker just call me Joe from now on."

"O.K. Joe," Billy responded with a broad smile. Billy then watched in awe as Joe demonstrated his skill with a six shooter hitting objects that were barely visible to the naked eye; shooting leaves off of trees without damaging the leaves. At times Joe would have Billy throw a pebble high in the air and then blast it to dust at twenty paces. Joe would also test his skill by shooting at flies in flight; and was successful in hitting them 30 percent of the time. There was no question in Billy's mind as to Joe's expertise with a six shooter. He was the perfect teacher for Billy.

Joe and Billy would head out to various shooting areas at least four times a week and they always had a pleasant outing: laughing, shooting, and telling stories, mostly of Joe's past adventures. Billy was learning fast and rapidly becoming a marksman in his own right. After a few months had passed, Joe couldn't help but notice the intensity and dedication that Billy was applying to his shooting lessons, which prompted Joe to ask,

"Billy you've come a long way in just three months, and I can't help but wonder why you're willing to sacrifice so much of your youth, on becoming an expert shooter; do you want to become another Simon Ganz some day to win fame and glory?"

"No!, No!," said Billy.

"I would like nothing better than to get married some day and settle down to an ordinary life and raise a family, but first I have a score to settle and the only way I can accomplish my goal is with this six shooter."

"Well," said Joe.

"Could you let me in on your little secret."

"Joe, you've been like a brother to me and I would trust you with my life, but right now it's still too painful for me to talk about it; but I promise you before I go out on my mission, I will tell you all of the gruesome details."

"O.K. Billy, then we'll leave it at that."

Their brotherly relationship and shooting schedules continued for another few weeks before Joe told Billy,

"You know Billy, I'm getting tired of us riding double on top of Thunder, so I think it's time for you to get a horse of your own."

"I would love to have a horse of my own Joe but I just can't afford to buy one right now."

"I know that Billy, so this is what I propose! On your next day off, we'll go out together and scour the Texas plain for a herd of wild horses; I think I know where we can find a herd and when we do, you can look them over and choose a horse of your liking. Then I'll lasso the beast and bring him or her into town where I can break the horse on Hank's ranch. How does that sound to you Billy?"

"That's music to my ears Joe,"Billy responded with a big smile on his face.

After the passage of a few days, Billy's day off came and Joe informed Billy that today they would ride out to the wide open Texas plains, in search of a herd of wild horses. Wild horses weren't all that difficult to locate on the Western plains and Joe had a pretty good idea where he could find a herd. They rode for an hour or so with the wind blowing up swirls of dust and tumbleweed; when Joe spotted a cloud of dust in the distance that was not due to the wind, and said,

"Billy, I think we found a small herd of wild horses and they're headed straight for us. Now all we have to do is stay put and watch them gallop by," which they did in a hurricane of horse flesh. It wasn't long before Billy spotted a beautiful sorrel mare with a white spot in the center of her head. In a fit of sheer excitement Billy pointed to the sorrel mare, indicating to Joe that she was the horse he would like to have.

"Billy you sure have an eye for good horse flesh; you wait here and I'll fetch her for you."

Joe road along side the herd for twenty minutes, trying to separate the sorrel mare from the rest of the herd. Finally, Joe succeeded in maneuvering the sorrel mare into a position where she could be lassoed. The mare showed a fierce defiance for being separated from the rest of the herd and resisted gallantly before being brought to bay. After Joe's long struggle with this beautiful animal he rested awhile before leading her into town; then headed straight for Hank's ranch where she would be broken.

All of the following week Joe was hard at work breaking Billy's sorrel mare, while Billy watched with keen interest. When Joe was not at work breaking the mare; Billy was developing a bond of friendship between himself and the mare, by offering her apples, carrots and some oats; and at the end of each day Billy would brush her down. When Joe finally broke the mare he saddled her and walked the mare over to Billy and said,

"Billy, this mare is now yours; have you thought of a name for her?"

"Yes, I sure have Joe, I'm going to call her Lightning."

Joe smiled and chuckled, saying,

"That's very imaginative of you Billy; Joe and Billy riding 'Thunder' and 'Lightning', that will certainly attract attention in this town, both laughing a bit."

Billy was as proud as a peacock with his newly acquired horse, and it gave him a renewed sense of freedom and independence. He especially relished running errands for Mr. Adam; giving Billy an opportunity to ride Lightning through town. At age fifteen, Billy was maturing rapidly into a strong young man. He stood at five feet, ten inches tall and displayed a crop of brownish hair somewhat lighter around the temples. His large brown eyes seemed to twinkle every time he smiled.

When working at the dry goods store Billy was always helpful and accommodating to patrons. Some patrons entering Mr. Adam's store weren't always in a good mood, but after talking to Billy for a while they became a little more pleasant. He had the ability to make people feel relaxed with his captivating smile and engaging manner; and they left the store in a more pleasant mood than when they entered. In the interim, working at the dry goods store and riding off with Joe to practice his shooting skills; Billy developed a warm and meaningful relationship with Rachel. He would see Rachel twice a week at the dry goods store; and while her mother was shopping they would enjoy each others company with lots of small talk and laughter. However, these encounters were far too short, and infrequent for Billy. Now that Billy had Lightning he could ride out to the Richardson place for one reason or another, just to see and talk to Rachel. Mrs. Richardson was always glad to see Billy who would never forget to bring her freshly cut flowers. They would sit on the veranda drinking lemonade and would talk about almost anything. Billy was fast becoming a frequent dinner guest at the Richardson household.

Billy would ride out to the Richardson house on occasion just to take Rachel for a ride on top of Lightning. She would sit on top of Lightning with her arms wrapped around Billy's waist, holding on tightly as Lightning galloped off. What Billy enjoyed most in taking Rachel for a ride was the feel of Rachel's arms around his waist. Rachel wasn't interested in owning her own horse or using the family horse to ride along side Billy; she much preferred riding on top of Lightning with her arms around Billy's waist; both sharing the same affectionate feeling. They would ride all around the countryside, absorbing all the beauty that nature had to offer. When arriving at the lake they would dismount and walk along its shoreline talking and laughing at every little thing as youthful lovers often do.

This state of affairs : courting Rachel, tending to his duties at the dry goods store and riding out with Joe for shooting practice continued uninterrupted for the next couple of years. Billy had developed rapidly in the past two years and he was now over six feet tall and as strong as an ox.

One hot and dry day Billy rode out to see Rachel and as usual they went for a ride along the lake. It was hot and getting hotter, and the water in the lake looked so inviting that Billy suggested they go for a swim. It was hard to reject Billy's suggestion with the temperature rising by the minute, so Rachel agreed. Both disrobed short of nudity and ran headlong into the water, swimming, splashing, diving, and having one hell of a good time. After a while they emerged from the lake a little exhausted seeking a cool spot under a tree, where they could rest and dry off. Rachel's wet garment clung to her body revealing every curve and contour of her beautiful and youthful figure. Billy couldn't help but notice, but tried not to make his glances appear obvious. They were alone and surrounded by shrubbery. After reclining for a minute or so Rachel turned toward Billy and said,

"Oh Billy, I have something in my eye."

Billy turned toward Rachel coming within six inches of her lips, when he gently lifted the upper eye lid to remove the foreign matter.

"I think I removed it Rachel, how does it fell?"

"Oh, much better Billy, thank you so much."

Vengeance

This little episode stirred the passion in Billy and he touched her check with his hand then looking her in the eyes and brought his lips on to hers and they melted into a passionate embrace. Their youthful passions stirring within; they were both virgins, exploring their sexuality. Billy ran his hand slowly down Rachel's back then upward along the side of her body until he began to feel the softness of her breast. Oh Billy, she murmured and pulled Billy tightly to her body and said,

"Billy, I think we ought to stop now, you know what will happen if we don't!"

"But Rachel, I love you!"

"I know that Billy, but if I get pregnant, I'll be disgraced and looked down upon and it would not only affect me but my mother too. I don't want to wind up as one of Rose's girls."

"That will never happen to you Rachel not as long as I'm alive."

Billy was breathing heavily and continued,

"I certainly understand your concern Rachel, and promise never to take advantage of you; look Rachel, we don't have to have intercourse in order for us to express our love for each other. Just leave it to me and trust me, O.K.?"

Rachel consented by her silence and they continued with their intimate relationship. In their passionate embrace Billy refrained from removing the last vestige of clothes from Rachel's body to avoid any uncomfortable feeling or embarrassment on her part. Billy too, maintained what little he was wearing, then he began to kiss Rachel on her lips and down her neck and on to her breast, while running his hand around the side of her body, exploring the vicinity of her lower extremities, this evoked a groan of sexual pleasure from Rachel and Billy knew that he had found a most sensitive area on Rachel's body. Rachel was doing her own exploring running her hands all over Billy's muscular body slowly edging down to his genitals. As soon as she touched him, he erupted like a volcano. It took Billy a few minutes to calm down and regain his composure, before embracing Rachel with renewed passion. He then began to kiss Rachel's breast, while his hands were gently touching the inner part of her thigh and moving in the direction of her vagina. When he touched a sensitive area she opened her legs like a flower. Billy realized he had found a sensitive spot. They were both overwhelmed with passion, taking liberties that under normal conditions would never have occurred to them. This foreplay continued awhile longer when suddenly she removed Billy's finger and hugged Billy tightly, echoing a deep moan of passion; she had reached her climax; then she relaxed in a state of abeyance in Billy's arms while the afterglow of her sexual experience slowly abated. After resting in each others arms for some time they found that their clothes had dried sufficiently for them to dress and ride back to the Richardson home. While riding home, they realized that they were both bond together for life and needed no marriage certificate to proclaim their union. They were happy and content. Their mirth and joy they felt was reflected in their dispositions, especially Rachel, who would promenade through town and greet everyone she knew with a smile and a big hello.

Rodney was observing Rachel's good humor and gaiety as he downed whiskey after whiskey, thinking evil and prurient thoughts that no decent man would contemplate or execute. Rodney Bean was a notorious recidivist and trouble maker who was in and out of Sheriff Rooney's jail dozens of times, having been jailed for all sorts of offenses ranging from disorderly conduct, to the molestation of women, both single and married and he would intimidate the men folks with his fists, or six shooters. He was big, husky, and always in need of a shave and definitely had a mean streak in him. The only two men in town he feared were Sheriff Rooney and Joe Young. When they were around he would be on his best behavior. He was also a frequent patron of the local saloon and would down whisky after whisky with his friends, while boasting of the women he had insulted or tried to seduce, which provoked considerable laughter amongst his cronies.

Rodney was now eyeing Rachel whom he and so many other men had admired with great admiration; but only Rodney harbored prurient and salacious thoughts and had the nerve and indecency to put those thoughts into action. Every one in town including Rodney, knew that Billy and Rachel were very much in love, but that fact did not phase or bother Rodney one bit, since he had no morels to guide his actions and had nothing to fear from a seventeen year old kid; this would be easy pickings. He studied Rachel's routine and knew that she would occasionally ride out to the lake alone in her horse and buggy, for a moment of peace and solitude. He knew her favorite location too, and on this particular day when he saw her move out in her horse and buggy he decided to follow her at a safe distance. When she arrived at the lake she lay down beneath the shaded tree where she and Billy often lay. When she shut her eyes and was deep in thought, Rodney slowly advanced to where she lay then awoke her, holding a knife to her throat.

"Now young lady," he said.

"Just relax and do as I say and you won't get hurt."

He couldn't very well rape her with a knife in his hand so he laid it down and ripped the top of her dress exposing her breast. She tried to fight him off the best she could by screaming and scratching his face. He responded by punching her in the face just below her left eye almost knocking her unconscious. He used this opportunity to lower his pants; Rachel returning to full consciousness and seeing what was about to take place, lifted her knee up so forcefully hitting him in the testicles. He rolled over in excruciating pain, giving Rachel an opportunity to escape from his diabolical attack of rape; then she ran and jumped frantically into her buggy and raced home to safety.

Rachel arrived home hysterical and in tears. Her mother tried to calm Rachel down in an attempt to find out what had happened. When Mrs. Richardson extracted the gruesome details of Rodney's attempted rape, she decided to report the rape attempt to Sheriff Rooney that evening. Two hours had passed, and Rachel was still trying to restore her composure from her traumatic experience when Billy rode up to the Richardson home. Mrs. Richardson greeted Billy at the door, explaining to him that something terrible had happened to Rachel. Without another word of explanation Billy rushed into Rachel's room to find her trembling, with tears rolling down her face and a large ugly bruise under her left eye. Rachel was too distraught to talk, so Janette took Billy aside and explained to Billy the terrible and cowardly act of rape that was attempted by Rodney. When Billy heard what had happened, he was furious and exploded in a fit of uncontrollable rage. Mrs. Richardson put her hand on Billy's shoulder to try to calm him down and told him that she was going to report this attempted rape to Sheriff Rooney this evening. Billy turned to Mrs. Richardson and said,

"No, I don't want you to report this incident to Sheriff Rooney. I'll take care of this matter in my own way."

"No, Billy, no; he's a grown man; you'll only get hurt, or worse yet you'll get yourself killed and what good will that be for Rachel?"

"I can appreciate your concern Mrs. Richardson, but don't worry about me I'm not going into the lion's den with a sling shot; I said I'll take care of this matter, and I will!"

Billy could not control his anger and rage and did not want to discuss the matter any more; then turned around and rushed out of the Richardson household heading for town in search of Rodney Bean. Arriving in town Billy went directly to the dry goods store and up to his room. He took the six shooter out of the top draw and strapped it to his right leg, then headed for the Gaylord Saloon where he was sure to find Rodney Bean. Billy had never been seen in town wearing a gun before and most folks thought that Billy didn't even own a gun, let alone know how to shoot one.

Sure enough Rodney was in the saloon boasting to his friends about his encounter with that little bitch of a Rachel. Surrounded by his friends with smiles on their faces, he went on to explain,

"I was just about to get into her pants when she kicked me in the balls and got away."

They all laughed heartily that little Rachel outwitted big Rodney. At that instant, Billy walked through the door just in time to hear him boast,

"She won't get away from me next time, I'm going to nail that little bitch."

"There won't be any next time, that's the last woman you'll ever molest!" shouted Billy.

Rodney looked at Billy in amazement and said,

"Well if it isn't Billy, Rachel's hero and he's packing a gun. Did you come here to defend Rachel's honor? Tell me, do you intend to use that gun, boy?"

His friends began to laugh, but Billy wasn't laughing. He walked up to where Rodney was standing looked him in the eyes, and said,

"You're nothing but a degenerate bastard prying on defenseless women to satisfy your animal instincts. I've met some depraved and immoral individuals in my life, but never have I ever encountered anyone as disgusting as you"

Rodney's face turned red, his lips tightened with anger as he rose from his bar stool and said,

"Boy, you now made me very mad, and you're not going to live to see your next birthday."

Billy had no enemies in town, everyone liked him and respected him. The bystanders in the saloon knew that and shouted,

"Let him be Rodney; he's only a kid."

"Yeah, he doesn't realize what he's saying Rodney; let him be."

Rodney wasn't the type to take advice, especially good advice and responded,

Vengeance

"He's a kid alright, with a big mouth and a six shooter strapped to his leg, and I'm going to put him to sleep and have Rachel all for myself."

Billy smiled and said,

"The only thing you'll have all for yourself is a pine box."

With that remark, Rodney called Billy a son of a bitch, drew his gun and pointed it at Billy, but before Rodney could pull the trigger Billy planted a bullet between his eyes scattering half his brains on the saloon floor. Billy blew the smoke away from the tip of his gun and put his gun back in his holster and walked out having no remorse for killing Rodney. Billy had a deep seated hatred for men who abuse women especially those with rape on their minds. The bystanders couldn't believe what they had just witnessed. Nice little Billy from the dry goods store had just laid to rest the biggest and toughest trouble maker in town. Folks in town still refer to Billy, as "Little Billy," since they still remembered him as a scrawny little twelve year old boy, working at John Adam's dry goods store just a few years ago, although he was now close to 6 feet tall and had a visibly muscular body. From now on no one would call him "Little Billy" anymore. The news of the encounter between Billy and Rodney spread through town like greased lighting. Billy was now a celebrated hero; everyone was glad that the town was rid of Rodney including the undertaker, since business was slow lately. Billy's celebrity did not affect his demeanor at all; he still went to work at the dry goods store and was as polite, courteous and cooperative as ever with the customers.

When Sheriff Rooney heard the news he was as shocked and bewildered as all the folks in town. Billy was in the clear since it was a case of self defense. Rodney drew on Billy. Rooney was secretly glad that Rodney was gone, a major headache was lifted from his brow. Joe Young was away herding cattle at the time when the showdown between Billy and Rodney took place. When he returned and heard the news of the encounter he was sure glade that Billy was able to take care of himself, remarking that,

"If anything had happened to Billy that scoundrel would have to face me."

Billy road out to the Richardson house to tell Rachel and her mother that Rodney would never again molest Rachel or any other women in town. They both knew what Billy meant, but most of all they were overjoyed to see Billy returned to them safely.

The social atmosphere in El Paso greatly improved, becoming more congenial since Rodney bit the dust. His cronies too evaporated into invisibility since they had lost their leader; they had become harmless and irrelevant. Outside of a little excitement at Rose's place, the citizens of El Paso went about their daily business free from unexpected violence, which meant that Sheriff Rooney could take an afternoon nap each and every day. The only business for the town's undertaker now was to bury those people who died from natural causes. This state of affairs continued happily for the next couple of years.

CHAPTER FIVE
COMING OF AGE

During these quiet years, the town's population was steadily growing along with the size and scope of the dry goods store. Mr. Adam was becoming a wealthy man, although he had lost his youthful gait and had a band of gray hair around his balding head. The duties and responsibilities of running a large store were becoming a little burdensome for Mr. Adam; he therefore delegated more of his daily responsibilities for running the store to Billy. The fame and size of Mr. Adam's dry goods store spread far and wide; people came from all over the general area just to shop there. The fame and prosperity of Mr. Adam's dry goods store also attracted the attention of outlaws.

There were three remaining outlaws from the Logan gang still at large and actively terrorizing local merchants and banks throughout Texas and Oklahoma. They had heard that people would come from miles around just to shop at El Paso's dry goods store. It didn't take Tom Sweeney the leader of this gang of three long to realize that the dry goods store in El Paso would be their next target. Sweeney was the oldest member of the original Logan gang, dating back to when they were at full strength, with ten desperadoes. During the passage of time, many of their members were either killed in the execution of their crimes or jailed by law enforcement. Now Tom Sweeney and his other two companions, Sid Gould and Gus Boyd sat at a table with a bottle of whiskey to map out a strategy for robbing the dry goods store. Their anticipation of a lucrative take from this establishment overshadowed the danger of a competent sheriff and a notorious bounty hunter named Joe Young. Their strategy would have to include the whereabouts of the Sheriff and Joe Young during the execution of their robbery.

They finalized their strategy as followers: they would occupy separate quarters while in town and keep a low profile; then they would wait till Sheriff Rooney was out of town on official business and Joe Young was indisposed, then make their move. They then put their plan into operation; each rode into town on different days so as not to attract attention and took up residence in the local hotel and waited. After two weeks had passed their opportunity came. Sheriff Rooney and his deputy would be out of town for two days on official business, transferring a prisoner from the El Paso jail to a jail in New Mexico to stand trail for murder. Joe Young would be at Rose's place for a couple of hours; that's when they would make their move.

So on a busy Saturday afternoon two of the Logan gang, Tom Sweeney and Sid Gould, walked into the dry goods store leaving Gus Boyd outside tending to the horses and as lookout. Mr. Adam was at the cash box checking out a customer when Sweeney walked up with a gun pointed at Mr. Adam and said,

"O. K. Mr., if you want to see another day put all that cash in this bag and make it quick."

Mr. Adam hesitated awhile in a semi-state of shock, when Billy chimed in,

"Do what the man said John!"

"Now that's one smart kid," replied Sweeney.

Mr. Adam still hesitated, so Billy nudged him aside and began filling the bag with all the cash they had.

"That's it Mr., that's all the cash we have," said Billy

"I know there's more cash around here someplace and you better get it quick before I start ripping up this place and your old man with it."

Billy's only concern was for the safety of Mr. Adam, so he went to another location, opened the draw and took out all the cash and put it in Sweeney's bag. Satisfied with their take, they left and rode off. Joe Young returned two hours after the robbery to find the store in disarray and Billy attending to Mr. Adam. Billy explained to Joe the details of the robbery. Joe Young knew every square foot of terrain within a 100 mile radius of El Paso and knew just about where they would hold up for the night, and said,

"The most likely place for them to camp out for the night would be a small enclave located near a stream and almost surrounded by trees and shrubbery, about fifty miles Northeast from here. I'm heading there right now before they break camp."

"Wait Joe, I'm going with you!" shouted Billy.

"No, Billy, You're not ready for this round up; it's much too dangerous, stay here and take care of Mr. Adam and the store."

Billy was insistent that he go along. But Joe was equally insistent that he stay behind, so Billy stayed.

Joe was gone for at least twenty minutes and during that time Billy was thinking, what if something should happen to Joe, he would need help. After all there are three against one and you never could tell what could go wrong; Billy was now convinced that he should follow Joe. Billy knew the place that Joe was referring to, so there was no guess work involved. Billy then rushed up stairs to his room, opened the top draw and strapped his six shooter to his leg. Scrambling downstairs at breakneck speed and out the door he went, jumping on Lightning and off he rode in pursuit of Joe.

It was over an hour's ride to the enclave, so Joe took his time; he wanted to give the bandits time to set up camp and relax before busting in on them. It was a slow ride and as Joe got nearer to the designated location he could see the smoke from their camp site rising from a distance. Joe dismounted from Thunder about a quarter of a mile from their camp site and went the rest of the way on foot. It was just about dusk with a full moon surrounded by a blue sky; as Joe approached slowly and silently toward their camp site. He now could hear them talking but could not see them, since the camp site was almost completely surrounded by trees and shrubbery. Joe heard one of the bandits telling the others how the old man was paralyzed with fear looking down the barrel of Sweeney's gun and how the kid saved the old man's life by pushing him aside and filling Sweeney's bag with the cash. Joe waited a while longer, then rushed in with his six shooters pointed at the bandits; when he noticed that there were only two of them there,

"Where's your other playmate," Joe shouted.

"Right behind you,"Sweeney replied.

"And drop your guns or you're dead on the spot."

Joe dropped his guns. Sweeney then informed the other two outlaws,

"Do you know who this guy is? He's Joe Young, the bounty hunter and he won't be hunting our kind any more."

Gus chimed in,

"How lucky could we be; all this loot and Joe Young too."

"Let's get rid of him right now and hang him high," said Sid Gould.

"That's a good idea," said Sweeney, as he detached his rope from the side of his horse.

Joe was angry at himself for not counting heads before jumping into the fire. He knew that his time had come and he would not see another day. Within a few seconds, thoughts of the past flashed through Joe's mind: Billy, the Adam family, Rachel, Rose and her girl, he would not see them anymore all because of a stupid mistake. Unbeknown to Joe, Billy was not far behind;

could he get there in time to save Joe?

Billy too saw the smoke from the camp fire in the distance, and as he got closer he saw Thunder tied to a tree. He dismounted and left Lightning next to Thunder as he moved toward the campsite. Billy sensed trouble and hoped that he wasn't too late. As he silently edged closer to the campsite he heard them talking, then listened. He heard one of them boasting how pretty Joe will look dangling from a tree. Sid and Gus were sitting on a fallen tree drinking coffee and waiting for the show to start. Sweeney tied Joe's hands behind his back as he sat on top of one of the outlaw's horse. Although it was dusk there was still good visibility as Sweeney approached Joe with the noose; stretching toward Joe he placed it around his neck, just as Billy appeared with his six shooter pointed at Sweeney, and said,

"Drop that noose and your gun belt too, Mr., and do it real slowly; make one false move to touch your gun piece and you'll never see another sun rise."

Sweeney did what he was told while Gus and Sid were eyeing Billy. Sid recognized Billy as the teenager who worked at the dry goods store. He had been intimidated by Sweeney enough to fill Sweeney's bag with cash while the old man watched. Sid whispered to Gus,

"We can take this kid; he's not going to shoot."

Then they both rose slowly from where they were sitting, and Sid said,

"Now son, be careful with that gun, you're liable to hurt somebody with it."

"That somebody will be you! If you take another step closer, you're dead."

They didn't heed Billy's warning but took that fatal step forward while drawing their guns. Billy discharged two bullets and the Logan gang was down to one.

"Now Mr., I want you to cut Joe loose and if you make one false move, you'll be as dead as your buddies."

Sweeney was smart enough to take Billy at his word and removed the nose from around Joe's neck. As soon as Joe was cut loose he went for his guns, strapped them on, and said,

"Billy, I never was so glad to see anyone in my life as I did you. You saved my life and I'll never forget it. I'm sure glad you didn't listen to me when I told you to stay in town and take care of Mr. Adam. You did a man's job and you can ride with me anytime. But as for now, we'll have to sleep here for the night; come morning we'll take these two stiffs and Sweeney back to town along with the money they stole."

Sweeney was looking for any opportunity to escape since he knew that if he was brought back to El Paso to face trial, he would be found guilty and hanged. Joe could read Sweeney's mind and took all necessary precautions to prevent his escape. Before Joe and Billy could go to sleep, they had to tie up Sweeney securely so he could not escape during the night. Joe did this by tightly tying a rope around Sweeney's ankles, then extending the rope to a position where he could tie both his wrists behind his back. Having secured both his feet and hands he threw the rest of the rope over a large tree branch and tied the other end of the rope to the ankle of his right foot. Any tugging on the rope during the night would alert Joe. With Sweeney safely secured for the night, they hit the sack.

At the first sign of daybreak, Joe and Billy rose from their slumber. Joe cut Sweeney loose and instructed him to tie up the dead bodies and throw them over the saddles of their horses. Joe made some coffee and prepared whatever rations the outlaws were carrying with them while Billy went for Thunder and Lightning. Upon Billy's return, he sat down with Joe for a cup of coffee and some biscuits before starting on their long trek back to town. In preparation for their journey, Joe told Sweeney to put his hands over his head while he put a rope around Sweeney's chest and under his arm pits and knotted the rope behind his back. The other end of the rope would be held by Joe; any attempt by Sweeney to escape, he would be yanked off his horse. When all was ready, Joe said, "O. K., let's head back to town."

It was a strange sight indeed to see five horses in tandem, the first lead by Billy on top of Lightning followed by the two dead stiffs across the saddles of their horses, then came Sweeney the last of the Logan gang with a rope around his chest, the other end of which was held by Joe on top of Thunder, like a man walking a dog.

As they neared town, the queue of five horses could be seen from afar. The citizens of El Paso began to gather, forming a crowd as the line of horses approached the outskirts of town. The town's people stared in amazement as they watched the line of horses saunter down main street; thankful that the last of the Logan gang was captured or dead. Never again would they terrorize El Paso or any other town in the Southwest. Joe stopped off at the Sheriff's office to unload the two dead bodies and have Sweeney put behind bars by the caretaker of the jail, in the absence of Sheriff Rooney and his deputy. The town's undertaker was waiting at the jail ready and eager to tag the two stiffs and prepare them for burial. Sweeney would remain in jail to await trial for robbery and a multitude of other crimes committed during his reign of terror. While Joe was attending to the incarceration of Sweeney, Billy brought the bag of stolen money back to Mr. Adam. The money was secondary to Mr. Adam; he and Molly were overjoyed to have Billy returned to them safe and sound; Billy was like a son to them since they had no offspring of their own. When Sheriff Rooney returned and heard from Joe what had happened, he was grateful to both Joe and Billy for putting an end to the Logan gang; but most of all he was shocked and amazed by Billy's courage and foresight in assisting Joe in the demise of the Logan gang. It was Joe who told Sheriff Rooney that if it had not been for Billy he would not be alive today and the Logan gang would still be at large. Sheriff Rooney again thanked Joe and Billy for watching over the town in his absence, and said,

"Fellows I don't know whether you realize it or not but there is a bounty of $8,000 on the head of each of the Logan gang, dead or alive and you two are entitled to the reward."

It came as a surprise to Joe and Billy. They knew there was a bounty on their heads, but they didn't realize it amounted to that much money. They took it in stride and accepted the money with big broad smiles.

After the public trial and conviction of Tom Sweeney, the judge sentenced him to be hanged by the neck within a fortnight. The hanging of Tom Sweeney had a calming effect on the town of El Paso; word had spread throughout the Southwest that El Paso was not a town in which to commit mischief. Criminals knew that the town had a no nonsense Sheriff, a famous bounty hunter and a teen age shooter who had already laid to rest a town's bully and two of the Logan gang. So for the next couple of years life in El Paso went on in a quiet and orderly fashion, thanks to Joe and Billy.

Time had passed, and Billy was now twenty years of age and he decided that the time had come for him to fulfill his mission and avenge the tragedy that befell his family. But before setting out on his journey, he had to seek out the whereabouts of Simon Ganz. Ganz was a warehouse of information on how to track down individuals; but more importantly he knew what to watch out for, in the way of traps and schemes which might be undetectable to a novice. Ganz was now retired, living a quiet and peaceful life somewhere in Northeast Texas; he had many Indian friends around those parts, so Billy had to be careful in his attempt to locate Ganz. He had to make clear that his intentions were friendly and not hostile.

Before leaving, Billy had to explain his hiatus from El Paso to Molly and John Adam, Joe Young, and most of all to Rachel. One evening when the day's business was concluded, Billy informed Molly and John that there was something of great importance he had to tell them. Molly and John couldn't imagine what could be so important and listened attentively as Billy explained: Billy told Molly and John that he would be leaving for a short time to attend to a matter that could no longer be postponed. Billy had to give them a reasonable explanation to justify his eminent departure. Without going into the gruesome details, he explained to his adopted parents the circumstances that brought him to seek employment at the dry goods store some eight years ago. It was still difficult for Billy to talk about the tragedy so long passed and without going into the frightful details, he said,

"Eight years ago, my parent's home was broken into and vandalized by three nefarious and immoral men from Astec, New Mexico; they stole $3,000 from my parents, then began to ravage my mother in such a way that provoked my father's anger; he came to her defense, but before my father could get up from his chair to help my mother he was shot dead. My eight year old sister and I were watching from upstairs in horror. My sister witnessing my father being shot, could not control her emotions any longer and oblivious to the danger, rushed downstairs to stop the slaughter, only to be shot dead before she reached the bottom step. In order to avoid being murdered I busted through my bedroom window and on to the ground below and ran as fast as I could into the surrounding woods. And as a final act of depravity they murdered my mother and burned our house to the ground."

Molly and John were nonplus and speechless, and could not argue against Billy's leaving; instead they told Billy that they would pray for his safe return. Mr. Adam told Billy that the dry goods store would be his some day when they departed this world. With tears in their eyes, Billy hugged and kissed both of them goodby and assured them that he would return as soon as possible. He was now off to explain his departure to Joe.

Joe Young was relaxing at home when Billy dropped in.

"Well Billy, it sure is good to see you; sit down and have a drink."

"I certainly could use a drink Joe, but I can't stay long because I just stopped in to say good by. I'll be leaving soon to take care of that matter that I had mentioned to you some time ago. At that time you were interested in knowing what my mission was and I told you that I would tell you in good time; well, that time is now"

Every time Billy retold his story his eyes would become watery. Billy then told Joe exactly what he had told Molly and John. As this horrific story unfolded, Billy could see the anger swelling in Joe's face and by the time Billy finished his explanation, Joe was as angry as a mad dog, and said,

"Billy, I'm going with you on your mission and don't give me any argument."

"No, Joe, this is a personal matter that I have to deal with, although I understand why you would want to join me."

"Billy, I won't interfere with your plans and I'll leave the fate of these men for you to deal with; I just want to tag along as a bystander and be there if you should need my help."

"Joe, you've been like a brother to me ever since I arrived in town, and you taught me everything I know; I can't in good conscience deny your request to join me."

With that settled, Billy explained to Joe, "I will be gone for a while, to seek the whereabouts of Simon Ganz. Simon Ganz is a warehouse of useful information and I would like to pick his brains for any advice he would offer. I would especially like to know the best way to track down these three scoundrels and what dirty tricks they might use against me. When I return from my visit with Ganz, we'll start off together, Joe, O.K.?"

Joe agreed.

Now the most difficult and emotional explanation of all would be to get Rachel to understand the necessity for Billy to leave town for awhile. While riding out to the Richardson home, he mulled over what he was going to say to Rachel. When he arrived, Rachel was waiting for him and greeted him with a big hug and lots of kisses.

"Rachel," he said, "I have to speak to you about a matter of great importance."

They sat down on the veranda, Billy paused for a while, still trying to think of the best way to explain his departure to Rachel. Then Billy explained: his explanation was basically what he had told to the Adams and Joe. Rachel understood but was in tears, worrying about the possibility of something happening to Billy and never seeing him again. At the very least he would be gone for a long time.

"I don't suppose I could talk you out of this vendetta?" Rachel asked.

"No, Rachel, I could never be a happy man knowing that these three villainous creatures still live and roam free. It would have a dire effect on my personality and eventually effect our relationship, so it would be best for me to settle this matter once and for all. By the way Rachel, Joe Young will be riding alone with me and that should make you feel a little better. And when I return, we'll be together forever, never to part again."

With tears in her eyes, she told Billy,

"Billy, please be careful; do what you have to do and return to me as soon as possible."

Billy felt a little choked up as he hugged Mrs. Richardson and said goodby. Janette was somewhat apprehensive concerning Billy's departure, realizing his life and Rachel's future rested on Billy's success. He then turned to Rachel and embraced her in his arms with an extended hug and kisses, with tears rolling down Rachel's face and Billy's eyes becoming a little watery; he then thought it best to make a quick departure. In the morning, Billy would be off in search of Simon Ganz.

CHAPTER SIX
THE LEGEND

Who is this man Simon Ganz? Where did he come from? How did he acquire such an awesome reputation? Where is he now? These are the questions most often asked by my readers, and I will try to answer these questions by stating the facts as I know them. It is not my intent to glorify, or portray Simon Ganz as a hero; although the better angles of his nature prevailed more often than not.

Simon Ganz was born in Western Pennsylvania in the year 1835, the only son of James and Lilly Ganz. They owned a large spread of land about 10 miles from the West Virginia border; and were true pioneers in the sense that they lived off the land and whatever nature provided. The area was heavily wooded, with a ruck of lakes and streams that added aesthetic beauty to the surrounding countryside. The woods abounded with wild life. Although the Indians and buffalo of the area were long gone, remnants of their previous existence were still in evidence by fragments of buffalo bonds and Indian artifacts.

The only domestic animals they housed were two horses used for travel and to plow the fields and a mongrel dog named Bandit, part collie and part German shepherd. Bandit was Simon's constant companion during his youthful years and he would rarely stray form his side.

The care and use of fire arms was an essential skill for human existence in the forests of Western Pennsylvania; Simon was taught that skill at an early age. It wasn't long before Simon mastered that skill and became an expert marksman.

A lake nearby was the home and breeding area for thousands of frogs. Their chirking could be heard from early evening and through the night; at first their chirking sounds would either lull you to sleep or keep you awake half the night, depending on your state of mind. After a week or two, Simon and his parents became accustomed to hearing their love calls, and henceforth became oblivious to the sound.

At age 10, Simon would walk down to the lake with his rifle and shoot frogs for target practice and viands. He would terminate his shooting session after accumulating several dozen frogs; he then would sever their legs at the hips and remove their skins as if to pull their pants off. The remains of the frogs were left on the ground as carrion for carnivorous forest animals to feed on during the night. The frog legs made a tasty side dish when roasted or fried; and Simon never killed more frogs than the family could consume for dinner. When Simon returned the following morning, the remains of the frogs were gone. The tell tail signs of the feces left behind indicated to Simon the kind of animal that had been feasting on the carrion during the night, most often it was a coyote, fox, or wolf. It didn't take Simon long to become bored with shooting frogs close to the shore line; it wasn't much of a challenge, so he moved a few feet back from the shoreline each day, rather than shooting frogs in the middle of the lake making them difficult to retrieve. Simon was such an excellent shooter with the rifle that the frogs did not have much of a chance for survival. So he decided to give the frogs better odd at survival and substituted a pistol for his rifle. The six shooter represented a greater challenge for Simon and gave the frog a chance to survive; but as he became more skilled in handling his six shooter, it too became boring.

In time, Simon took to hunting larger game such as turkey, quail, ducks, deer, and bears. Simon loved wild creatures and felt a little remorseful after killing one. He would never kill an animal for the sake of killing, but only to put food on the table. His personal code of ethics governed his hunting forays and he would never shoot a bird or mammal at rest or in a compromising position. He realized at an early age that the only defense a wild animal has is to fly or run from danger, and he would give the animals the opportunity to flee. With Simon providing the meat for the family and his parents tilling the soil, the Ganz household was well fed.

While Simon and his parents were eking out a living in the wilds of Southwestern Pennsylvania, they maintained a keen interest in the country's state of affaires. Although they did not have access to a daily newspaper, they frequently visited the nearest village of Uniontown, 10 miles to the east' to replenish supplies, and update their knowledge of current events. All members of the Ganz family looked forward to their frequent trips into town as a pleasant diversion from their daily routine. The country was growing and so was Simon. While Simon was at the lake shooting frogs and developing his skills with the rifle and pistol, President James Polk signed into law the "Annexation of Texas," making Texas the 28th state to be admitted into the Union. Simon grew from youthful adolescence into manhood during the years of 1840 to 1855 in an atmosphere ranging from relative tranquility to violent confrontation. During that fifteen year period, the country became more polarized, embellished in polemic oratory, social upheavals, and insurrection. Most of the men in town would congregate at the local watering hole to discuss the current topics of the day, and James was always an active participant in these discussions. The slavery question and the disposition of the lands in the Western territory were the main topics discussed and passionately debated.

The slavery question was the most contentious and emotional issue in the nation. Everyone had an opinion, and James was no exception. He viewed slavery as an evil and sinful institution, having no place in a civilized society; the degradation of human beings was odious and disgraceful to him.

James was a free soil Democrat and advocated that states seeking admission to the Union from newly acquired territories as a result of the Mexican War should be admitted as free states. The overwhelming majority of Northerners were free soil people, but this did not translate into abolitionism. The population in the North was by no means united in thought or philosophy, as to the disposition of the slave question. Some were indifferent to the South's peculiar institution, others demanded total abolition of all forms of servitude, but most of the Northern population simply opposed the extension of slavery into the new territories of the West beyond the boundaries where it already existed. To this end, the leading statesmen and protagonists of the country added their voices to the National debate, each of whom had their supporters and detractors.

The abolitionist had an eloquent and tenacious spokesman in the person of William Lloyd Garrison, editor of the "Liberator" newspaper. His arguments solid and his following substantial, he editorialized the institution of slavery in the most damnable terms, as a diabolical system that relegates the Negro to the level of a farm animal or a thing, to be bought or sold like a piece of furniture. His daily diatribe against those who would hold the Negro in bondage made him the most hated man in the South.

Another eloquent and influential person was Senator Henry Clay of Kentucky, recognized for his ability to mediate controversial political problems; he established the "Colonization Society," advocating the voluntary return of free Negroes back to their native Africa or Haiti. The plan was not popular amongst free blacks and proved to be too expensive to execute. However, thousands of free Negroes, unhappy with their social status in America, accepted the re-colonization offer and emigrated back to East-Africa and founded the Republic of Liberia.

However, the most debated and controversial legislation in Congress was the doctrine of "Popular Sovereignty," the brain child of the "Little Giant," Senator Stephen A. Douglas, of Illinois. The doctrine proclaimed that the people of the territory should decide whether to admit a state into the Union as a free or slave state. Unfortunately the legislation received little support from both sides of the political spectrum. The Northen representatives in Congress viewed the legislation as creating conditions for civil unrest and violence as free soil and slave state immigrants vied for control of the territory. Representatives from the South protested that "Popular Sovereignty" violated the property rights of Southern settlers and did not guarantee the extension of slavery into the new territories.

The representatives in the Congress of the United States were turbulent in manner and antagonistic in speech toward each other; that precluded any rational compromise to be consummated on the subject of slavery. Congress was a microcosm of the country. The subsequent tensions and animosities that prevailed in Congress resurrected talk of cession, which echoed through the halls of Congress. The present and future events during the 1850's were ever present on the mind of Simon as he grew from adolescence into manhood.

While the Kansas-Nebraska territory was in a constant state of social and political upheaval, the Ganz family was living a happy and serene life, free of violence and confrontation. However, the year 1854 ushered in a change of circumstances that had a profound effect on the Ganz household. On a hot summer day, while Simon was out hunting and James working the fields, Lilly was busy preparing the noon day meal. Suddenly Lilly felt a sharp pain in the lower right side of her abdomen and she paused till the pain subsided, then resumed her chores. When the pain returned, she thought it best to lie down till she felt better. Lunch time was always a pleasant affair when James, Simon, and Lilly would share their thoughts and any unusual happenings of the day. On this particular day, James found Lilly prostrate in bed complaining of abdominal pain and soreness. He sympathized with Lilly, and advised her to remain in bed till she felt well enough to resume her normal activities. Simon entered a few minutes after James and was equally concerned for his mother's condition and assured her that they would take care of things while she was resting. Both James and Simon were of the opinion that her malady was caused by indigestion and she would be fine in a day or two. However, the following morning brought no relief for Lilly and the pain persisted throughout the day; that evening Lilly developed a slight fever, which James attributed to a cold. The next morning Lilly was burning with fever accompanied by nausea and weakness. James now realized that Lilly's malady was more serious than indigestion or a cold; he told Simon to ride to Uniontown and search out Dr. Myers and bring him to their home. Simon left immediately, arriving in Uniontown in late evening. After locating Dr. Myers, he explained his mother's condition, and beseeched Dr. Myers to come to his mothers aid immediately. Dr. Myers told Simon that he had a few more patients to attend to that evening and by the time he finished making his rounds, it would be to late for him to travel to his homestead. He assured Simon that he would be at his homestead at the break of dawn. With that, Simon left for home; arriving home, he explained to his father the reasons why Dr. Myers was unable to come that evening and assured his father that Dr. Myers would be there at the break of dawn. James then went to Lilly's bedside, and assured her that Dr. Myers would be at her bedside early in the morning; then he tried to make Lilly as comfortable as possible during the night. True to his word, the next morning shortly after the sun appeared on the horizon, Dr. Myers arrived at the Ganz farm and was immediately escorted to Lilly's bedside. He proceeded to examine Lilly while James and Simon were in the next room nervously awaiting Dr. Myers's diagnosis. He concluded his examination by lightly touching her lower abdomen which evoked a painful moan from Lilly. He then made her comfortable and retired to the next room to speak to Mr. Ganz.

"Well, James, it's just as I suspected; she has acute appendicitis, I'm sorry to say, but there's not very much that medical science can do for her. I can give her medication to ease the pain, but her faith is now in God's hands."

Those words coming from Dr. Myers saddened both James and Simon, who would become more despondent in the coming weeks; but for now they were determined to display a sanguine appearance in Lilly's presence. They made her as comfortable as possible and attended to her every need right to the end; it wasn't long before peritonitis set in and Lilly slipped away into the hereafter.

James made a simple wooden casket and laid Lilly's body within, then sealed the lid shut. James wanted to give Lilly a decent burial and thought that the cemetery in Uniontown would be an appropriate place to put her body to rest. Early next morning, James and Simon loaded the casket onto their wagon and rode into Uniontown. James made arrangements to have her body interred at Christ Cemetery; then he placed a wooden marker, with a small cross on top, with an inscription that read,

"Lillian Anderson Ganz
Rest in Peace
1815-1854"

Lilly's death had a profound effect on James's and Simon's dispositions. Their enthusiasm and desire to operate the farm was substantially diminished. And their home lost its vitality and attractiveness; every room was a reminder of Lilly's absence. To ward off their anguish and despondency, they would visit Uniontown several times a week, stopping off at Lilly's grave site to pray; then on to the town saloon, where they would discuss topics of local and national importance with fellow patrons.

About two months after Lilly's demise, a friend of James heard of a proclamation by the "New England Emigrant Act Co." that would provide aid to farmers from Eastern and mid-Western states, to promote free soil settlements in Kansas. This news peaked James's interest, and he decided to investigate further as to the conditions and requirements for a land grant. James read the details of the land grant offer several times and viewed it as an opportunity to rid his mind of the haunting and disastrous memories of the past few months and start a new life in the Kansas territory. Before James made a final decision, he would have to talk it over with Simon; they sat down at a table in the local saloon to discuss their present situation and the land grant offer. They talked for hours while imbibing cold beers, and the more they talked, the more interested and excited they became in regards to their Western adventure. The first order of business was to sell their farm and use the proceeds to finance their Western trek. James put an add in the Uniontown newspaper for the sale of his house and property; and within three weeks, he was able to negotiate a price $1,800 for the sale of his farm. After settling his affairs in Uniontown, he wired the bulk of the funds from the sale of his farm to the Territorial Bank of Kansas City. Now that everything was in order, they were ready to travel West; but first they went to the local saloon for a brief farewell celebration; James said good-by to his friends, then he and Simon rode to Christ Cemetery to pay their final respect to Lilly and say a pray at her resting place. Arriving home they loaded the wagon with all the necessities for the long trip. With renewed enthusiasm and interest, James and Simon began their trek West to the Kansas-Nebraska territory and the unknown.

CHAPTER SEVEN
THE CHALLENGE

James and Simon left their old farm at 5 A.M. on a hot summer day and never looked back. They traveled all that day and into the early evening, until they came upon lush grass land at the confluence of the Ohio and Scioto rivers. They considered the surrounding area an ideal spot to graze and water their horses before heading for the nearest town of Portsmouth, Ohio, five miles to the west where they could replenish their supplies and get a hot meal and a comfortable bed for the night. While the horses were grazing on sprouts of new grass, James and Simon were relaxing under an old oak thee; suddenly they heard the piecing sound of a scream coming from the woods to the rear about one hundred yards in distance. The screams were sounds of pain and were repeated at intervals of four to five seconds; their curiosity was aroused so they decided to investigate the source of those terrifying sounds. When they arrived at the scene they were shocked and horrified to see a young Negro boy tenaciously holding on to the trunk of a tree while a big husky man was laying the lash of the whip to the boy's back. To be a silent witness to such brutality was beyond the scope of human tolerance for James and Simon and James interrupted the brutal beating by imploring,

"What possible reason do you have to justify such a whipping."

"Well, if you must know this nigger is a run-away slave and I was hired to return him to his rightful master."

"You mean you're going to return him to 'God' by beating him to death?" James replied.

"I mean he's going back to the plantation in Kentucky where he ran away from and I advise you gentlemen to mind your own business if you know what's good for you."

"Well Sir." said James, "I don't approve of such cruel treatment so I'm going to make it my business and ask you to stop whipping that boy."

"How do you propose to stop me? I see you're not packing a gun and that shit heel next to you doesn't look like he knows how to use his gun."

Simon now entered the conversation, "You're right; I am packing a gun but as to whether I know how to use it or not remains to be seen, so I'll ask you for the last time to stop whipping that boy."

The big man smiled with a sneer of defiance as he raised his whip over his head for another strike at the boy's back. Such arrogance prompted Simon to draw his gun and shoot the whip from his hand. The blood from his wounded hand was running down his arm as he pulled out a bandana to wrap around his hand while shouting,

"You'll pay for interfering in something that is none of your business; this isn't the end of the story."He retreated, mounted his horse and rode away. Simon walked over to the Negro boy who could not have been more than sixteen years of age, and asked,

"Boy, let me ask you a foolish question. Why did you run away from the plantation?"

"The Master worked me from sun rise to sun set, six days a week, and if I stopped to rest the overseer would whip me; I couldn't take it any more, I rather die than live like dat, so I runs away."

The welts on the boy's back attested to his inhumane treatment.

"I understand why you're running away but where are you running to?" Simon asked.

"I is running to Cincinnata, there is an underground railroad there that will take me to Canada and freedom."

"Cincinnati is a good fifty miles from here, so we'll give you something to eat and a clean shirt, and you could leave at will."

The boy did just that, he eat the food voraciously, put on a clean shirt, then thanked James and Simon and took off like a rabbit for Cincinnati and hopefully freedom.

In the meantime, James and Simon were getting hungry and decided to head into the nearest town a few miles away for a hot meal and a comfortable bed. Arriving in town they registered for a room at the only hotel in town, The Boar's Head. After cleaning up they went down stairs for dinner and while enjoying their first hot meal in two days, who should walk in to interrupt their meal but the big husky one with his hand still wrapped in his bandana and accompanied by a gun slinger friend of his. They looked around the room and as soon as the big husky one spotted James and Simon having dinner he smiled and walked over to their table, and said,

"Well look who's here, now Mr. Busybody you're going to pay for interfering in something that was none of your business; to start with there was a fifty dollar reward for returning the nigger boy to the plantation and his rightful owner and since he got away you're going to pay me the fifty dollars."

"And how do you propose to get the fifty dollars?" Simon asked.

The husky one frowned with half a smile on his face, saying,

"I can't handle a gun since you bloodied my hand, but my friend here is mighty skilled in its use; so let me put it to you another way, are your lives worth fifty dollars?"

"They certainly are, but your lives are worth nothing dead, so I suggest that you leave now while you can still walk out in one piece."

James interrupted, saying,

"Simon, let's pay the fifty dollars; you know you're not shooting frogs at the lake now."

"Don't worry father the frogs were much more of a challenge and had more dignity than these two unprincipled mercenaries standing before us, especially the big fat ugly one with his arm wrapped up like a sausage."

"Why you dirty son of a bitch," replied the gun slinger and he drew his gun, but Simon beat him to the draw and planted two bullets in his chest, dropping him to the floor like a sack of potatoes.

"And as for you, you ugly bastard, you can bury your gun slinging friend; and if I ever see your ugly face again you'll meet the same fate as he."

The husky one stood over his friend's dead body staring in disbelief, then dragged him out with his one good hand. James and Simon finished their dinner and retired for the night.

The next morning, both father and son were up and about by 7 A.M. Having had a substantial breakfast under their belts, they continued their journey westward. Shortly after their departure James suggested to Simon that they were entitled to a little relaxation and entertainment and the place for that was Cincinnati; the suggestion brought a smile to Simon's face indicating that he too was ready for a little diversion.

"A cold beer and the sight of a few females wouldn't hurt a bit," Simon added.

They arrived in Cincinnati around 11 A.M. and checked out a stable where they could leave their horse and wagon before locating a suitable hotel. The best way to survey the town and find a suitable hotel would be on foot. They walked from one end of the town to the other, observing the many different types of stores, hotels, casinos, saloons, churches and a variety of other establishments that were the lifeblood of the city. During their perambulation they came upon the Royal Hotel, located in the center of town where most of the action is and booked a room for the night. It was a pleasant room with a large bed and a window facing Cincinnati's main drag. They were a little tired and dirty from traveling all morning and decided to bathe and shave before napping for a couple of hours. When they awoke from slumber in the early evening they were fully rested and energized, ready to explore the town.

"Simon, before we leave I would like to talk to you about things in general, which I've been meaning to do for some time now. You know Simon, I've lived a long time and I've learned a great deal; I made some mistakes in life and had some accomplishments, the biggest of which is when I married your mother. Unfortunately, the mistakes you make in life people never forgotten, while your accomplishments are rarely remembered. I would like to mention some of the situations and pit-falls you may encounter during your journey through life so that you may avoid making the same mistakes. My counseling may or may not seem relevant at this time, but should you encounter certain situations when I'm no longer around you may recall your father's advice. The first thing I would like you to remember is never trust anyone when it come to money; now I know there are many honest people in this world, but it's difficult to distinguish the honest from the dishonest. So to play it safe mistrust everyone till proven otherwise. And since we're on the topic of money, the money I received for the sale of our farm was sent to the Territorial National Bank of Kansas, in Kansas City, Kansas, registered in both our names; and I withheld just enough money to see us through to our destination. Finally, when going out for the evening never take more money with you than you intend to spend for that evening's entertainment; that way you'll never regret the following morning any misjudgements you may have made the night before. Even if you follow my advice you're still going to make plenty of mistakes, but at least you'll avoid some of the big ones."

"When I think back to the days of my youth before I met your mother, I was quite a cut up in town, a frequent patron of the local bars and in constant pursuit of loose women; that was the extent of my philandering. Early in life I discovered there are two types of women who frequent bars; the first type are just like us, out for a good time; the other type are those who work for the house, whose job it is to separate you from your money. It doesn't take much to recognize this type since their flamboyant style is apparent to most patrons. These women will cozy up to you and make you think you're something special and agree to be your drinking companion for the evening. I can readily recall during my youth being duped by this type of woman, for my first and only time. This gal and I sat there talking while the waiter kept serving us round after round of whisky. I couldn't understand why I was getting high, while she remained as sober as a judge; it finally dawned on me to switch our drinks in a moment of distraction. I discovered that she was drinking tea, while I was drinking the house's rot gut. I'll never forget the expression on her face when she downed the whiskey; with her eyes wide open she started to cough and gasp for air, then looked at me in an unfriendly manner. That was the end of our coziness; it was an expensive lesson and I got off easy. This is the type of world we live in Simon. And now that I have finished my sermon let's get out of here and do the town."

They walked downstairs and into the gaiety of the town, walking from one end of town to the other, while observing the many different stores and activities that a large town has to offer. They worked up a sizable thirst during their walk tour and were lured into the Golden Nugget Saloon to quench their thirst. They sat down at a table and ordered two beers and two whiskeys. While drinking their boiler makers, Simon caught the eye of a young lady sitting at the bar who returned his glances with half a smile; and within minutes he walked over to her and introduced himself and offered to buy her a drink. She accepted Simon offer and both engaged in a conversation of pleasantries. It was obvious that she was on the make, so Simon asked,

"Tell me do you work for the house or are you free lancing."

"No," she replied, "I'm here strictly on my own."

The conversation then became more serious and intermit. After they both had a few drinks, Simon exclaimed,

"You know alcohol makes me very passionate and seems to bring out the animal in me."

"Well you should do something about that," she replied.

"What would you suggest?" Simon retorted.

"Is $10 an hour too much for you?" she questioned.

"No, I think I can handle that," Simon said.

"Then follow me," she responded.

Before they both retired to a room upstairs which she rented by the month, Simon walked over to his father and told him,

"Pop, I'm going to disappear for an hour; will you still be here when I return?"

"I may or may not son; if not, I'll be back at the hotel, so you have yourself a good time and be careful.."

After she escorted Simon to her private room she locked the door behind her and they both began to disrobe to signify a formal business arrangement. After consummating their love making they both lay side by side in a state of repose. Simon gave the impression that he was dozing off. She sensed the ease at which Simon slipped into slumber and after ten minutes she stirred from her bed causing Simon to notice her departure. Simon partially opened one eye to see what was afoot and observed her riffling through his trousers and dislodging the remaining money from his pockets. Simon jumped out of bed, shouting,

"Put that money back before I lose my temper and forget you're a woman!.."

Startled, she looked at Simon, with her mouth half open, and said,

"I just thought you were going to stay longer than an hour."

"If I wanted to stay longer than an hour you would be the first to know about it! No, you were just trying to hustle me, then do a disappearing act. If I were less than a gentleman I'd give you a good swift kick in the ass and throw you out. Now get dressed and get the hell out of here."

They both began to dress themselves, but she was a lot faster since she had a greater incentive to do so and beat Simon out the door. Simon left the room with his father's sermon ringing in his ear, and returned to the hotel to find his father fast asleep. He replicated his father's action and both got a good night's sleep.

They made an early start the following morning, their destination for the day being Vandalia, Illinois, a distance of two hundred miles. The events of that day revealed no surprises just a hot and dusty drive westward. Their only companion was the blazing sun and a constant thirst. After traveling all day they arrived at their destination, Vandalia, while there was still plenty of daylight left.

They found a town buzzing with excitement over a shooting tournament scheduled for that evening. It was open to all comers who could pay the $20 registration fee; the person who could demonstrate superior skill in the art of shooting his six shooter would be the winner of the contest and would claim the jackpot minis $50, to defray expenses. The contest certainly appealed to Simon and without any hesitation he slapped down his twenty bucks and registered for the shoot out. The contest was scheduled for 6:30 that evening which gave Simon and James ample time to book a room at the "Lady Bird Hotel" and cleanse themselves of the dirt and grime which their had accumulated during their long trek westward. After cleaning up, Simon readied himself for the 6:30 contest by cleaning his six shooter and resting for an hour.

The contest was held just outside the town of Vandalia, and Simon and his father were there waiting for the action to start, along with eighteen other contestants. While Simon was mulling around waiting for the tournament to start one of the spectators engaged Simon in conversation.

"You're new to this contest aren't you Mr.? I don't recall seeing you around town or at any of the previous shootouts."

"Yeah, I'm just passing through and I thought I'd try my luck at this shootout," replied Simon.

"Well, I wish you luck stranger. The guy to beat is Hank Hawkins he's won these contests every time they were held which is every other year for the past ten years so I guess you're out twenty bucks."

"Well, maybe so, we'll just have to wait and see how it turns out."

A committee of five citizens from Vandalia would state the rules of the contest, decide on the targets and declare the winner. The shootout began when a member of the committee placed a target the size of an apple at a distance of fifty feet and gave each contestant five shots at the target. Any shooter missing the target more than once would be eliminated. If all the contestants missed the target more than once, they all would repeat the shootout till some were eliminated. The first round caused four individuals to be sacked. The second round required that they draw and shoot within one second, missing the target more than twice was grounds for elimination, unless everyone missed the target twice. At the end of the second round, six others bit the dust. Now the committee decided on a moving target; they had some purple plums and tied a string around each, then suspended each plum from a tree branch. A committee person announced to the contestants that whoever hit the target three times or more would remain for the finale; the rest of the contestants would be congratulated for their effort and sent packing. Of course, if no one emerged as a winner hey would have to try again. At the end of the penultimate shootout, only Simon and Hank Hawkins remained both of whom hit the target five times. The committee huddled for a few minutes; then the spokesman for the committee announced that the finalist would have to have his back facing the target, turn around, draw and shot; any hesitation on the part of the shooter would be counted as a miss. Hank was the first to shoot. As the plum started to swing he turned around and got off a shot, hitting the target. He then repeated his performance four more times with the same results. However, during his first two shots he hesitated long enough to disqualify those two shoots making his score three out of five. Hank's performance put plenty of pressure on Simon; he knew if he could maintain his composure he would win the contest. Simon's father was silently watching with heightened anxiety as Simon prepared to shoot. The plum started to swing; Simon turned around and fired without hesitation blasting the plum out of existence and repeating that performance four more times. The committee huddled for less than a minute before declaring Simon the winner of the shootout and presenting him with the $310, jackpot. Hank walked over to Simon, and said,

"Congratulations Mr. Ganz, I never thought there was anyone as good a shooter as myself. You put on a splendid performance."

"Thank you," replied Simon. "You put on a pretty good show yourself and had me worried for a while; I thought that I had finally met my match."

During their exchange of pleasantries, Simon invited Hank to join him and his father for dinner that evening at the Lady Bird Hotel which Hank graciously accepted.

"Fine, I'll see you there at nine this evening," said Simon.

"I'll be there," Hank replied

For dinner that evening they dined on prime rib of beef and washed it down with cold beers; during the course of their conversation Simon mentioned his desire to purchase a horse and saddle and asked Hank if he knew of a reliable dealer.

"Yes, I sure do," Hank replied. "There is a stable on the outskirts of town named the Double 'A' Corral that has a fine collection of horses at a reasonable price. Tell Arnold you're a friend of mine and he'll treat you like family."

After dinner they continued their conversation accompanied with a plenitude of liquor. As the hands of the clock approached midnight, Hank thanked Simon for his hospitality and wished Simon and his father good luck on their journey westward, then left for home.

Early the next morning, Simon visited the Double "A" Corraland introduced himself to Arnold. He told Arnold that he was a friend of Hank's and he would like to purchase a horse and saddle.

"Any friend of Hank is a friend of mine; come this way and I'll show you some fine horses."

Arnold displayed several fine horses and told Simon that they were the cream of the crop and he would sell any one of them to Simon for just $200 plus $75 for the saddle. Simon liked what he saw and decided on a brown mare; he gave Arnold the $275 and told him to saddle her up.

With his mare tied to the rear of their wagon, Simon and his father continued on their journey westward to Jefferson City, Missouri, a distance of one hundred and sixty miles. After traveling a good part of the day, Jefferson City came into view. They noticed that the traffic going into the city was steadily increasing as if a convention or celebration was about to take place. When they stopped to water their horses, James asked one of the travelers going into the city what was going on! He replied,

"The Reverend Gabriel Jones is holding a revival meeting in town this evening; and people are coming from all over the state to hear his inspiring sermons."

Sure enough, as James entered Jefferson City people were pouring into a large building that was usually reserved for conventions or political rallies. James scratched his head in amazement and was overwhelmed with curiosity as to what Reverend Jones could possibly say to inspire so many people to travel such long distances to hear him preach. To find out, he and Simon decided to attend the revival meeting. James believed in God but was not a church goer. His credo and belief was simple, do good, respect the rights of others and lead a good Christian life; that's all that could be expected from any individual. Besides, he had seen too many so called "religious people" who were the antitheses of Christian behavior.

So James and Simon took their seats and patiently waited to hear Reverend Jones. Before Rev. Jones appeared his assistants came on stage to warm up the audience with inspirational singing. When the people in attendance were sufficiently warmed up, Rev. Jones appeared. He was a tall man a little on the chubby side with thick brown hair, sunken eyes, and prominent jowls, wearing a white shirt open at the collar. He first asked his flock to pray with him and when the prays were concluded he began to speak. Softly at first, then gradually increasing the sound and pitch of his voice while walking back and forth on the stage with the Bible in one hand

and gesticulating with the other. He beseeched his audience to cast the devil and temptation aside and seek salvation in the arms of Jesus Christ our savior. Only through Him can we live and die in peace and reap the rewards of heaven. Then he got personal with his audience by declaring,

"Is there someone in your family who is disabled or inflicted with a terrible disease or in financial difficulties or having experienced any other catastrophic problem? If so, then pray to Jesus Christ for help and salvation and give to His temple of hope."

He kept repeating the same theme over and over again with slight variations of intonation; give whatever money you can to support our crusade and you will be rewarded by the Lord for your sacrifice here on earth and in the hereafter. His histrionics lasted for forty five minutes before his ushers began to pass bucket size containers through the aisles. The money poured in from his congregation, some individuals who looked liked they could ill afford to give anything, were the very same people who gave the most.

James and Simon walked out of the revival meeting uninspired and unimpressed. As they walked toward their hotel, Simon told his father,

"What impressed me most was Rev. Jones's constant reference and connections between God and money as the solution to all their problems. Give money to Rev. Jones and through him God will take care of you and lead you out of your difficulties. I don't recall from my reading of the Bible that Jesus Christ ministered to the poor, the afflicted and the hungry by asking them to give Him money. But I have to admit that Rev. Jones is a very good salesman who could probably sell buffalo meat to the Indians."

Simon also realized that Rev. Jones had a very well organized business operation which was making him a very wealthy man; becoming wealthy is especially rewarding when preaching on the subject of religion, a philosophy that most people want and need, making his job much easier, like offering water to a thirsty man. By now they had reached their hotel where they would bed down for the night in preparation for their final journey west to Lawrence, Kansas.

CHAPTER EIGHT
CONFLICT

After arriving in Kansas City, James went directly to the Federal Land Grant office to lay claim to a parcel of land a half mile outside the town of Lawrence, Kansas. After completing the paper work and receiving the necessary documentation of ownership, they road out to take possession of their land and to start a new life. They would have to travel into Lawrence for all their supplies and needs. The town of Lawrence, Kansas, was a newly established town, only ten months old founded by free soil Northerners from the Midwest and New England. The town itself was built mostly of brick and stone structure, especially the hotel with its thick brick walls, resembling a fortress. Lawrence was the stronghold of the free soil settlers whose intent was to prevent the spread of slavery beyond the Missouri border; a town well organized and well run. The very appearance and existence of the town of Lawrence was anathema to the pro-slavery residence, living along the Pottawatomie Creek outside the town of Lawrence. There had been brawls, shootings and killings in and around Lawrence ever since its inception.

James and Simon went about their business building their new home not realizing at first that they were square in the middle of a confrontational area between the pro-slavery settlers and the free soil folks of Lawrence. After completing the structure of their new home, they set about planting crops to sustain them through the severe winters that the Midwest was known for; they settled down to a routine life style and enjoyed a degree of respite. During the following eighteen months, James was periodically visited by pro-slavery residents to gauge his political leanings. James made it clear that he was not in favor of slavery but neither was he an abolitionist; he also made it clear that he was not interested in politics, he just wanted to be left alone to go about his business. In the ensuing months it became increasing clear that the whole country, as well as Lawrence, was becoming more polarized and violent. The town of Lawrence became a symbol of what the rest of the territory might become and its importance spread beyond the border of Kansas.

One terrible week in May 1856, a series of violent acts eruption from Lawrence, Kansas, to the Senate floor of the United States. On May 20th, Senator Sumner of Massachusetts delivered an eloquent anti-slavery speech; it changed no minds and didn't intend to. The next day, unrelated to Sen. Sumner's anti-slavery speech the town of Lawrence was sacked. About one thousand "Border Ruffians" mostly from Missouri crossed the border into Kansas with five canons and invaded Lawrence. The town's people offered little resistance while their town was being decimated. They dumped the printing press into the river and set fire to the hotel, homes and businesses. In their rampage of destruction the "Border Ruffians" killed five people and injured many more in their crazed rowdyism. Lawrence became the symbol of "Bleeding Kansas" and there would be many more violent outbreaks in the ensuing years as a prelude to Civil War.

The following day in the Senate chamber of the United States, Representative Preston Brooks of South Carolina was so offended by Sen. Sumner's anti-slavery speech that he attacked Sen. Sumner at his desk; beating the Senator over the head with his cane repeatedly till the cane broke in two; Sen. Sumner lay bleeding in a state of insensibility, almost to the point of death.

Two days later, when John Brown got the news of the sacking of Lawrence his temper erupted in a fit of madness. He was bent on avenging the destruction of Lawrence and the murder of five of its citizens; "an eye for an eye and a tooth for a tooth!" he shouted and began to assemble his raiding party. He gathered four of his sons and three other supporters and spent the evening sharpening their broad swords and planning their attack. In the dark of night they descended on the pro-slavery conclave at Pottawatomie Creek and hacked to death five pro-slavery inhabitants from three different families, including one of their leaders. The axiom, "Who lives by the sword, dies by the sword," was never more appropriate.

In the wake of John Brown's raid the pro-slavery inhabitants were now intent on eliminating all free soil settlers in and around Lawrence; which meant that the Ganz homestead was on their list for removal. About a month after the sacking of Lawrence, four of the pro-slavery settlers from Pottawatomie Creek led by their leader Leo Smith rode to the Ganz homestead and engaged James in conversation; the essence of which was to inform James that free soil settlers were not welcomed in this part of Kansas and that James should make arrangements to move out of the area. When James heard his ultimatum he was irate and told him straight out that he did not take kindly to threats or ultimatums; and he had a legal right to his property; furthermore, he had no intentions of moving anywhere and then ordered him off of his property and told him to stay off! The pro-slavery men were very fortunate that Simon wasn't present during that conversation, for if he had been present I'm sure there would have been a shootout, leaving four dead pro-slavery men. The pro-slavery people had little respect or fear from dirt farmers tooting guns; up till now they pretty much had their own way and succeeded in driving off the free soil people from the surrounding area. Those four men were well known to James and Simon since they had visited the Ganz homestead on several occasions since their arrival in Kansas, but under less confrontational circumstances. After hearing James's defiant reply, Leo Smith retorted,

"That's too bad; I'm sorry to hear that!" and he rode off.

The pro-slavery men went into conference to decide on the best way to dispose of the Ganz homestead. They had been successful in the past with one family by burning their home to the ground; that in turn frightened two other families to pack up and leave the area. They concluded that this was the best way to handle the Ganz homestead. The pro-slavery settlers now made plans to burn down the Ganz home; they knew that James never packed a gun and Simon probably couldn't shoot straight. And to make their crime less obvious and to avoid a shootout with Simon, they decided to wait until Simon was in Kansas City buying supplies before moving on the Ganz household to commit their nefarious deed.

They had the Ganz homestead under surveillance, waiting for Simon's departure. A week after James's contentious confrontation with Leo, Simon prepared his wagon for the trip to Kansas City to replenish supplies. Now the four unscrupulous pro-slavery men had their opportunity and prepared their villainous attack on the Ganz homestead. With flaming torches they rode up to the Ganz place shouting to James to leave or be cremated inside his home. James rushed out toward one of the men carrying a torch and attempted to dislodge the torch from his hand; while the brawl was taking place Leo pulled out his gun and shot James. James fell to the ground helpless and mortally wounded as he watched his home go up in flames and burn to the ground. Their heinous work complete, they rode off knowing that Simon would probably seek retribution. They weren't really that concerned with Simon's rage, since they were ignorant of his expertise with a hand gun and returned to their homes satisfied and complacent. Simon returned a few hours later to find his home burned to the ground and his father lying beside the ashes mortally wounded. He held his father in his arms and with tears in his eyes he heard his father murmur,

"It was the four,....it was the four....pro-sla...."

And he slipped away out of earthly existence. Simon knew exactly what had happened and was filled with overwhelming anger and rage, but tried desperately to keep his emotions under control and not do anything hasty or foolish. His first thought was to provide a decent burial site for his father before wreaking havoc on those responsible.

Simon gently wrapped his father's body in a sheet and placed it in his wagon for the journey to Kansas City for burial. After arriving in Kansas City, he made arrangement with the local undertaker to have his father's body interred at the Good Shepherd Cemetery; then he went to St. John's Lutheran Church to ask Pastor Brady if he would say a few words at his father's internment. Everyone was most cooperative and within a few hours they were at the grave site. Pastor Brady gave a heartfelt eulogy, then James was laid to rest. Simon remained at the grave site for a few minutes after everyone had left. Looking down at his father's grave; it's hard to say what he was thinking.

Simon lost interest in farming since there was nothing now to bind him to the soil or homesteading and he panned to leave Lawrence and travel further west into Indian territory to start life anew. But now it was time for retribution for those morally bankrupt scoundrels who murdered his father, an unarmed old man in cold blood. Simon contemplated his next move; he would sell his wagon and two horses then withdraw enough money from the Kansas City Territorial Bank to last him a few months. After completing the sale of his wagon and two horses as well as some minor business transactions, he walked to his horse preparing to leave Kansas City for Lawrence. When he was just about ready to mount his horse he spotted one of the four desperados who murdered his father. Simon watched with keen interest as his heart began to beat a little faster and his face flushed with anger; he paused, thinking that maybe he might lead him to his cohorts. Simon followed him a short distance to the edge of town where he entered the

Shamrock Saloon. He waited a few minutes, then walked in; sure enough there was another one of the deadly quartet. Simon was now packing two six shooters and was as adroit with two as he was with one. He rarely packed two guns only on special occasions and this was indeed special. He walked up to the bar and stood about ten feet from the two of them, watching them drink and laugh as if to celebrate some important event. Simon stood there staring at his father's murderers; it wasn't long before the two caught Simon's penetrating stare and immediately recognized him. Their laughter and smiles quickly changed to dead pan expressions, knowing full well the meaning of Simon's presence. They realized that there was no escape; they would have to face him down. They huddled together for a few seconds to decide their strategy; then agreed the best way to face Simon would be if they both drew at the same time. After they acknowledged Simon's presence, Simon walked over to the two men and asked,

"Tell me, you brave men, how does it feel to murder an unarmed old man and burn down his home? Surely that event calls for a celebration. So let me celebrate with you by buying you a drink, since it will be the last drink you'll have on Earth!"

The two men became apprehensive and slowly separated from each other by a distance of three feet. A showdown was eminent; and a dead silence enveloped the room as the patrons at the bar receded to the background, removing themselves from the feuding trio.

"Well, go ahead and draw; let's see how well you can defend yourself against someone packing a gun," Simon goaded.

They paused for five seconds, then both men drew simultaneously but not fast enough. Simon dropped the first blackguard with a bullet through his heart and shot the gun out of the hand of the second man. The wounded man in fear and desperation, extended his hands over his head and began to shout,

"Don't shoot, don't shoot; I'm unarmed, I'm unarmed."

"You sure are, just like my father was."

Simon paused for a few seconds, giving him time to sweat a bit then let loose with both guns blazing emptying both barrels of his six shooters into his body as he fell to the floor like a piece of Swiss cheese. Simon then drank a shot of whisky, paid the bartender, bid him good day, and left.

Simon had $2,600 in his account at the Kansas City Territorial Bank but had withdrawn only $500, enough to carry him over during his westward travels. The balance would remain in the bank; it was much safer there. He now set out to settle the score and gun down the other two scoundrels.

The news of the shooting at the Shamrock Saloon spread like wildfire through Kansas City and all the way to the settlements at Pottawatomie Creek, where Leo Smith receive the news with trepidation. Leo now was aware that Simon was no ordinary gun carrying dirt farmer but a shooter to be reckoned with. He summoned his conspiratorial buddy to discuss their defense against Simon who was sure to show up at any time. They did not want to face Simon in a face to face shootout despite the fact that there would be two against one; so they made plans to bushwhack him. Leo told his buddy Gus, that there was only one road leading into their settlement and Simon would have to traverse the road to reach them. Leo went on to explain that one mile north of our settlement there is a portion of the road that bends sharply, with large and small conifers growing on a rocky incline on both sides of the road. That would be a perfect location for an ambush, both men agreed and decided to put their plan into operation immediately. It was early afternoon when both men loaded their six shooters, packed ample ammunition and headed for the designated location. Upon their arrival, Leo told Gus to take one side of the road while he took the other side; and when Simon comes within shooting range we'll blast him to kingdom come.

With his affairs settled in Kansas City, Simon set out for Pottawatomie Creek to execute his idea of justice. He could not depend on the law for justice as presently constituted in Kansas City; that would be futile since a jury trial would be long and cumbersome and the result uncertain, since most of the jurors and legal officials had pro-slavery leanings. Simon had to settle this matter in his own way.

During Simon's long ride back to Lawrence, then continuing on to Pottawatomie Creek, he had plenty of time to think and mull over in his mind the different scenarios that might unfold in his pursuit of Leo and Gus. He knew that a face to face confrontation was unlikely; knowing their past history they would formulate a devious or stealthy plan to assure their survival. They might try shooting me in the back from behind a rock or ambush me from within a concealed area; anything is possible save a vis-a-vis confrontation. By now Leo and his buddy probably heard of the shootout at the Shamrock Saloon and were awaiting my arrival. Simon had intended to attack their homestead in the dead of night to even the odds. As he got closer and closer to their homesteads, Simon came within sight of the bend in the road with its ruck of conifers growing on a rocky incline. He realized instinctively that it was an ideal location for an ambush and decided to investigate. Simon dismounted from his horse about one hundred yards from the bend in the road and tied her to a tree out of sight in a heavily wooded area. He would now survey the area on foot; if he found no human presence he would then camp there till dark before proceeding further. However, if Leo and his buddy were hiding in this cluster of evergreens he would finalize his search by making them fodder for vultures; that is if he could outsmart them in this deadly game of chess.

Simon began his search by clinging to the edge of the rocky incline, slowly and quietly working his way toward the dense underbrush. Simon would pause every few seconds to listen for any unfamiliar sounds. About fifteen minutes into his surveillance he heard a human voice coming from across the road; it was Leo, calling to Gus,

"Gus, are you ready? He should be passing through here in an hour or two."

"I'm as ready as I'll ever be; as soon as he comes around the bend in the road and shows his face I'll start blasting away," replied Gus.

"That's good; from here on in Gus, no more talking till this job is done." Now Simon knew where Gus was about on hundred feet from him. Simon began slowly edging toward Gus, approaching him from behind, steadily advancing toward him till he was only a few feet from Gus when he made his presence known.

"Gus, are you looking for me?"

Gus turned around and looked up at Simon in frightful astonishment and he started to crawl backwoods on his elbows while still looking at Simon. His only chance for survival was to reach for his gun before Simon did. Simon gave him a despicable look and said,

"I have no qualms in killing you right now, so why don't you go for your gun and give yourself a fighting chance! I'm giving you more of a chance than you gave my father."

That's exactly what Gus was trying to do, so with every tug backwards his hand came closer and closer to his sidearm, finally when his hand was within an inch from his gun he went for it; but before he could withdraw his gun from its holster, Simon withdrew his gun and filled him full of lead. By killing Gus Simon also gave away his location; but Leo wasn't sure who survived, Simon or Gus. Leo waited a few seconds hoping to hear from Gus; since he did not hear Gus's voice he assumed that Simon prevailed. A pause of a few seconds was just enough time to give Simon a chance to change locations. Within the densely covered area of shrubbery and evergreens it was difficult to determine a man's location; both men had that problem. Simon wasn't certain that by throwing a stone at a particular area would draw fire from Leo, revealing his location. No, he didn't think it would work, it would only indicate to Leo the immediate area of Simon's location. He had to think of something new and deceptive. And finally came up with an idea that might work; if he tied a string or cord to a shrub and extended the cord along the ground for a distance of ten to fifteen feet, he would then be able to twitch part of the shrub indicating the presence of a person or animal. That might be enough to draw fire from Leo from across the road revealing his location. But Simon had no string or cord to execute his plan. He thought for a while and came up with a solution; if he didn't have a cord , he would make one; from Gus's pants. Simon went back to Gus's dead body and stripped off his pants, saying,

"Gus, I'm taking your pants, as you won't be needing them where your going. You're performing a better service to mankind dead than alive."

Simon then proceeded to strip the pants off of Gus's dead body then withdrew his knife and shredded his pants into long thin pieces of cloth; tying the ends together till he had a nine foot long blue cord that would blend in perfectly with the green grass. He then tied one end of the cord to a large conifer shrub and extending the remaining cord to a location behind a large rock and laid prostrate on the ground. Simon tugged gently on the cord at first hoping to attract Leo's attention, but no gun fire response from Leo; maybe Leo wasn't looking in the right direction. He waited a minute or two, then tried again. This time Leo spotted the movement of the shrub and let loose with a barrage of gun fire. Leo gave away his position but could not be certain whether he had shot Simon or not, or if Simon was behind the shrub. Now that Simon was aware of Leo's location he let loose a barrage of gunfire of his own, then quickly moved to another location. Simon wasn't aware that he had winged Leo in the leg which slowed him down considerably as he began to moved to where his horse was tied. Simon moved in the opposite direction concealed by evergreens in an attempt to cross the road and be on the same side as Leo. After crossing the road Simon moved quickly and cautiously in Leo's direction, when he came upon a pool of blood indicating that he had hit Leo. Simon was now hot on Leo's trail realizing that he was trying to reach his horse. It wasn't long before Leo came into view. He was at a lower elevation than Simon, crouched behind a tree with his gun in his hand waiting for Simon to appear. Simon slowly approached Leo from the rear, as he did Gus till he was practically on top of him, and said,

"Drop your gun, Leo."

Leo dropped his gun and turned around to face Simon with an expression of shock and fatality, knowing that he was looking at his executioner. Simon hovered over Leo with his gun pointed at Leo's head. Leo looked tired, dirty, sweaty and bloodied from his leg wound and didn't say a word to Simon. What could he possibly say? Nothing he could have said could mitigate the fact that he had murdered Simon's father. He just sat there waiting for Simon to pull the trigger and end his life. Simon hesitated in pulling the trigger, his thirst for vengeance could not be quenched with Leo's quick death. Under normal circumstances Simon was a decent and considerate man, willing to aid anyone in distress but this was not a normal circumstance. He was looking at the man who murdered his father whom he loved dearly. As he stood there pointing the gun at Leo's head, visions of the past flashed through his mind; of holding his dying father in his arms as his life drained from his body; a man who never carried a gun and never harmed anyone. "He wouldn't even kill an animal, that's why I had to do all the hunting," Simon said to himself,

"No, Leo won't get off that easily; I don't know if there is a heaven or hell, but Leo's hell is going to be here on earth."

There is an element of savagery in all humans lurking beneath the surface, quiet and dormant, waiting for an emotional or tragic event to ignite the venom of hate and revenge. And this was such a moment. Simon marched Leo who stumbled along in pain from his leg wound to where his horse was tied. Leo knew his time had come but wasn't sure what Simon had in mind. When they reached Leo's horse, Simon dislodged the rope from the side of his horse and told Leo to lay prostrate on the ground; by now Leo surmised his fate. When Simon told him to keep his feet together and outstretched Leo was reluctant to comply. But when Simon let loose with a swift kick to Leo's ribs he became more cooperative and complied. Simon then tied his two feet together ever so tightly then tied the other end of the rope to the saddle of Leo's horse. Simon then gave Leo a minute or two to contemplate his fate, as he squirmed around on the ground like a snake trying to shed its skin.

"Well, I guess it's time Leo; enjoy the ride."

Vengeance

And with one strong swipe on the horse's rump accompanied by gun fire, Leo's horse took off at breakneck speed in the direction of Pottawatomie Creek as Simon watched the trail of dust and blood left in its wake. His business in Kansas now consummated Simon set his sights on the open plains of Texas and the New Mexico territory.

CHAPTER NINE
THE UNKNOWN

 imon left Kansas in the spring of 1859, with a well established reputation as a gun slinger and sharp shooter which would be further enhanced in the ensuing years. When Simon left Kansas City, he did not have any predetermined destination in mind nor did he have any particularly desirous life style. He was just going to live life as it came and not worry about the future. During the subsequent years his travels would cross paths with farmers, homesteaders, cattle ranchers, bankers and the poor living in hovels. The West was still growing and the vastness of its open plains and grasslands was sparsely populated with human inhabitants. Simon could travel one hundred miles or more without crossing paths with another human being and that was often the case. Quite often his landlord was mother nature; he would sleep under a blanket of stars and a refulgent moon with the fragrant night air flowing through his nostrils.

At days end, if he came in contact with human dwellings he would knock on their door and ask for quarters, offering cash or labor for room and board. More often than not, the homesteaders or ranchers were more than willing to accept his labor, since there was plenty of work to be done and they didn't have the means to hire help. Labor for room and board was a perfect arrangement for Simon since he needed the exercise after being in the saddle all day. This arrangement would last from two to ten days in most instances, depending on the family's need and Simon's restlessness to move on. Simon received a room and three meals a day, sometimes four; that's all Simon wanted and that's all he would accept. Simon was extremely versatile from his own experiences as a farmer and homesteader; he could mend fences, round up and brand cattle, shoe horses and was "Mr. Fix It" around the house. In almost every case, the owner of the farm or ranch would ask Simon to stay longer or offer Simon a salaried job. But that wasn't part of Simon's plan and when it was time to leave Simon thanked the owner for his hospitality, said good-by to the family and was on his way.

Knocking on doors to ask for quarters in exchange for his labor was an act of diversion and physical necessity for Simon and did not constitute his main intent during his trek westward. These mundane activities were periodically interrupted by exciting and dangerous interludes of adventure, exemplified by his stop over at Abilene, Texas.

The topic of conversation in town was that of the notorious "Jack Gang" Jack, Jake, and Jim. During the course of eighteen months they had robbed six banks and terrorized the community with the death of four innocent bystanders. The town's people were fearful of leaving their life savings in the Abilene National bank while these desperados were still at lodge. Simon had been living in Abilene for two days and was sympathetic toward the people's concerns, which aroused his interest in bringing these bandits to justice. It represented a challenge he could not resist. The element of excitement had been missing from Simon's diet for the past few months; bringing the Jack Gang to heel would make everyone feel safe and more at ease. But Simon didn't know where they were nor when and if, they would hit the Abilene National Bank. He thought about this problem off and on for the next few days; and finally he formulated a plan that he thought had a reasonable chance of success to terminate the "Jack Gans's" activities permanently. But first he wanted the approval of the Abilene Sheriff to execute his plan. He walked into the Sheriff's office and introduced himself; the Sheriff looked up in amazement and stared at Simon for a second or two, then said,

"You mean you're the same Simon Ganz of Kansas City fame?"

"Word really travels fast, doesn't it! Well, for better or worse that's me."

"Well, well, well, Mr. Ganz what brings you to Abilene and why have you come to see me?"

"To answer your first question: I was just passing through on my westward journey and thought I might rest awhile in a civilized community such as Abilene before moving on. To my surprise, the only topic of conversation here was about the 'Jack Gang'; the folks in town are obsessed with those bandits and my reason for seeing you is that I have a plan to capture or kill the members of the 'Jack Gang.' "

"Well, Mr. Ganz, you can stay in Abilene as long as you like; now tell me what is your plan?"

Simon then explained to the Sheriff that the Jack Gang was sure to hit the bank in Abilene sooner or later, and when they do I'll be in the bank waiting for them.

"You mean to tell me that you're willing to stay in that bank day after day waiting for the 'Jack Gang' to rob the Abilene bank, not knowing if they would ever show up?"

"Well, it's not that simple Sheriff just give me a little leeway in town and leave the rest to me."

"If it was anyone else making such a request I would say he was crazy, but I know you're not mad or reckless, so I'll give you a free hand and wish you luck. If you're successful there's a $5,000 reward for each of them dead or alive waiting for you; if not we'll give you a decent burial."

With that settled and having Sheriff Philips's blessing and cooperation, Simon was on his way to speak to the President of the Abilene National Bank to explain his plan. Upon entering the bank Simon told the clerk that he wished to speak to Mr. Moore. When asked what business he had with Mr. Moore, Simon replied,

"It's a matter of bank security."

After conveying that message to Mr. Moore, and getting his consent, she escorted Simon to Mr. Moore's office. Mr. Moore was a short man, standing five feet, four inches tall and at fifty five years of age he displayed a pot belly and a bald head. His face had a reddish complexion and on top of his nose sat a pair of steel rim glasses that made his baby blue eyes appear larger than they actually were. After the customary greetings and salutations they exchanged some pleasantries, then got down to business. Simon explained his plan to capture the "Jack Gang" to Mr. Moore who listened intensely to what Simon proposed.

"In your bank Mr. Moore, there's a small closet size room at the far end, about thirty feet from the entrance, where I could sit and observe people entering the bank, as well as patrons within the bank whose movements and actions could readily be observed through a small hole in the closet. If I should detect any abnormal or suspicious movements by patrons within the bank, I would be on high alert and ready to take any action necessary to protect the assets of your bank."

Mr. Moore sank back in his chair scratching his head, and said,

"It sounds plausible but there are a few aspects of your plan that bother me. You mean to tell me that you're willing to occupy that cramped quarter day after day waiting for the 'Jack Gang', who may never show up? And if they do show up there are three of them against you!"

Vengeance

"Those are reasonable questions Mr. Moore and let me say straight out that I don't intend to stay in that closet for an extended period of time. What I would like you to do Mr. Moore, is this: take out a full page ad in the Abilene Gazette newspaper, boasting of the bank's quarterly profits and that business has never been better with a record number of new bank depositors."

"But that's not true; business is actually very bad and my customers are withdrawing their money from my bank in fear of this bank being robbed by the 'Jack Gang.' "

"I know that Mr. Moore! But the 'Jack Gang' isn't aware of your financial difficulties and when they read this ad in the Abilene Gazette, they'll think that your bank is a gold mine and make plans to rob it; which they surely will do sooner or later anyway. If I'm successful and I'm sure I will be, if they attempt to rob your bank; the 'Jack Gang' will be out of business and your bank will be back on the road to solvency with people putting their money back into your bank"

Mr. Moore frowned and paused for thirty seconds before exclaiming,

"I don't like it; I don't like it; if your plan is unsuccessful my bank will be out a fortune, or worse, I'll be bankrupt! You're going up against three experienced bank robbers; and one thing more how do I know that you're not part of the gang, which would make things real easy for them."

"Tell me Mr. Moore, have you ever heard of Simon Ganz?"

"I sure have; everyone around these parts has heard of Simon Ganz; he has a reputation for being the quickest sharp shooter in the West. He has won a king's ransom just in shooting tournaments. His exploits are well known too, especially the four desperados he bagged at Pottawatomie Creek."

"Well Mr. Moore, you're looking at him."

His eyes could not have opened any wider, with his mouth open exposing his gold fillings, as he stared Simon down, and said,

"You mean, you mean, you're Simon Ganz?"

"I'm afraid I am Mr. Moore, and I would like to help you."

"Well, if you are who you say you are it's a deal. But first you'll have to prove to me that you are really Simon Ganz. I don't want to be too skeptical, but a man in my position as guardian of the people's money, I can't be too careful."

"Fair enough Mr. Moore, I'll give you some of my personal

information including where my father is buried and the balance on my bank account at the Kansas City Territorial Bank in Kansas City. You can contact the bank and other sources by telegraph for verification. In the meantime, I'll be at the Sheriff's office waiting to hear from you. Good day, Mr. Moore."

Mr. Moore stood at the door still in a state of shock as Simon walked out. Mr. Moore was an extremely cautious man by nature, an essential quality for a good bank president. He spent the balance of the day and the next, making the necessary inquires into Simon Ganz's statements. When he was convinced that Simon was the real McCoy, he sent word to Simon that he was ready to execute his plan.

To fulfill his end of the bargain, Mr. Moore rushed to the office of the Abilene Gazette and asked the editor to run a full page ad boasting of the record profits of his bank and the growing number of new depositors. The advertisement would run every other day for the next eight days.

It wasn't long before the news of the record profits of the Abilene Bank reached the ears of the "Jack Gang" held up in the town of Throckmorton, seventy five miles northeast of Abilene. With broad smiles on their faces they read the ad in the Abilene Gazette newspaper over and over again. They immediately began making plans for a raid on the Abilene Bank; they thought that this would be a golden opportunity for them to make a killing and hit the jackpot. They sat down together and meticulously planned every detail of the robbery; the plan was to send Jim into Abilene to case the bank and map their escape route. Jim was to wait outside the bank, to tend to the horses and to ready their escape while Jack and Jake terrorized the patrons within and gathered up the loot. Their escape route would be through a narrow ravine a few miles out of town which the posse would have to pass through. At the exit end of the ravine they would hide a box containing sticks of dynamite to be used against the posse while the posse was passing through the ravine, then all three men would dismount from their horses and throw stick after stick of dynamite into the ravine decimating the posse and every living thing in the ravine; the dynamite blasts would dislodge boulders from the bedrock and cause a cascade of falling rocks and splintered trees to rain down over their dead bodies. That surely would give them enough time to escape into Oklahoma even if they were to walk the entire distance. They sat around a table drinking whisky and congratulating themselves on a fool proof plan. What they didn't realize was that Simon Ganz was in town and it wasn't their plan; it was Simon's plan.

Vengeance

Simon waited six days before taking his position in the bank closet, he wanted to give the Jack Gang time to read the advertisement in the Abilene Gazette newspaper and make plans for their assault on the bank. He thought it might be a little premature to occupy the bank closet only six days after the release of the advertisement, but Simon was taking no chances; he wanted to make sure that he was in the bank when the fun started. Simon spent the next seven days in the bank's closet emerging periodically to stretch his legs and walk around when the bank was empty or had only a few women customers. There was an opening at the top of the closet wall forming a twelve inch long and a one inch wide slot that admitted fresh air. Simon sat there day after day becoming more bored with each passing day, but it was his idea so he kept his complaints to himself. Finally, after seven days in the closet and thirteen days after the first release of the bank's advertisement, he observed three men through the peep hole in the closet riding up to the bank. They were dusty in appearance and their horses looked like they traveled a long distance, which in itself aroused Simon's suspicion. While observing these three men he noticed that only two of them dismounted and entered the bank while the third man stayed outside with the horses. That scenario set off alarm bells in Simon's head and he was pretty much convinced that these fellows were the "Jack Gang" and readied himself for the confrontation that was about to unfold. There was only three people in the bank when the two drew their guns; Jake was standing by the door while Jack was at the teller's cage and yelled,

"This is a stickup; anyone causing a problem will not see......."

At that point, Simon busted out of the closet. When Jack turned to look he got a bullet between his eyes and simultaneously hit Jake twice, mortally wounding him. When Jim who was waiting outside with the horses heard the gunfire he was uncertain what had happened, until he saw Jake tumble through the door of the bank covered with blood and falling to the ground. Realizing the bank robbery had gone awry, he quickly mounted his horse and galloped off. Simon knew that his job wasn't complete until the third member of the gang was captured or killed. He quickly left the bank, jumped on his horse and was in hot pursuit of the third bandit. Simon was never far behind in pursuit. As they passed through the ravine Simon noticed that Jim dismounted his horse, jumped behind a tree and grabbed something out of a box; as he got closer he saw it was a box of dynamite.

Simon yelled to Jim,

Vengeance

"Come out with your hands up or I'll blow that box of dynamite up and you along with it."

Jim had no intention of going to jail, nor did he want to be blown up, so he emerged from behind the tree with his hands held high but still holding on to a stick of dynamite with a burning fuse in his left hand, so Simon shouted,

"Stop right where you are and pull the fuse from that stick of dynamite."

Jim paid no attention to Simon's instructions and kept coming closer; he figured that Simon wouldn't risk blowing himself up along with him. Jim didn't know what to expect from Simon but that was his only option to avoid a certain hanging if brought into town alive. Simon knew what Jim had in mind and jumped behind a large rock hugging the ground while shooting the dynamite from Jim's hand. The blast shattered Jim's body all over the ground. Simon then had to search the surrounding ground looking for any artifacts that could identify the victim. He meticulously inspected the entire area, then spotted a shiny object, it was a belt buckle with the initials J. K. engraved prominently on the back of the buckle. It was Jim Keen's belt buckle alright, and not too far from the belt buckle was a piece of paper showing the layout of the bank. That was sufficient proof that the victim was indeed Jim Keen, the third member of the notorious "Jack Gang."

The people in town were elated over Simon's success in bringing an end to the "Jack Gang." They had seen Simon race out of town in hot pursuit of the third member of the gang and anticipated his return by congregating on the outskirts of town, anxiously awaiting his return. Their waiting came to an end when they saw a lone rider appear in the distance and as he came a little closer, they recognized him as Simon; but where was the third bandit? When Simon got within range, the crowd spontaneously erupted in cheers of thanks and gratitude for his service to the community. Simon acknowledged their greetings then went to the Sheriff's office to explain the circumstances of Jim Keens's demise. The Sheriff thanked Simon for formulating and executing a brilliant plan to terminate the activities of the "Jack Gang," and added,

"Frankly Simon, I never thought your plan would succeed, but it did and we're all thankful for that, especially Mr. Moore who can breath easy knowing he can serve the people's needs without fear of being robbed. By the way Simon here 's your well earned $15,000 reward."

Vengeance

"Thank you Sheriff, I think I'll put it in Mr. Moore's bank for safe keeping"

Simon decided to stay in town for the next few days to unwind, relax, and seek a little entertainment. His first stop was the Good Will Saloon, where the local gentry gathered to discuss the current topics of the day. Simon grabbed a beer and walked over to where a group of men were discussing the possibility of the Southern states seceding from the Union. It was a hotly debated subject in the Congress of the United States and throughout the country. It seemed to Simon that the rhetoric was being elevated to an inflammatory level; if continued to escalate it surely would precipitate a civil war. Although the pro- slavery people out numbered the free soil folks their contentious debates did not foster harmonious relations between the two groups.

What was becoming clear to Simon was that the opinions of both groups on the subject of slavery and secession were so polarized that their opinions were set in stone; and any further discourse along those lines would be an exercise in futility, since reason and compromise became an alien concept in their discussions. It was very depressing for Simon to listen to such foolish and fatuous talk of forming two countries each weaker than the former. They should think more about the cost in human life, the destruction of homes and property and the financial burden on the population at large. No, Simon was through with such self destructive talk and left the Good Will Saloon to find a more congenial atmosphere.

As Simon casually promenaded through the main section of town he came front and center with a classy haberdashery store. The manikin in the window caught his eye; he became mesmerized by the elegance of the latest Western style dress on display. The manikin was clad in a fancy blue shirt with white piping around the collar and running down the front of his chest to his belt buckle and also around the cuffs of his shirt, topped it off with a fancy design over each of the pockets of the shirt. It wore black dress pants and a pair of black leather boots with a gold design on the upper end of the boots. And on the manikin's head was a black felt hat about six inches in height. Simon was mightily impressed in what he saw and kept staring at the manikin.

Ever since Simon left Western Pennsylvania he wore the clothes of a typical Western farmer: a plaid shirt and blue jeans and a nondescript hat. Simon decided then and there that he was going to change his dress style;

from now on he would look like that manikin in the window and be attired in this new Westerner style for all occasions.

Simon walked into the haberdashery store and was greeted by an attractive young lady standing six inches shorter than he, with dirty blond hair and gray eyes. She was just plump enough to be sexually exciting, full breasted and wearing a low cut dress revealing two inches of cleavage. She greeted Simon with a broad seductive smile and said,

"Good afternoon Sir, what can I do for you?"

"Well Madam, I would like to buy a new outfit, just like the one the manikin is wearing in the window, something real fancy that would attract a young lady like yourself."

"You don't need fancy clothes to attract women, you're quite handsome with the clothes you're wearing."

"That may be, but I still want to buy that outfit the manikin is wearing."

"O.K., but it's quite expensive it's the latest in Western fashion and cost $130 with the hat and boots included."

"I'll take it! Do you go with the sale price?"

"Well, you come right to the point don't you? How do you know I'm not married?"

"I didn't see a ring on your finger, so I assumed you weren't married; Are you married?"

"Well it so happens that I'm not married, although I had been married twice before, but both marriages were a disaster so I decided to remain single."

"Really, you don't look old enough to be married twice; you can't be over twenty five years of age."

"Who are you kidding, you know as well as I that I'm over thirty years of age."

"I don't care how old you are, you look like an angel with your sparkling eyes and irresistible smile and a figure that should be on the cover of a fashion magazine."

"You really have some line and I don't believe a word of it."

"Let me tell you something young lady! Yes! It is true that it's a line, but in order for me to make such grandiose statements I have to be inspired and you are the source of my inspiration. So I wasn't too far off my mark."

"O.K., you can pick me up after work, right here at six; now let me complete this sale and where do I send this outfit to?"

"I'm buying two additional shirts one white and the other black, I'll wear my new clothes and send the extra shirts to the hotel that I'm staying at and you can throw my old clothes away; by the way what is your name?"

"My name is Mae, Mae Bender and what is your name and the name of your hotel?"

"The hotel that I'm staying at is the Grand Plaza and my name is Simon Ganz."

"SIMON GANZ, oh my God, you mean you are Simon Ganz?"

"Yes Madam, I mean Mae."

"How do you like that, I've been flirting with Simon Ganz all this time and didn't know it."

"Well I'll see you tonight Mae and we'll flirt some more, that is if you haven't changed your mind."

"Oh no Simon, I'll be waiting for you"Simon then walked out with a half smile on his face. Both Simon and Mae were anxiously anticipating their six P.M. rendezvous. Simon rented a horse and buggy for the evening; and at the appointed time he arrived wearing his new Western outfit. Mae was waiting for Simon outside the haberdashery store in a new red dress. They made a handsome couple. Simon escorted Mae to the buggy, helped her in and off they went. He rode the buggy out of town to a nearby stream then stopped to listen to the sound of the water rushing by and other sounds of the night. It was a clear night with a three quarter moon shining down on Mae accentuating her beauty. Mae was curious about Simon's past exploits and her inquiries began the minute they left the haberdashery store. Simon was most patient and accommodating; he described some of the less gruesome and bloody events; he did not want to depress her spirit but attempted to put her in a receptive and jovial mode. After a while, Simon turned the table on Mae and asked her about her two ex-husbands. It didn't take much to loosen Mae's tongue as she went on to explain, "My first husband wasn't an alcoholic but he did like the bottle too much. When we first got married, all was wonderful and we had a great sex life for the first few months. Then gradually during the course of eighteen months I had competition, not from another women but from the whisky bottle which became his companion and first love. I tried my best to correct his behavior, with no success. When I realized he wasn't going to change his ways, I divorced him. The same was pretty much true with my second husband, only instead of whisky he was addicted to gambling which is just as bad as alcohol. I don't know why I can't find a man with a stable and normal temperament. After my disappointing experience with two failed marriages I decided not to marry again."

"That's really too bad Mae, a beautiful woman like you should have a man."

"Oh, I have my men all right from time to time, I just don't marry them."

That sounded encouraging to Simon and the rest of the evening involved frivolous talk mixed in with a few laughable jokes. All things considered, they had a very pleasant evening and then they decided to ride back to town. Upon their arrival in town Simon invited Mae to his hotel room for a good night drink. Mae smiled and said,

"Why you devil, I was wondering when you would get around to inviting me to your room. Since you won't be in town all that long why beat around the bush; sure I'll come up for a drink."

And up they went. The minute the door closed behind them they melted in each others arms. While their lips met, Simon's hands were busy exploring Mae's body. Mae lifted Simon's shirt from his pants while Simon slowly began disrobing Mae, till she was down to the last vestige of clothes that separated her from nudity. What became palpable to Simon was the intensity to which Mae reacted to their foreplay. A minute or two after their first embrace, Mae began to moan, groan, and squirm in Simon's arms; he thought that Mae might have an orgasm before they reached the bed. While still holding Mae in his arms, he walked her over to the bed. Once in bed it didn't take long before Mae took the initiative and made contact with Simon, both reaching the ultimate peak of ecstasy at the same time. After their heavy breathing subsided, they rolled over and rested in silence.

After thirty minutes elapsed in silent repose, Simon was just about to doze off when Mae snuggled close to Simon and ran her hand over Simon's chest and down between his legs. Simon couldn't resist her tender caresses and responded to her wake up call. As Simon became fully engaged he couldn't help but think,

"I have one hot potato here."

At the height of their love making, suddenly Mae fainted; Simon became alarmed, not knowing if she had fainted or died. Simon jumped out of bed and started to put his pants on to get help if necessary. Then Mae opened her eyes and said,

"What are you doing?"

"I didn't know what had happened to you, I thought you might need a doctor."

"Don't be silly; get back in bed."

Simon took his pants off, jumped back in bed and resumed where he had left off. After completing their second round of love making, Mae said,

"Simon you're some Romeo; I haven't had a man like you in a very long time. Go to sleep now my love, I'll wake you in the morning."

As Simon dozed off he began to think, maybe Mae's two ex-husbands really weren't that fond of whisky or gambling after all; but used it as an excuse to avoid being called upon to perform beyond their capabilities.

Sure enough come morning and Simon was awakened by Mae's warm body next to his, he knew what was coming next. Simon wasn't adverse to Mae's sexuality and willingly accommodated her in their third round of love making within the last twelve hours. That was about as much as Simon could take and decided to get dressed and go for breakfast before Mae got other ideas. While Simon was getting dressed, he casually said to Mae,

"Mae, since you enjoy sex so much have you ever thought of going into business?"

"Oh no Simon, I could never do that! It would mean I would have to take on all comers; I couldn't make love to a man I didn't find attractive or desirous. Besides it would take all the pleasure out of sex. No, I'm happy at my job and being free to chose my partner."

With that said, they left and went for breakfast. After a hardy breakfast they walked out and Simon told Mae,

"Good-by Mae, and thanks for making my evening so enjoyable; I won't forget you."

"Good-by Simon, It was a real pleasure sharing your company and if you ever come this way again, please look me up."

"I will indeed Mae, good-by."

With those parting words they went their separate ways. Simon learned from the young men in town that Mae was a popular young lady, not only as a salesperson. Simon rested all that day; in the morning he would be on his way further west into the New Mexico territory.

Chapter Ten
Indian Country

Not having any definite destination in mind Simon headed in the direction of the plains of western Texas and eastern New Mexico. After traveling for almost two days through the plains of Texas, he found himself in the middle of a dry and arid mesa in New Mexico surrounded by small mountains. He kept riding, but those distant mountains never seemed to get any closer. The temperature kept raising draining his limbs of strength, the exposed parts of his body were encrusted with a layer of dirt and grime and his clothes were the same color as the ground. Simon was very thirsty and the water in his canteen running low, he had no other option but to keep moving as a feeling of desperation began to enter his mind; he was dirty, tired and thirsty. After another hour or so, he found salvation when he emerged out of the mesa into a different world with a few conifer trees and some green bushes bearing eatable berries. His throat was parched and on his body were small patches of dried mud on his face and hands formed by his sweat catching the sand particles stirred up by the wind, and his canteen was now empty. He dismounted, walked over to the berry bushes and he and his horse ate some of those luscious berries, then moved on. Another half hour ride from the mesa and his eyes feasted on a verdant scene so beautiful and enticing, with a stream of water one hundred and fifty feet wide as clear as crystal and in rapid transit; for a while Simon thought he had died and gone to heaven. There was only one thing on Simon's mind as he observed the clarity of the rushing water; how fast could he get into that stream of water and wash off the encrusted dirt from his body and feel the cool water enter his mouth and down his throat. Simon spent a full hour frolicking in the water and diving after fish before deciding to wash his clothes and hang them up to dry. Amazingly, his clothes dried in 15 minutes in the hot and dry air of New Mexico; he then shaved himself, put on his clean clothes and felt like a new man. Simon then stretched out under a large pine tree, put his hands behind his head and dozed off. While in a semi-state of sleep, he was awakened by the sound of youthful voices coming from up stream not more than fifty yards away; children doing what he had been doing previously, enjoying the cool rushing water. He recognized them as two Indian youths, a boy of about thirteen and a girl of ten or eleven, bathing with what little clothes they had on. Simon smiled in recognition of their youthful exuberance and went back to sleep. While Simon was resting, two men appeared driving an empty wagon in a downstream direction. They both probably were in their 40's, the man driving the wagon had a black, but short, full beard with a cigar planted in the middle of his face. The other fellow was clean shaven, with a crop of reddish hair that was starting to turn gray. Both had a disheveled appearance, wearing dirty work clothes and deformed hats ready for the garbage heap. The two horses pulling the wagon were old and emaciated and didn't look like they had much life left in them. They stopped to admire the two beautiful stallions, one black and the other brown with a white patch on his chest that were tied to a tree and belonged to the Indian youths. They also admired the artistic handy work that was prominently displayed on the leather saddles of the horses. It didn't take them long to decide to steal the horses, since the two defenseless youths wouldn't pose much of a problem, this would be easy pickings. As they proceeded to tie the two horses to the back of their wagon, the Indian youths saw what was taking place and immediately emerged from the stream and desperately tried to prevent their horses from being stolen. The boy put up a hell of a fight, until the tall husky red head hit the boy in the face, sending him crashing to the ground with blood gushing from his lip. His sister came to his defense and sprang into action, attacking the two men the best way she could, kicking and scratching, but she was no match for these fellows. Finally, the one with the black beard said to his buddy,

"Let's teach these Indian rabble a lesson."

Now their intent was to commit a sadistic act of cruelty by strapping the boy to the spokes of the wagon wheel; they lifted his knees till they almost touched his chin and tied them in place. Then dragging the little Indian girl to the opposite side of the wagon and subjecting her to the same fate as her sibling, by tying her to the wagon wheel as they did her brother. Their intention was to drive the wagon as long as it takes until the youths were dead; and to assure their deaths, they tied ropes around their necks and through the spokes of the wagon wheel. All this commotion aroused Simon from his slumber. He was curious as to what was going on and glanced down the road just as the two youths were having their necks tied securely to the spokes of the wagon wheel. What he witnessed shocked him and his sense of justice required his intervention. Simon jumped on his horse and within seconds he was upon them, just as their were ready to commit their ruthless and senseless act of cruelty. The two youths were in a state of semi-consciousness after being beaten and tied to the wagon wheels. After observing the surrounding area and after seeing how the two Indian youths were brutalized and their horses tied to the rear of the men's wagon, it didn't take Simon long to figure out what had happened. Simon's usual easy going demeanor was not apparent on this occasion; they would witness his unmitigated fury as he shouted with obvious anger in his voice,

"Mr., I want you to cut those two Indian youths loose, and I mean right now."

"Why are you interfering in something that is none of your business? They are just two riffraff Indian kids,"

"They may be riffraff to you, but they're not riffraff to their parents and I would rather share bread with them, than with the likes of you two scoundrels and if you don't want to stand trial for horse theft, I'd release those two Indian kids now."

At that moment, his black bearded buddy, who was sitting in the wagon heard enough of talk and decided to draw his gun, not knowing who he was up against. Simon's peripheral vision detected black beard's arm movement and within a split second Simon drew his gun and put a bullet through his right and left shoulder. He then turned to the other scoundrel, saying,

"I'm beginning to lose my patience, so if you don't want a bullet between your eyes, I suggest you release those two Indian youths now."

Realizing that he meant business and that he was no match for the stranger, he did what he was told at break neck speed. The two Indian youths struggled to their feet, looking pretty much beaten up and disheveled. Simon told the two Indian kids to take their horses and ride back to their tribe. In their weakened state, they barely had enough energy to climb onto their horses. Both looked at Simon gratefully, then the boy asked Simon his name,

"Simon Ganz," he replied.

And off they rode. Unbeknown to Simon, he had just saved the lives of the son and daughter of the Comanche Indian chief, Flying Eagle. The two in the wagon were in a state of shock, realizing that they went against Simon Ganz and lived to talk about it. They rode off more humbled than when they started. Simon satisfied with the outcome, returned to the large pine tree to finish his snooze for he had a busy day and deserved a little uninterrupted sleep. He remained in the immediate vicinity of this serene environment for the balance of the day, enjoying his surroundings; at night he slept under a blanket of stars and listened to the wild creatures going about their business.

The following morning, when the sun peaked over the horizon to start a new day, Simon continued on his journey. A mile or two into his travels he noticed someone standing at the side of the road, and as he got closer, he discerned the figure to be an Indian brave. Simon didn't know what to make of it, but as soon as he got within speaking range, the Indian said,

"How, you Simon Ganz?"

Simon acknowledged that he was. Then the Indian brave said,

"Comanche chief, Flying Eagle, want to have 'Pow Wow' with you."

The Indian brave wasn't armed, spoke in a friendly manner and his statement was in the form of a request, not a demand; if there was any danger or evil intent, they wouldn't invite him to their compound. Simon always one for adventure and curious as to what this was all about, agreed. They rode a good distance before reaching the Comanche Indian compound. As they entered the Comanche camp, Simon noticed that the path leading to Chief Flying Eagle's dais was crowded on both sides with men, women and children, staring at Simon as if he were a hero or villain; the smiles on their faces suggested the former. At the far end of the compound sat the Comanche Chief, Flying Eagle, his son and daughter sitting at his right and an interpreter on his left. As Simon approached Chief Flying Eagle, his eyes were actively surveying his surroundings, absorbing bits of information of the environment he had rode into; when suddenly his eyes rested on the two Indian youths he had rescued from certain death. When their eyes met, they smiled at Simon and he in turned smiled back. Simon surmised that this pow-wow was initiated to thank him for saving the lives of the Chief's son and daughter. Chief Flying Eagle had indeed prepared a feast in Simon's honor in recognition of his bravery and sense of justice. To celebrate these qualities in a white man was most unusual for Comanche Indians, or any other Indian tribes of the American South-west. These Indian tribes in the past have been the recipients of broken treaties, stolen lands, mistreatment and abuse resulting in mutual slaughter between whites and Indians. Indians have no love for the white man, only a deep rooted mistrust. That's what made Simon so different and the subject of their curiosity.

Chief Flying Eagle greeted Simon warmly and placed him in a seat of honor on his left before the ceremony and festivities began. The men of the tribe put on a flamboyant and ritualistic dance to celebrate friendship and good will; while the women paraded past Flying Eagle and Simon with baskets of viands containing buffalo meat and indigenous foods that were grown along the river bank: maze, squash, beans, sweet potatoes and freshly picked berries and pine nuts. The celebration lasted well into the night, keeping the interpreter busy while Simon and Flying Eagle smoked their peace pipes. The moon was now high in the sky while the festive ebullience slowly faded, giving way to peaceful slumber and physical repose. Simon too was feeling a bit drowsy and somnolent and decided to retire for the night. After thanking Chief Flying Eagle for his hospitality, Simon was escorted to his hogan.

Δs Simon lay in his hogan on top of blankets of buffalo skins, the teepee like hogan was illuminated by the light of a full moon entering through a small hole at the top of the hogan. He glanced around the interior of the hogan and was fascinated and curious as to its construction. He noticed that the main support came from three twelve foot long straight poles that were forked at one end and interwoven at the top to form a tripod. The door posts were supported by two straight poles that were laid against the tripod; and a number of long straight poles were set up around the frame forming a cone-shaped teepee like structure. The spaces between these poles were filled in with bark and sealed with mud. Simon admired the simplicity and sturdiness of their dwellings.

Simon rested well that night and was awakened early the following morning by the sounds of ritualistic dancing in preparation for a hunting foray. Simon was invited to join the hunting party, which he readily accepted. He was well versed in the art of hunting wild game from his early days in Western Pennsylvania and was eager to learn the Comanche method in tracking down wild game. The hunting party rode to a wooded area, then dismounted and continued on foot. As they walked through the woods, his Indian guide pointed out telltale signs on the ground, on trees and on shrubbery of the passing of different kinds of animal pray; and on other occasions he was taught to trap beaver and down buffalo. In the subsequent days and months that Simon sojourned with the Comanches, he greatly admired their way of life and learned their culture, language, costumes and social structure. He would in time come in contact with other Indian tribes, especially the Kiowas, allies of the Comanches and their neighbors to the north. To his surprise he discovered that the Kiowas spoke a different language than the Comanches. Simon had to adjust to the cultural differences he was thrust into.

While recording the relationship between Simon Ganz and the Comanche Indians, Harry Dillon deemed it appropriate to uncover and explain to his readers a little historical background on the Indians of the American Southwest. He reserved a whole column in his newspaper to this end, which read,

"....Hundreds of years ago, the Comanche, Kiowas, Shoshone, and Apache Indians all descended from a common ancestry. The Indians occupied the lands where Montana is located and emigrated south along the peneplain east of the Rocky Mountains and on to the western plains of what is now Oklahoma, Texas, New Mexico, and Arizona. During the course of hundreds of years, these Indians gradually dispersed into various tribes. Each tribe developed its own language, indistinguishable from one tribe to another; this was true of all Indian tribes of North America. Therefore, communications between tribes was facilitated mostly by sign language.

Simon never intended to stay more than a day or two with the Comanches, but one day lead to two days and two days expanded into four days and eventually his sojourn with the Comanches lasted almost a year. His extended stay with the Comanches was probably due to his keen interest and fascination with their culture, life style, as well as an amorous relationship with a young Indian squaw. During the course of that year, Simon learned as much about the Indians as the Indians knew about themselves.

The Indians owned no land in the legal sense, for the land itself was their home and the sky their ceiling. They lived in an egalitarian society, having no written laws or governance. The pow-wow was their forum, where the chief and braves would decide on issues of importance by consensus. In their society, the qualities most admired and respected in individuals were bravery and wisdom. An Indian brave would have ample opportunity to display his wisdom during the many pow-wows preceding hunting forays, wars, or deciding on tribal matters of survival. Bravery was always a key element in Indian society, especially in the pursuit of dangerous animals, such as wild boar or buffalo. The Indian brave who best fulfilled these qualities was sure to achieve prominence and possible Chiefdom.

In the weeks and months that followed, Simon participated in many of the cultural and ritualistic aspects of Indian society, especially on one notable occasion during a hunting expedition. While hunting with his Indian companions for most of the day, Simon was in awe and astonished by the seemingly inexhaustible display of energy and strength that the Indians possessed; he was particularly amazed with their ability to deny themselves water and food during extended periods of time; it seemed almost superhuman. Simon later discovered that their seemingly superhuman display of stamina and endurance was due to their use of opiates. Simon was relieved to know that he was quite normal by not competing against Indians who had a different body chemistry.

The use of opiates was frequently used by the Indians of the American Southwest. They were used in both religious and secular ceremonies, but the most frequent use of opiates was in the cure and prevention of disease, as practiced by their shaman or medicine man. They would use it to ease the pain from wounds or to create a feeling of euphoria and well being. The secular use was during their hunting forays, to allay hunger, thirst, and fatigue when performing strenuous tasks; and it was also frequently used during the pow-wow.

The opiates used by the Comanche Indians were almost exclusively from the peyote cactus-like plant. This plant grows underground like a carrot or tuber. As the plant breaks the surface of the ground, a rounded button like appendage appears; this button is cut off and dried and is known as the "peyote button," which is then chewed or made into a tea to release the many alkaloid compounds responsible for its euphoric and pain killing effect. One of the more potent alkaloids in peyote is mescaline. I sometimes wonder whether peyote encourages the many ceremonial and festive affairs or if their ceremonies require the use of peyote; most likely both are contributing factors.

One summer evening, a few days after Simon's arrival Chief Flying Eagle and his braves gathered at the ceremonial grounds to celebrate a very successful hunt; they had killed five buffalos and three wild boar. In preparation for this event, the women of the tribe were busy most of the day roasting buffalo meat and other native viands. The aroma of which permeated the air.

It was at this ritualistic gathering that Simon first noticed the presence of a beautiful young nubile squaw, who could not have been older than seventeen years of age. Those present were seated on the ground forming a circle, while the center was reserved for ceremonial activities. Simon's eyes kept wondering in the direction of this gorgeous creature, and soon her eyes made contact with his; she returned his glances with a Mona Lisa smile in acknowledgment of his interest in her. There was no doubt that she possessed in abundance all the essential female qualities that could increase the cadence of a man's heartbeat to an audible sound. It soon became apparent to Flying Eagle and all in attendance that they were engaged in a silent flirtatious affair. At the next ceremonial gathering, in recognition of their mutual interest for one another, Chief Flying Eagle invited the young squaw to sit next to Simon, introducing her to Simon as Sun Flower. All that evening Simon focused his attention on Sun Flower, attempting to teach her some English words and phases. It was obvious they were having a pleasant evening and enjoying each other's company to the fullest, often displaying broad smiles and audible laughter. The high regard that Simon was held in the eyes of Chief Flying Eagle and his Indian companions tacitly sanctioned their union, if it was to be.

One evening after a successful buffalo hunt, Simon returned to his hogan for a well earned rest. After an hour or so of relaxation, Simon joined the rest of the Indians in a feast of buffalo meat and freshly picked beans and sweet potatoes. After they had eaten their fill of buffalo meat a soporific feeling enveloped their bodies, as their eye lids occasionally dropped to closure; one by one they drifted toward their teepee's to close out the day in slumber. Simon sat there alone in silent contemplation and watched the sun's refulgence disappear below the horizon to be replaced by a blanket of stars that lit up the sky; while a chorus of crickets replaced the silence of the night. It was a beautiful evening, with Simon sitting there and staring up at the stares, albeit feeling a bit lonely; unaware that he was being watched by Sun Flower, when he decided to retire for the night.

In his hogan, Simon lay down on a blanket of buffalo skins; the light of the moon filtered through the hole at the top of his teepee, partially illuminating the interior of his hogan. He was just about to close his eyes in slumber, when he heard a slight sound at the entrance to his hogan; it was Sun Flower standing at the entrance. She stood there silently staring at Simon in a seductive manner. In the past Simon was reluctant to pursue an intimate relationship with Sun Flower, due to her age, but there she was standing before him. Simon felt the blood rushing through his veins and his heart pounding in his chest, he could not, or would not, suppress his feelings any longer as he beckoned her to come closer. She slowly advanced toward Simon, slipping off her outer garments as she approached, revealing a figure that was molded to perfection. With her long black hair partially concealing her firm round breasts, she slowly walked over to Simon and lay down beside him. They looked each other in the eyes and slowly embraced, melting into each others arms as their warm lips made contact. Simon's hands began to explore her warm body, as she did his. After some time of foreplay, Simon sensed that she was reaching fulfillment; while foundling her breast he entered her body. After their passion had come to fruition, Sun Flower rested in Simon's arms while her sexual intensity slowly subsided. Finally, they rolled over and rested side by side, content, happy, and enthralled with each other. As the hours of the evening passed and the night grew older, once again Simon was aroused by the warmth of Sun Flower's body next to his. Simon's uncontrollable passion that he felt when first he touched Sun Flower's body, was now more controllable to the extent he now approached Sun Flower with less impetuosity and more deliberate and tender feelings; she responded in kind and both engaged in unrestrained passion; their love for each other continued at that level of intensity for the next couple of months, before waning to a level of moderation. The fact that Simon stayed with the Comanches for almost a year, was due in no small measure to Sun Flower and his love for her.

Simon was now involved with every aspect of Indian life and attended most of the Pow-wows, where his voice was added to the many. One day a pow-wow was called by Chief Flying Eagle to try and solve the mystery of the disappearance of some of their horses. Within the past month some thirty horses were missing and Flying Eagle suspected that renegade Indians from the north were stealing their horses. They weren't sure, but they suspected that the Apaches were engaged in stealing horses and live stock from neighboring Indians, as well as from the white settlers in the east. Simon suggested that he go and talk to the white settlers concerning their loss of live stock before they decide on retaliatory measure against any Indian tribes. The consensus in the pow-wow was that Simon had the knowledge and understanding to deal with the white man's temperament, and he should be the one to approach the white settlers. The following morning, Simon said good-by to Sun Flower; explaining that he would be gone for a day or two. He started out at the break of day, for the two hour journey to the white settles homesteads. It was a hot and dry day; as he approached the white settlement, he could see from a distance a man chopping wood about fifty feet from his home. Simon road up to the settler and said,

"Good morning."

"Good morning to you sir." he replied.

"I've heard that you settlers have been losing some horses and live stock as of late."

Ben Bowmen replied in no uncertain terms.

"You heard right stranger, and the responsible party are those dam Indians; and we settlers are preparing a raiding party to teach those red skins a lesson."

"Well, before you go off half cocked, I suggest you make sure that your targeting the guilty Indian tribe."

"How do you know so much about those Indians stranger?"

"My name is Simon Ganz, and I have been living with the Comanche Indians for over six months now and I can vouch for the Comanches. They are not doing the stealing, as a matter of fact they too are victims like you folks. The Comanches have lost over forty horses in the past month; and their allies to the north the Kiowas also have been losing horses. The Comanches in this part of the country are a peaceful tribe and would like to remain so."

"So, your Simon Ganz; I've heard a lot about you, and so have my neighbors. If anyone else but you told me such a wild tale as that, I would have though him crazy. Do you mind if I ask you a personal question?."

"You can ask anything you like, but it doesn't mean that you'll get an answer," replied Simon.

"Well I'm just curious as to why you're living with the Comanches?" asked Ben.

"Yeah, I can answer that question for you. Briefly, I did a good deed by saving the lives of two Comanche youths; they happened to be the son and daughter of Chief Flying Eagle, and as a result Flying Eagle sought me out to invite me to his compound and thank me for saving the lives of his children. Chief Flying Eagle treated me royally, with a plethora of food and entertainment. I really didn't intend to stay longer than a day or two, but as things turned out, two day lead to a week, then a month, so here I am six months later. Does that answer your question?"

"It does indeed. Your life has been a series of good deeds, along with plenty of killings. It seems to me that your actions are a bit contradictory;

how can you explain them?"

"I never killed any man who didn't deserve it, or didn't ask to be killed by his heinous behavior. I don't relish, nor am I proud of killing any human being, but there are times when it cannot be avoided, no matter how hard you try. It's like warfare; kill or be killed. Now let's get on with the business that brought me here, the mystery as to who's responsible for stealing horses and live stock. The Comanches think it might be renegade Apache Indians; but we should not move against them unless we're sure that they are the guilty party. If the Apaches are the guilty party, then we should unite our forces as one. The Apaches are a war like tribe and they outnumber each individual group. Our only chance of success would be to unite the two Indian tribes, the Comanches and Kiowas, with you settlers to form an overpowering force."

Ben realized the wisdom of Simon's remarks, and agreed to consult with his fellow settlers as to their willingness to form a united front against the Apaches. While Ben was in consultation with his neighbors, Simon was given quarters and food while awaiting the decision of the settlers. The following morning, Ben and two other members of his group consulted with Simon, Ben explained,

"The settlers are in agreement with your plan, and we could add about one hundred men to this fighting force; these men all have the latest model of Springfield rifles, which will make up in part for our lack of numbers," Ben went on to explain,

"The Indians left in their wake some artifacts clinging to trees, bushes or found on the ground. Maybe the Comanches could identify the Indian marauders by examining their feathers, beads or arrows left behind."

Simon looked at the artifacts and said,

"They sure don't look like anything the Comanches wear. I'll take them back with me and let the Comanches examine them; maybe they could identify the tribe they belong to. If and when we make a positive identification, I'll get back to you and arrange a meeting at the Comanche compound to explain my plan of attack."

Simon gathered the half dozen or so artifacts the marauding Indians left behind; said good-by to the settlers and set out on his way back to the Comanche compound. Simon had been gone for only two days; yet as he rode through the compound, the Indians gathered outside their tee-pees and greeted Simon back with a sea of smiles and hand waving, signifying their delight in his return. No one was more happy than Sun Flower, to see Simon return. She greeted him with a smile of deep affection. Simon knew that Indian women don't display their love openly in public. He put his arm around her shoulder and they walked to their hogan.

The women of the tribe were preparing a welcome back feast for Simon; but Flying Eagle had more pressing matters on his mind and scheduled a pow-wow for the next day to discuss Simon's findings and gauge the thinking of the white settlers. The feast commenced early in the evening as the Indian men began imbibing their peyote cocktails in preparation for their ostentatious dancing. The festivities lasted well into the night, and around about midnight, the participants with their full stomachs and drunk on peyote cocktails were becoming lethargic and somnolent. The most subdued and suber couple there were Simon and Sun Flower. Gradually, each family began to retreat into their own tee-pees in a slow and deliberate disappearing act. Simon and Sun Flower were the first to depart, they had a rendezvous with love and once behind closed buffalo skins, they tenderly embraced each other and continued where they had left off, before Simon departed for the white settlement.

The next day, Flying Eagle and the elders of the tribe gathered for the pow-wow; Simon was already in attendance when they arrived. When all were seated, their eyes focused on Simon, anxiously waiting to hear what he had to say. Simon explained to the Indian council,

"The white settlers were frustrated and angry and were ready to attack any Indian settlement they came upon. I convinced them by attacking innocent Indian compounds wouldn't solve their problem, since we had to identify the Indian tribe responsible for this mischief. They then handed me the artifacts they had collected in the wake of the last Indian raid."

Simon displayed the artifacts to the council; Flying Eagle scrutinized them, then passed them around to each of the elders for their examination and assessment. The evidence was damming and undeniable to each member of the council. All came to the same conclusion; it was the Apaches who were stealing the horses and live stock.

Now that they had identified the guilty party, the discussion evolved around how to deal with this problem. One impetuous brave suggested an outright assault on the Apache compound. Simon immediately interjected his opposition to such a scheme, declaring, "The Apaches outnumber the Comanches and it would be too costly a conflict in terms of bloodshed, with no assurance that we would prevail." No, he continued, "We must take them by surprise with overwhelming force. The Apaches are a warlike tribe, with a fighting force of one hundred and fifty worriers; while the Comanches have eighty worriers, and our allies to the north, the Kiowas, have only about sixty five braves. If I could convince fifty of the white settles to join us, with their new Springfield rifles, it would augment our fighting force to a hundred and ninety five. Then we could spring a surprise attack on the Apache compound and put an end to their marauding ways, with a minimum of bloodshed on our side."

The elders in the pow-wow consulted with one another for a half hour, then unanimously sanctioned Simon's plan and had him work out the details of the assault.

The following morning, Simon set out for the white settlement with the express purpose of presenting his plan to the white settlers, and to find out if they were willing to join the Comanches and Kiowas Indians in a combined attack on the Apache compound. In the West, stealing horses is a serious offense, whether it's one horse or a heard of horses; and the Indians understood that as well as the white man. After arriving at the white settlement, Simon sought out Ben Bowmen the apparent spokesman for the white community, and greeted Ben,

"Good morning Ben, I have some news for you concerning the ownership of those artifacts you gave me for identification; the Comanches were able to identify those artifacts as belonging to the Apache tribe. Now that we know who the guilty party is, the hour of decision for action is now. As you well know, the Apaches are a formidable fighting force and in order to subdue them we should combine our forces; the Comanches, their allies the Kiowas and fifty of your riflemen. That's what it will take to defeat them. Are you willing to join us?"

"Well, it sounds reasonable, but I'll have to discuss your plan with the rest of our committee; so why don't you make yourself comfortable, get something to eat, sleep over and we'll let you know in the morning."

"That sounds good to me, if you do decide to join us then you and two other members of your group are invited to join us at a pow-wow one week from today at the Comanche compound, at which time I will explain the details of our attack." The next morning Ben walked to Simon's quarters and said,

"Good morning Simon, were your accommodations satisfactory?"

"They were just fine Ben, have you fellows reached a decision?"

"Yeah Simon, we'll listen to your plan and anything else you have to say, but I can't promise you our participation."

"Good enough Ben, I'll see you and the other two members of your group a week from today at the Comanche compound; so long for now."

While Simon was consorting with the white settlers, Flying Eagle sent an emissary to the Kiowa tribe to inform them that the Apaches were the guilty party responsible for the thief of their horses, and that Chief Flying Eagle was forming a warring party to attack the Apaches, and would like the Kiowas to join the Comanches in this attack. The Kiowas listened attentively to what the emissary had to say, then retired to decide whether to join the Comanches in a combined assault on the Apaches. After several hours of deliberation, they decide to join forces with the Comanches and put an end to the Apaches's thieving ways. The emissary then asked the Kiowa Chief, Shooting Star to attend a pow-wow seven moons from today at the Comanche compound, along with his elders, to learn the details of the attack. Chief Shooting Star told the emissary he would attend the pow-wow with his elders.

During the interim between Simons visit to the white settlement and the scheduled pow-wow meeting, the white settlers had several discussions amongst themselves concerning Simon's proposal of a combined offensive operation. The consensus of the white settlers was that they would join the assault group if they agreed with Simon's plan. Prior to Simon's visit, the white settlers were driven to despair and were preparing to attack any Indians they encountered; that would have been bad for Indians, and catastrophic for the white settlers who knew nothing about the Indians and their culture.

In times of tension and anxiety, time passes slowly. When the time of the pow-wow did arrive all three parties were in attendance and a large hogan was filled to capacity. The Kiowa Chief and his elders were seated, as were Simon, Ben Bowmen and his two committee members. After a congenial greeting by Chief Flying Eagle, Simon was introduced to explain his plan. Simon stood up to addressed those assembled.

"I'm sure you're all curious as to why the Apaches resorted to such a despicable acts as stealing horses and live stock from their neighbors. They would never have made these raids if they didn't think they had immunity from retaliation; since their numerical superiority as a fighting force was greater than any of their neighboring tribes. What they did not realize, and never could imagine was white settlers uniting with smaller Indian tribes to form an overwhelming force against them and bring an end to their nefarious raids. If we do unit we can be successful. Now this is the situation as I see it. The Apaches reside in a shallow basin surrounded by small hills ranging in height from thirty to seventy-five feet. The largest of these hills is located at the entrance to their compound, which will work to our advantage. The white settlers with their Springfield rifles, will form a semi-circle on both sides of the entrance to the Apache compound. Half of the Kiowa braves will occupy a lower tier of the hill to the right of the entrance, and half of the Comanche braves occupy the tier left of the entrance; a combined party of twenty to thirty Comanches and Kiowas will round up the horses and live stock and lead them out of harm's way. There are bound to be a few Apache sentries guarding their compound, they will have to be silenced before we commence operations. The corralling of the horses and live stock will be the signal to begin our attack. Since our assault will start as soon as the sun breaks the horizon, it may be difficult for us to distinguish our Indians allies from the Apaches, especially for the white settlers. I therefore suggest that our Indians wear red scarfs around their necks, to prevent any accidental killings by white settlers. One thing more, I do not want any women or children killed in this raid. Are there any questions?"

One of the white settlers asked,

"What if they concede defeat, does that end the fighting?"

"That's a good question, yes it does! I didn't formulate this battle plan to kill all Apaches, we just want them to realize that there is a price to pay for stealing horses and live stock. Now if everyone is in agreement, we'll meet again four days from today at the Comanche compound for our day of vengeance.

The day of retribution had arrived, and the attacking parties advanced in the dead of night toward the Apache settlement. Before the arrival of the main Indian and white combatants, a small contingent of Comanches quickly and silently disposed of the Apache sentinels surrounding their compound. The Comanches and Kiowas were the first to arrive on the scene; they could approach the Apache compound as silently as a deer moving through the woods. The white settlers with their Springfield rifles were the last to arrive, since it was uncertain as to whether they could move into position as quickly as their Indian allies. All combatants were now in position and patiently awaiting daybreak.

Vengeance

As the first rays of sunlight displaced the darkness of the night, Simon gave the signal to release the impounded horses. The Comanches and Kiowas released the horses and live stock from their confinement and corralled them out of harm's way. The thundering sound of horses hooves alerted the Apaches to action, emerging from their tee-pees en mass. That was the signal for the Springfield rifles to go into action; the deadly sound of rifle fire echoed through the morning air, causing great havoc and bloodshed. After the riflemen decimated a portion of the Apache warriors, the Comanches and Kiowas rode into the Apache compound in a deadly assault on the stragglers. It was a fierce and bloody encounter with a heavy loss of life on both sides. The Apaches at the far end of the compound regrouped and launched an assault on the hill where the gunfire was coming from. This assault on the riflemen was the fiercest and bloodiest encounter of the battle; the riflemen could not reload their rifles fast enough to repel the onslaught. The white settlers were saved from certain death, only by the intervention of the red scarfed Indians attacking from the rear of the compound; dispersing and hacking to death the Apaches. That attack saved the day and ended the battle. The remaining Apaches fled the scene of battle, leaving behind a field littered with dead and dying Indians, staining the ground red with their blood.

The victorious combatants having vanquished the Apaches, corralled the stolen horses and live stock and distributed them to their rightful owners. Peace and harmony was now restored to the Indian communities and the white settlement, and a sense of normalcy prevailed.

Peace and normalcy was not part of Simon's evaluation as he lay in his hogan, and silently relived the events of that terrible day. The rampant slaughter and bloodshed was still fresh in Simon's mind. The sight of Comanches wheeling tomahawks to the skulls of Apaches, splitting their heads in two and exposing their brains, could not be easily forgotten. There were no real winners in this conflict, in a sense everyone lost. Yes, the Apaches were punished for their rapacious disregard of their neighbors property; sacrificing the lives of fifty of their young braves. The Comanches and Kiowas retrieved their stolen horses; losing sixteen and thirteen of their braves respectively, and the white settlers lost eleven of their men. Although this war was a necessary exercise in justice, to Simon it couldn't be considered a worthwhile outcome for anyone.

The Apaches, in their predacious desire for wealth, in the form of horses and livestock, decided to use their superior manpower to steal from their weaker neighbors. It was clear to Simon that the greed and miscalculation on the part of the Apaches, were responsible for the unnecessary loss of human life and the diminution of their property. Simon's last thought before dozing off was, if only mutual respect and understanding could replace greed and suspicion; how much better off we all would be.

Chapter Eleven
Drums of War

From time to time Simon would visit the white settlers in western Texas located a couple of miles from the New Mexico border. This fledgling community spread its wings over the landscape for several square miles; its fertile land and grassy plains beckoned people from diverse sections of the country to migrate to Texas at the end of the Mexican War. Habitation was slow for the first ten years, but increasing as of late, and now home to over one hundred families with a population of four hundred and twenty five whites, and seventy five black slaves. This community was indeed a melting pot of people with different religious faiths, political views, social upbringing and training. A hotel was now under construction with a saloon at its base and currently in operation. It was known as the Long Horn Saloon and was the focal point for socializing, smoking strong cigars and drinking hard liquor.

The topics most frequently discussed were the extension of slavery into the newly acquired territories of the U.S. and secession of the Southern states from the Union. Embroiled in these debates were pro-slavery people, free soil folks, secessionists, unionists and even some pro-slavery unionists. Simon made his views known on secession in no uncertain terms, calling it the diminution of central power in the Union; by creating two separate countries, each weaker than the former Union. If the Southern states had the right to secede from the Union, then each Southern state had the right to secede from the Confederacy and that would be self destructive, since each Southern state was "Too small for a country and too large for an insane asylum." Others weren't shy in expressing their opinions, and did so. Their diatribes were vehemently expressed and hotly debated but their opinions never elevated to the point of physical confrontation. They realized that they needed each other for their survival and would always depart with a smile and a hand shake. That's what made this community so different from the rest of the country.

Simon had made arrangements to stay overnight at one of the guest houses which was hastily constructed as temporary quarters, pending completion of the Long Horn Hotel. Prelude to Simon's retiring for the night he spent the evening at the Long Horn Saloon, smoked cigars and drinking his share of whisky while trying to solve the country's domestic problems with words. After this debating society had spent the better part of the evening talking, Simon decided to call it a day and retire for the night; but before he exited the Long Horn Saloon a rider came roaring up to the saloon shouting, "It's war, it's war between the states. Fort Sumter, in Charleston Harbor has been bombarded into submission by Confederate forces."

A moment of silence enveloped those in the saloon, then chatter of war was on everyone's lips. Some of the patrons were smiling and obviously glad that war would settle the question of secession. Others were somber, aware of the dreadful impact war will inflict on the country. Simon said nothing and retired to his cottage despondent and dejected, to think that it had came to this. Early next morning, Simon set out for the Comanche compound worried and concerned over the faith of his country. He had once heard a myopic politician predict,

"The amount of blood that would be shed in a Civil War could be wiped up with a handkerchief." It bothered and bemused Simon that the destiny of our country rested in the hands of such fatuous politicians. His prediction missed its mark by a light year.

Before leaving he flagged down Ben Bowmen to say good -by,

"Good-by Ben, I'm not sure how quiet things will be around here since war is now a reality."

"As you probably know Simon, Texas is one of the states that will seceded from the Union; since I'm a Texan, I'll have to go with my state. I and forty others from this settlement are leaving tomorrow morning to enlist in the Confederate army that is being formed under Gen. John Hood, in Austin. I've also heard that there are about fourteen settlers who will be on their way to join Federal forces in the North. With all of these men leaving for the army it will certainly create a manpower shortage in some quarters. I'm sure glade I don't have a wife or kids to worry about. I hope this war won't last very long so we can resume normal relations again. Well, Simon, I guess it's time for us to part company, It's been a real honor and privilege knowing you; I know you're thinking on secession and I respect it. We've fought the Apaches together and I hope we will never meet on the field of battle in this conflict. So I'll just say good-by and the best of luck to you and hope that we both survive this war."

"Well Ben, as I said so many times before, I don't think anything, least of all slavery can justify the formation of two countries. Now that all this talk of secession is over, I'm afraid the shedding of American blood begins, I do hope you survive this war in one piece Ben, so for now I'll say good-by and good luck."

And off Simon rode.

Riding back to the Comanche compound Simon's thoughts were focused on the war and its ramifications. There were some politicians in high places who thought that the war would be of a short duration, but most Americans including Simon feared a long and bloody conflict, leaving in its wake misery and destruction with families torn asunder and bereft of love ones. For now, Simon would sit tight and watch events unfold; if the war appeared to be a long and bloody contest he would then enlist for the duration of the war to defend the Union against all who seek its destruction.

Once a week Simon would ride out to various outposts on the frontier seeking information on the progress of the war, including rides to the white settlement. The initial reports were not encouraging, and the first battle of the war between green troops occurred at Manassas, a railroad junction in Northern Virginia about thirty miles west of Washington. At this junction is a gap, the gateway to the Shenandoah Valley, a fertile and productive land mass used to grow crops and livestock, known as the "Bread Basket of the South."

Prior to the battle of Manassas, the Washington newspapers were replete with detailed information of the operation and strategy of the Federal army at Manassas junction. To no one's surprise these newspapers found their way to Richmond, to the delight and satisfaction of the Confederate War Department. The Washington reporters inadvertently acted as the eyes and ears of the rebel army. Consequently, the battle of Manassas ended in a disaster for the Federal troops who retreated in a disorderly route, discarding their rifles and anything else that would impede their flight back to Washington.

This was not what Simon wanted to hear as he road back to the Comanche compound. As Simon continued to live and hunt with his Indian companions, his comfort level dropped and continued to drop after each passing month as he began to realize that this war would not be consummated in six months. If it weren't for Sun Flower he would have departed the Comanche compound long ago, his love for her was the only reason for his continued presence there and he continued to struggle between his love for Sun Flower and duty to his country. In addition to his low comfort level, a guilt complex began to take root and overpowered his desire to stay with Sun Flower and his Indian companions, knowing that his fellow countrymen were engaged in a life and death struggle to prevent the dismemberment of his country. As he remained deep in thought, Sun Flower walked in. He looked at her affectionately and decided that he could no longer remain a bystander in this monumental struggle.

He walked over to Sun Flower, placed his hands on both of her shoulders and looked her straight in the eyes, and said,

"Sun Flower there is something important I must tell you; tomorrow I must leave you to join the Union army in the North. I can no longer stand by and watch as brave men shed their blood to preserve this Union. Ever since this war began I've been slowly sinking into a state of despondency knowing that while I'm living in comfort and safety here with you, my fellow compatriots are engaged in a noble struggle, spilling their blood, and leaving their arms, legs, and mangled bodies on the battlefields of this land. If I don't leave to join these brave men in their righteous struggle to preserve this Union, I would be of no value to you or anyone else. I can no longer stay here and maintain my honor and self respect. Do you understand what I'm saying Sun Flower?"

She had noticed his decline in spirit and energy for the past few months and realized the wisdom and necessity for his decision to leave and tried to remain stolid while tears rolled down her checks. She would not try to dissuade Simon from leaving, since staying here with her would be worse than leaving. She knew that Simon gave considerable thought to his decision to leave before finalizing it into action.

"Yes Simon, I understand. You are a noble warrior, you fight for your country like you fight for the Indians. Go, and return to Sun Flower when you finish war."

With that said, they both lay down beside each other in silence. Simon with watery eyes and Sun Flower with a heavy heart and a nagging resolve not to show Simon any weakness. Before retiring for the night Simon informed Flying Eagle of his decision to leave the Indian compound and join the Union army.

The next morning as Simon prepared to leave, he embraced, caressed and kissed Sun Flower good -by and promised he would return after the war. Finally, it was time for Simon to leave and as he and Sun Flower emerged from their hogan, the entire Indian population headed by Flying Eagle was waiting to bid Simon farewell and happy hunting. Most of the women in the compound were trying to conceal their wet eyes and muffled sobs. Simon thought it best to make a quick exit, kissing Sun Flower good-by, hugging Flying Eagle, then mounting his horse and waving to the crowd, Simon was off to war.

CHAPTER TWELVE
THE BLUE AND THE GRAY

 imon pointed his horse in a northeasterly direction and stayed the course. After several days of travel he learned from the local population that a big battle had been fought on the Tennessee and Cumberland Rivers, in Tennessee. He was traveling through rebel country and each person he spoke to gave a different version of the conflict. In order to obtain a better assessment of the battle he talked to a dozen or more people and read the details of the engagement in the newspapers. He was now able to piece together the details of the battle, which appeared to be a glorious Union victory. This is what he had learned:

On the 6th of February, 1862, Gen. U. S. Grant with fifteen thousand troops traveled up the Tennessee River, landing eight miles north of Fort Henry, while Admiral Foote's gunboats opened fire on the rebel batteries. After two hours of exchanged canon fire most of the rebel batteries were disabled or destroyed. The defendants of Fort Henry having lost half their men, killed or wounded, realized their plight hopeless and retreated to Fort Donelson to make their stand. When Gen. Grant arrived at the fort, he found a white flag atop Fort Henry. Gen. Grant's troops were spared the effusion of blood due to Admiral Foot's gunboats that blasted the rebels into submission. Fort Henry represented an important strategic outpost on the Tennessee River.

While Fort Henry was a relatively easy conquest, the same would not be true for Fort Donelson which was three times as strong as Fort Henry and mounted on a bluff one hundred feet high overlooking the Cumberland River, with twenty one thousand rebel troops defending the Fort. In the morning, the Union artillery arrived, followed by Adm. Foote's four ironclads and two wooden gunboats. The gunboats maneuvered too close to Fort Donelson and overshot their mark, while the gunboats were in a perfect location to receive rebel fire. The resulting exchange of fire proved disastrous for Adm. Foote's gunboats, the rebel cannoneers ripped the iron plates off the ironclads and inflicted serious damage to the rest of the fleet. After several hours of exchanged fire, Adm. Foote was wounded and the fleet pulled out of action.

Adm. Foote sent for Gen. Grant and while conferring aboard one of his gunboats, Adm. Foote suggested to Gen. Grant that it might be best to abandon the attack on Fort Donelson.

"No!" said Grant.

"The army will do it alone, outnumbered that we are."

Fort Donelson was commanded by Gen. John Floyd (Sec. of War, during the Buchanan administration) and a wanted man in the North for fraud and alleged transfer of arms to Southern arsenals. Floyd committed eight thousand men against Gen. McClernand's division on the right, they fought gallantly against overwhelming Confederate forces, till they were subdued and rendered inoperative; Floyd followed his success with an attacked on Gen. Lew Wallace's division. Grant had heard the sound of battle and rode up to assess conditions; he sensed that all of Floyd's strength was on his right flank and ordered Gen. Smith to attack the Fort on its front at once. Grant was right, Floyd had drawn out most of his force to the right in an attempt to escape to his left. Gen. Smith led the charge in person, vanquishing the whole line of fortification on his front. By the end of the day, with McClernand's division blocking the road of egress and Grant placing his artillery on the high ground that Gen. Smith had taken, Grant was in position to blast the Fort to pieces. The Fort could no longer be defended and Floyd was afraid he would be hanged for his past activities if captured and turned over command of the Fort to his second in command, Gen. Pillow. Pillow had no desire to be captured either and turned over command to West Pointer Gen. Simon Buckner, who wrote to Grant asking Grant for terms of surrender. Buckner had known Grant in the old army. When Grant was discharged from the army, Buckner had given him money for transportation home. But no such kindness exists in war.

Grant replied, "No term except an unconditional surrender can be accepted. I propose to move immediately on your works."

Buckner then surrendered his whole army of seventeen thousand men, sixty five guns and the Fort. Simon read every newspaper article, squib, or commentary on the Battle of Fort Donelson; when he read Gen. Grant's "Unconditional Surrender" reply to Gen. Buckner, he proclaimed,

"That's the General I want to serve under."

And he set out looking for Gen. Grant's army. Simon traveled north along the eastern side of the Mississippi River, then turned due east about fifty miles south of Memphis. After riding a good portion of the day he came upon a small contingent of Federal troops who were obviously a scouting party. He flagged them down to inquire as to the location of the nearest recruiting station. Simon was told that about five miles north of here, along the Old Post Road he would find temporary headquarters for recruitments and a Sergeant Dunn would answer any questions he might have. Simon thanked the troopers and headed north. It wasn't long before the recruiting station came into view; he rode up to the tent, dismounted and walked inside, asking,

"Is this where you sign up for military service?"

"Yes, you've come to the right place. All you have to do is sign on the dotted line and indicate how long you wish to serve and you'll be in the Army; but I would suggest that you read the enlistment form before signing."

"I'm signing up for the duration of the war," replied Simon.

"That's great; that's the kind of men we need," handing Simon the enlistment forms.

Simon read the enlistment papers, then signed them and handed them back to Sergeant Dunn. The Sergeant examined the enlistment papers for completeness, then noticed the name Simon Ganz. He paused and said.

"Simon Ganz; that name sounds familiar," He paused again and thought a while, then blurred out, "Are you the Simon Ganz of Abilene and Kansas City fame?"Simon smiled and said,

"Yeah that's me."

"Well, well, well, I'll be dammed! Never thought I'd see Simon Ganz at an Army recruiting station. One thing is for sure, the Army won't have to teach you how to handle fire arms. As a matter of fact, you would make an excellent instructor for these new enlistees; you would have a safe job and the rank of Sergeant."

"Now listen here Sergeant, I understand that somebody has to drill recruits and shuffle paper but that's not for me. If I wanted a safe job I would have stayed where I was. I can't ask a poor farm boy from Minnesota to shed his blood while I'm given a safe job because of my name. No, I'll take my chances fighting with Gen. Grant."

The Sergeant's face turned red, realizing he had offended Simon by offering him preferential treatment over the common soldier, then replied.

"Of course you're right Mr. Ganz, I mean Priv. Ganz, I should have known better and I do apologize. Here is a copy of your enlistment papers, just travel north along the Tennessee River and you'll find Gen. Grant's army, and the best of luck to you."

"Thanks Sergeant, I understand you meant well and if I had more time I'd be happy to have a drink with you, but I'm afraid this war won't wait."

Simon mounted his horse and rode north to where the war was.

Simon road fast and hard after receiving his orders. That evening he arrived at Gen. Grant's headquarters at Pittsburg Landing along the Tennessee River. He walked into the largest of many white clad tents and was greeted by a Lieutenant Jones. Simon introduced himself and presented his enlistment papers to Lt. Jones. After inspecting the papers and finding them in order, he shook Simon's hand and said.

"Glad to have you Private Ganz, the Quartermaster will issue you your uniform; I see by your papers you have quite a reputation out West as a sharpshooter and a law enforcer. Since you have your own horse, I'll assign you to Gen. Prentiss's Division as a surveillance scout where you'll be the eyes and ears of his Div. Now grab yourself something to eat and get a good night's sleep, you can report to Gen. Prentiss in the morning. Incidentally Ganz, the rank of Sergeant goes with that job, so you are now Sgt. Ganz."

"Thanks Lt., at that rate I should make General in a week."

Gen. Grant was reinforced with twenty five thousand green troops, many of whom had never fired a rifle before, bringing his total force to forty five thousand men. These troops were scattered over an area of twelve square miles, south and west of Pittsburg Landing, from Shiloh Church, across one mile of peach orchards to a country road worn down by many years of travel and erosion revealing its bed a couple of feet below the surrounding ground. The twelve square mile area was blanketed with white tents where the troops resided. The troops reflected a happy and vacation like attitude and after morning drills off they went to swim in the Tennessee River. Both Gen. Grant and Gen. Sherman were complacent and thought there would be no fighting for the next day or two; at least not until Gen. Don Carlos Buell arrived from upper Tennessee with his army to reenforce Grant.

Not far from Shiloh across the border in Mississippi, lies the busy town of Corinth, an important railroad junction connecting the East to the West and the North to the South, where supplies and materiel would enter or depart for various locations in the country. Gen. Beauregard had joined forces with Gen. Johnston at Corinth, augmenting their army to 45,000 men, for an assault on Grant. Albert Sidney Johnston was a seasoned veteran of the Mexican War and had many victorious battles to his credit. He was regarded as the best general in the Confederate army by both the North and the South and was in command in the West.

The troops he commanded were equally green civilians, thrust into ill fitting uniforms to look like soldiers. Like their Union counterparts, they were barely out of their teens and had never fired a rifle before. There was a scattering of veteran soldiers in both camps; but not since the battle of Manassas, was there such a collection of civilians disguised as soldiers. The next few days would test their manhood and separate the boys from the men. Those who would stand and fight and survive the battle can rightfully be called soldiers. Gen. Johnston was well aware of Gen. Grant's intention to attack Corinth as soon as he was joined by Gen. Buell. He decided to strike first and he readied his troops for an attack on Pittsburg Landing.

Meanwhile, Sgt. Ganz was roaming the countryside, scouting the terrain for signs of rebel troop movement from the town of Shiloh to Shiloh church, across the peach orchards with the trees in their full spring dress of pink blossoms and east toward the Tennessee River. Stopping at various Union outposts to chat with the sentinels on duty. He lingered awhile at one outpost and engaging Pvt. Anderson in conversation, while chatting he noticed a faint sound and movement of leaves in the nearby bush; Simon was experienced enough to recognized subtle movements that would alert him to danger and was sure there was someone hiding in the shrubbery and alerted Pvt. Anderson to be on guard; both drew their weapons and Simon yelled out,

"Come out from behind that bush or we'll start blasting away."

Suddenly a Confederate soldier emerged with his hands held high.

They both looked at the Confederate soldier in amazement; why he was just a boy who could not have been more than fourteen years of age, clad in an ill fitted Confederate uniform.

"Well, what have we here?" asked Simon,

"What's your name soldier? Where are you from? And did your mother give you permission to join the army?"

The boy looked a little bewildered not knowing what to expect, then replied, "My name is Pvt. James Potts and I'm from a small town five miles south of Birmingham, Alabama. My mother is a widow woman and she cried and pleaded with me to stay home with her, but I told her that I had to join up and fight for the glorious defense of the Confederacy before the war ended."

"How come they signed you up, they surely knew you were underage."

"Maybe so, but I told them I was eighteen, they scratched their heads and looked at me for awhile, then signed me up and gave me a uniform and a rifle."

Simon decided to interrogate the boy rather than send him to the rear, since time was more precious than military procedure, besides he would only wind up in a prison camp and probably wouldn't survive.

"Tell me soldier what are you doing hiding in the bushes?"

"I'm a scout, looking for Yankees!"

"Well you found two of them, now tell me how many men has Gen. Johnston got in Corinth, and does he intend to retreat or fight?"

"I don't know how many men we have but there sure is plenty of them. Retreat, hell no, we're getting ready to drive every damn one of you Yankees into the Tennessee River."

Simon got as much information as he could from the soldier and knew that he was being truthful, he was much too young and unsophisticated to be deceptive or reticent. They still had to decide what to do with this soldier, they couldn't let him go free and they didn't want to send him to a prison camp where his chances of survival would be slim. They thought for a while, then Simon said,

"Tell me soldier, are you a God fearing man?"

"I sure am, I carry my Bible with me at all times and read it every chance I get."

"That's good," replied Simon.

"Now I'll tell you what we'll do. We'll let you go free, if you take an oath on that Bible of yours to return to your mama and not take up arms against Union forces or aid the Confederacy in any way for the duration of the war."

"Oh, I can't do that! You're asking me to desert the glorious course of our Confederacy and run away."

"No! I'm asking you to save your ass, if we send you to a prison camp you'll never see battle and you'll never see your mother again, and you'll probably die there of dysentery, disease, or malnutrition. So what will it be? Prison camp or home to mama?"

The boy soldier looked sad and broken hearted and after pausing a good while he realized that he had no other alternative but to accept Simon's offer.

"O.K. I'll take the oath."

Simon had the boy place his hand on his Bible as he administered the oath of a noncombatant. With that settled, the boy took off for home where he belonged.

Simon then turned to Pvt. Anderson and said,

"You know private, some day that boy will be a man and he'll look back on this episode in his life and be grateful for the choice he made. Well, I guess I'll be on my way now."

A few hours after Simon's encounter with the boy soldier he found himself in the area of the peach tree orchards, admiring the beautiful pink blossoms caressed by a warm spring breeze. Everything seemed so peaceful, it didn't seem like a bloody battle was about to erupt into deadly combat. Simon was just a little east of Shiloh church when he heard the rebel yell echo through the peach tree orchard, breaking the silence of a spring day as thousands of Confederate soldiers emerged from the thick underbrush. The enfilade of rebel troops saw Simon and let loose a volley of rifle fire; fortunately for Simon, they were poor marksmen which allowed Simon to put a little distance between himself and the invading force before having his horse shot out from under him. He had barely made it to the sunken road where Gen. Prentiss's Div. was stationed. The Federal troops were awakened by the loud yells of the advancing Confederate force and they scrambled into position to await the enemy.

Rest no more soldier boy, for this battle will be the bloodiest in American history up till now. Some of the green soldiers in both camps panicked and fled to the rear. Despite the runaways, those who remained fought with brave determination and resolve. All day long the battle raged throughout the once peaceful country side. The fire was so heavy at times that the pink blossoms rained down from the peach trees before the peach trees themselves were blasted into wooden missiles. The area of the sunken road was where the bloodiest and most contentious fighting took place. All day long the rebels attacked and each time were driven back. The Southerners labeled this piece of real estate as the "Hornet's Nest." They had assaulted this ground so many times that the defenders lost count. The ground along the entire length of the sunken road turned red with the blood from both the Southern and Northen soldiers. The area was littered with body parts, legs and arms ripped away from living tissue, heads severed from mangled bodies exposing their white ribboned brains. Most of the line had collapsed from constant bombardment and rebel assaults. One Division still holding its ground was that of Gen. Prentiss, who was becoming an indomitable force of resistence. Most of the officers in his division were either killed or wounded and to fill the gap, Simon took command of a company of men and directed their fire. A Confederate general commandeered sixty artillery pieces and zeroed them in on the "Hornet's Nest." After being pulverized with cannon fire for most of the afternoon, Gen. Prentiss realized he could do no more and surrendered the remainder of his force. His brave and tenacious stand saved most of Grant's army.

Not far from the sunken road near the peach tree orchard a catastrophe unfolded. Gen. Albert Sidney Johnston while directing field operations on top his horse, took a bullet in his leg severing a major artery. Although he did not realizing the severity of his wound, the blood gushed forth filling his boot. He dismounted his horse and rested under a peach tree. At that point in time a tourniquet could have saved his life; but lacking medical attention he slowly bled to death.

Behind the Union lines complete chaos rained. All along the road leading to Pittsburg Landing were disorganized men, teamsters, reserve artillery, and ambulance details bringing back the wounded. By late afternoon, neither army was hardly recognizable as an organized fighting force. The Confederates had gained much ground but were in no better shape than the Federal defenders. One more assault on the Union forces might have ended in a Confederate victory, but darkness had descended; if there were to be a final assault it would have to wait till dawn. The Confederates just could not fight any more without a good night's sleep. While they were sleeping, Buell's army had arrived.

Gen. Lew Wallace could have reversed the fortunes of war that day if he had not been wrongly directed from Crump's landing. He had arrived at midnight with his seven thousand men to fill Grant's weakened right flank and at 2 A.M. "Bull" Nelson reported with his 1st Div. of Buell army, at 2:30 that morning Crittenden arrived in river boats with another of Buell's Div., at 3 A.M. McCook followed with his 3rd Div. and by 4 A.M. Grant had all his troops in place to go on the offensive.

The Federal soldiers who were taken prisoners by the surrender of Gen. Prentiss's troops at the sunken road were lined up and marched south to await transfer to a Confederate prison encampment. Sgt. Ganz was among those soldiers marching south. While walking, he recalled the advice he had given the boy soldier he had captured concerning the deplorable conditions that existed in prison camps. The more he thought about it, the more determined he became not to languish in prison to live a subhuman existence for the duration of the war. His mind began to think of possible means of escape. Suddenly an opportunity presented itself. They were marching in a queue that was parallel to the nearby woods. The woods were a good distance from the line of march, but Simon noticed that a quarter of a mile ahead the wooded area came within twenty five or thirty feet from the marching prisoners. At that point, he decided to make a run for the woods and if successful he might be able to evade his pursuers and make it back to the Union lines. The nearest guard from Simon was thirty five feet away, if he was a poor shot he might make a successful run of it. He had to take that chance and as soon as he approached the elected spot, Simon bolted out from the line of marchers as fast as his legs could carry him. The guards fired at Simon missing him twice, he came within five feet of the woods before being hit in the leg by a bullet from one of the guards. Simon fell to the ground unable to move while the blood from his wound stained the ground around him. The sentry realizing that he was hit and bleeding profusely, decided to leave him there, they couldn't be bothered with a wounded soldiers. So Simon was left to his own device.

That morning Gen. Grant's army was in position and poised to take the offensive with Lew Wallace's Div. leading the charge. As they advanced forward from Pittsburg Landing, they drove the Confederates back across the ground they had gained the previous day and beyond, driving them from the field of battle and into rebel lines. As the Union forces moved forward they passed through the dead and dying of the blue and the gray soldiers from the previous day's battle. Arms, legs and shattered bodies peppered the battle field for miles, bodies twisted in grotesque forms, horses blown apart with their internal organs mingled with the human dead, broken equipment and implements of war were scattered about. The stench of rotting flesh was starting to permeate the air and the depressing sight of this killing field was a terrible reminder of the high price paid for war. Gen. Beauregard, realizing the battle of Shiloh was lost retreated all the way back to the ramparts of Corinth, in Mississippi.

As Simon lay helpless and bleeding on the ground he saw a mass of blue uniforms approaching in the distance. The sight elevated his spirit knowing that he would not be left to die, but now had a fighting chance for survival. The mass of blue uniforms was followed by a contingent of ambulances, gathering the wounded from both sides. When they reached Simon he was somewhat incoherent from the loss of blood, but the medics weren't listening, their only concern was placing him in the ambulance and transport him to the nearest medical facility.

Simon was taken to the bank of the Tennessee River at Pittsburg Landing where a hospital ship was waiting to transport the wounded soldiers to a general military hospital in St. Louis. Before boarding the hospital ship, Simon had to be evaluated by the army surgeon to determine if amputation was necessary before being transferred to a military hospital. If amputation was required, the patient was forwarded to a large tent where the wounded limb was severed from the soldiers body. When Simon's turn came to be examined, the doctor took one look at it and said,

"Sgt., we'll have to cut part of your leg off from below the knee."

"No Doc.!, please don't remove my leg, I don't want you to amputate!"

"But Sgt., it's in your best interest to have part of your leg removed, since the consequences of not removing your leg might result in gangrene setting in then we would have to remove the entire leg, putting your life in danger."

"I understand that Doc.! And I'm willing to take my chances, but please don't remove my leg."

"Well, I don't have time to argue with you Sgt., there are too many wounded soldiers who need my attention. But if that's what you want, I'll bandage you up as best I can and send you on your way."

Simon was relieved that his body would remain whole for the present and hopeful that his leg would not have to be removed in the future, he then boarded the hospital ship, very much in pain.

CHAPTER THIRTEEN
A NEW VIEW

The boat traveled up river for a distance of about fifty miles and docked at a hospital way-station where soldiers were reexamined to determine their fitness to travel to the Army General Hospital in St. Louis. Those soldiers who were too sick to travel and needed immediate medical attention stayed at the way-station's make shift hospital to receive additional treatment. The rest of the wounded who were deemed travel worthy were sent on to St. Louis. After examining Simon, they couldn't do much for him other than to change his bandages, then the doctors tagged him well enough to travel.

The hospital steamer was not a place of comfort; broken bodies were strewn all over the floor of the boat and moans of pain could be heard echoing throughout the passage way. After Simon traveled many long hours in pain and discomfort the steamer docked at St. Louis, where a line of ambulance wagons were waiting to transfer the wounded to the Army General Hospital. A crowd had gathered at the dock to gape at the disfigured bodies as they were carried off the boat, witnessing the human tragedy and cost of war. To add to the discomfort of the wounded, the ambulance had to traverse a bumpy road for the fifteen minute ride to the hospital.

The hospital was terribly overcrowded with the sick and wounded and beds were at a premium. Only the sickest and most severely wounded had beds to rest their weary bones. The rest of the soldiers had to lie on the floor of the corridor, lined one after another, waiting for someone to attend to their needs. As Simon sat on the floor, he glanced down the long column of sick and wounded men and noticed that some of the soldier were shivering as if cold, when actually it was quite warm in the hospital corridor. Others lay there with bloody stumps where limbs had been. The stench of blood and healing wounds permeated the air and was almost overpowering. A large percentage of soldiers sleeping on the floor were sick with measles, mumps, diarrhea, and dysentery. It resembled an asylum for the suffering, rather than a hospital.

The hospital administrators realized the inadequate facilities available for the many wounded and sick soldiers who were arriving by the hundreds, on a monthly basis. At present a construction project was under way to add an additional wing to the hospital, scheduled for completion in a week or two. When the additional wing of the hospital is completed, it would double the capacity of the hospital and those soldiers who were lined up in the corridors of the hospital would be transferred to the new wing and have beds to sleep in. The ward that Simon was eventually transferred to had ten beds on each side of the ward. Doctors would make their rounds each morning to examine and evaluate the condition of each patient. They changed the bandages on Simon's leg every couple of days and although the wound looked hideous, there was no sign of infection or gangrene which Simon interpreted as good news and indeed it was. Simon was now certain he would not lose his leg. He continued to languished in this ward for months, with the unpleasant odor that permeated the air from the wounds of newly arrived soldiers; eventually Simon got used to the smell and was hardly aware of it anymore.

Life became a little more comfortable with the arrival of Mary Livermore of the Chicago Sanitary Commission and her army of women volunteers. They brought the soldiers fresh fruits and vegetables, tended their wounds, but most of all they made the soldiers smile again. Most of the women were elderly with a few younger women in their thirties.

Simon had been in this hospital ward for over five months, when the attending physician informed him that his leg was healed and there wasn't anything more they could do for him, he would be transferred to a convalescent facility in Southern Illinois. That sounded good to Simon. For a man that had been active all his life, the five months confinement to a hospital ward was depressing and had a deleterious effect on his health. However, when informed of his departure from the hospital Simon was infused with a spirit of optimism, since it gave him a chance to exercise his leg and get some much needed fresh air.

It was a beautiful warm September day in 1863, when he departed the Army General Hospital for the rehabilitation center located fifty miles south of Quincy, Illinois. The boat ride was a pleasant four hour journey up the Mississippi River. As the boat tugged along up river, he could see Arcadian fields of green pastures that came into view and slowly disappear as the boat traveled on. For a while he had forgotten that a horrific war was still being fought somewhere in the country. When the steamer docked, the large white rehabilitation center could be seen from a distance, sitting majestically on top of a mound overlooking the Mississippi River. He disembarked with five other soldiers whose needs were the same as his. An ambulance wagon was waiting to take them to the rehabilitation center; as they approached the ambulance a gentle autumn breeze carried the fragrance of the surrounding flowers and grass past Simon's nostrils and he inhaled deeply with great delight. Simon arrived in front of the big white building which seemed to beckon him to come in. As he stumbled forward using his crutches to support his awkward gait, Simon could smell the odor of freshness in each and every room he passed; finally the orderly informed him that room 126 was his, which he would share with three other patients. The room had a large closet, a desk and two large windows providing a view of the Mississippi River where boats could be seen traveling up and down the river.

Breakfast was served from 6-8 A.M. in a large dining room, followed by physical therapy from 9 to 12 noon and another hour of physical therapy commencing at 2 P.M., then the patients were free for the rest of the day. There was a recreational hall where patients could go to play cards, games, or participate in other forms of entertainment. A library was on the premises where Simon preferred to spend his leisure hours. It was well stocked with books on all subjects, magazines and newspapers, both old and current, from all over the state of Illinois.

Upon entering the library, Simon went directly to the section displaying newspapers. The scribes and editorials of these newspapers gave their opinions and analysis of current events. He read the newspapers with keen interest eager to obtain as much information as possible on the progress of the war and the country at large. There was one newspaper in particular Simon found most informative, The Springfield Sun. This newspaper had a syndicated columnist named Peter Conway, who wrote a bi-weekly column on the history, development and ramifications of the Civil War. Simon read his current articles, then searched for back issues of the scribe's columns. By doing so, Simon was able to piece together the genesis of this terrible war.

Conway's first article described the social and economic differences between the Northern and Southern section of the country. The economy and social fabric of the Northern states were largely based on industry and manufacturing that required a vast network of railroads that crisscrossed the North. The densely populated North relied on free labor for its industrial production and economic growth. Then compared it to the South.

Vengeance

The Southern economy was drastically different from that of the North; agrarian by choice with a climate conducive to the growth of the cotton plant. Its economy was primarily basted on "King Cotton," cotton was the major export to England, France and other European countries, providing the wealth that flowed back into the coffers of the Southern plantation owners that made possible their luxurious life style. At the bottom of this pyramid of wealth was the slave who planted, picked and processed the cotton for export, providing an uninterrupted and continuous flow of money to support the plantations and their masters. It is a sad commentary on human nature, when "man" is given a choice between moral rectitude or ill gotten financial gains, "man" invariably chooses the latter.

And so it was with the nabobs of the South who insisted that their peculiar institutions should be extended westward to the Pacific Ocean. The Southern politicians reasoned: If the lands of the Western territories were admitted into the Union as free soil states, their representation in Congress would be diminished to an irrelevant voting block.

The irrepressible obstacle that obstructed any reasonable compromise to prevent disunion between the Northern and Southern states was the extension of slavery into the newly acquired Western territories. The government could not and would not agree to the extension of slavery beyond the borders where it already existed. The firebrand Southerners who had been at odds with free soil Northerners for years over this issue, had become uncompromising and inexorably opposed to anything less than the establishment of new slave territories in the West. The elements of mistrust and animosity were so ingrained in the psyche of the Southern population, along with the government's opposition to the extension of slavery, that the Southerner deemed separation from the Union as the only practical solution to this vexing problem, eventually jumping from the frying pan into the fire.

When Simon returned from the library he sat quietly in his chair deep in thought, contemplating that which he had read, wondering when and how this terrible war would end. He was presently sharing the room with two other rehab. patients. One of the soldiers sharing the room with Simon was Thom Selinsky, a handsome young man of nineteen years of age, slim in build, about six feet in height with brown eyes and brown hair, he came from eastern Tennessee where Union sentiments ran high; Tom lost a leg in battle, six inches above the knee. He was a reticent young man, hardly ever spoke a word, only when asked a direct question would he respond, if at all and with as few words as possible. It appeared to Simon that his wounds were not all physical.

The other rehab. soldier occupying their room was Frank Gordon, medium height, brown eyes, black hair and sporting a goatee extending two inches below the chin. He was a gregarious young man of twenty two years, he lost his right hand up to his wrist and was having one hell of a time learning to use his left hand. He seemed to adjust well mentally to his physical impairment.

Simon's progress was very slow, after two months he was able to discard his crutches in lieu of a cane. He was no longer in any pain, but walked with an obvious limp to his gait. One afternoon when Simon and Frank were returning from the recreational facility with a chuckle and a laugh as a by-product of their conversation, Simon opened the door to their room and stood in horror at the sight before them. It was Tom lying in a pool of blood with his wrist slashed open.

"Get the medics!"

Simon shouted to Frank as he attempted to stop the bleeding. Within minutes the doctor was there examining Tom's limp body; the expression on the doctor's face said it all, it was too late, Tom was dead, another casualty of the war.

After the passage of time Frank Gordon was now well enough to be released from the rehab. center and discharged from the army. He embraced Simon and bid him farewell and a speedy recovery. Simon watched Frank till he disappeared from sight, then returned to his room. Simon was destined to stay at the rehab. center for another couple of months. During that period of time he progressed to the point where he no longer needed a cane, but still walked with a pronounced limp to his gait. One day during a medical evaluation of his condition, the attending physician informed Simon that they could do no more to improve his walking ability and he would have a permanent limp for the rest of his life. The diagnoses had an ambivalent effect on Simon, he was disappointed to bear the burden of a limp for the rest of his life, but overjoyed to leave the rehab. center. So after nine months and two weeks of rehabilitation, Simon was to be released from the rehabilitation center and discharged from the U.S. Army. The commanding officer of the rehab. center thanked Simon for his service to his country and presented him with his discharged papers from the U.S. Army.

After receiving his discharge papers he left the rehab. center and closed the doors behind him, pausing to take a deep breath of fresh air with the sweet smell of freedom filling his lungs. He walked to the nearby pier and boarded a steamer for a trip up the Mississippi River to the town of Quincy, Illinois, where he would outfit himself with civilian clothes, then purchase a horse and a pair of six shooters. Soon after his arrival in Quincy he stopped a pedestrian to inquire as to the location of a haberdashery. He was told that a fine clothing store was only a block away. Simon thanked the stranger and went in that direction. He walked in and was greeted by the proprietor. Simon explained to him the type of garments he was interested in and other items of wear. The owner told Simon that he had a large selection of shirts and pants in stock for him to choose from and proceeded to lay them out before Simon. Simon chose that which was similar to what he wore before enlisting in the Army; a black shirt with white piping, navy blue dungarees and a black felt hat. He paid the merchant for his selection and ask him to roll his uniform up in a tight bundle for easy transport. After completing his business at the haberdashery, he asked the merchant where he could purchase a horse and the location of a gunsmith shop. Equipped with that information he set out for the town's stable.

The stable was known as the "Horse Academy," located just outside of town. When Simon arrived, there was no one in attendance so he walked down the long lane of stalls, looking and examining the horses; they were all fine specimens of horse flesh. Finally, someone did come to ask if he could be of service. Simon told him that he was interested in purchasing a horse and saddle and since all of his horses were fine animals it came down to appearance. He was attracted to an all white stallion and asked the price for him. The owner replied that all his horses had the same price tag, $250 and $150 for the saddle.

He was beginning to look like his old self again but there was one thing still missing, a pair of shooting irons. Simon mounted his white stallion and was the picture of elegance in his attractive civilian clothes as he road through town in search of the gun smith shop. Just about in the center of town he spotted a large store displaying a sign that read, "Johnston's Gun Emporium." When inside, he was favorably impressed with the large and varied display of fire arms and associated paraphernalia, from pistols to automatic weapons. Simon's elegant appearance attracted the attention of one of the salesmen, who walked toward Simon and asked if he could be of assistance.

Simon replied, "I would like to see the latest state of the art six shooters you have."

The clerk replied, "Yes sir," and went to a draw unlocked it and withdrew two beautifully crafted shooting irons, manufactured by Remington Corp. It didn't take Simon long to realize they were high quality precision made instruments and said, "I'll take them."

He also bought two holsters for the six shooters, then strapped them to his waist. Simon was going west where many renegades and army deserters roamed the country side preying on disabled veterans and defenseless individuals. Completing his business in Quincy, he headed westward to the Comanche territory to renew old friendships and his relationship with Sun Flower.

CHAPTER FOURTEEN
THE RETURNING WARRIOR

Simon left Quincy, Illinois, at 6 A.M. in early September 1864, on a hot and sultry day and rode down to the pier where he boarded a ferry for transportation across the Mississippi River. When reaching the other side of the river in the state of Missouri, he pointed his horse in the direction of Kansas City. It was a return visit for Simon, the last time he entered the city was ten years ago when he and his father established a homestead site in Lawrence, a few miles south of Kansas City. The unpleasant events that followed were still fresh in his memory, but this time his visit to Kansas City was strictly business and would be of short duration, just long enough to withdraw sufficient funds from the Territorial Bank of Kansas City to carry him over to his final destination in Southwest Texas, boarding New Mexico. After traveling a good portion of the day, a distance of two hundred miles he arrived in Kansas City in late afternoon just before the closing of the bank. In short order he consummated his financial transaction, then rode to the local stable to have his horse fed, groomed and cared for during the night.

Kansas City had changed dramatically since last he walked its streets. Now it was under Federal control, with Union soldiers everywhere, in saloons, restaurants, shops and hotels, roaming the streets from one end of town to the other. Some of the officers and men were stationed in Kansas City, others were there on leave for "Rest and Recreation." Everyone was in a jovial mood, celebrating and having a good time. Simon was curious as to the course of this levity and entered a saloon to find out. He engaged a captain in conversation by introducing himself as a veteran of the Shiloh campaign and offered to buy him a drink which he readily accepted. As they stood at the bar drinking whiskey with beer chasers, the captain brought Simon up to date on the latest events of the war. He told Simon that Gen. Sherman had taken the city of Atlanta on Sept. 2, destroying its infrastructure and the railroad depot by ripping up the rail road tracks and heating them over bond fires till red hot, then twisting them around trees, forming what has been called "Sherman Bow Ties." His troops destroyed everything of value to the Confederacy: factories, bails of cotton, cotton mills, warehousers, business establishments and they ransacked food supplies needed for his army. Anything that could not be used or carried away was destroyed, leaving Atlanta in a burning inferno.

The latest information we have is that his army of sixty thousand men is somewhere in the heart of Georgia living off the well stocked Georgia countryside, cutting a swath of destruction sixty miles wide and burning whatever they can't consume or carry away. Their destination as I understand it is Savannah, a distance of two hundred and eighty-five miles from Atlanta. There doesn't seem to be any Confederate force capable of stopping his army. This to Simon sounded like the death knell of the Confederacy. He stayed in Kansas City that night and moved on the next morning.

Simon was always an early riser, starting off at daybreak and by nightfall was in Wichita, Kansas. While riding through town he spotted a boarding house between Pine and Maple Street where he decided to bed down for the night. He much preferred the friendly atmosphere and sociability of a boarding house, rather than the austerity of a hotel. After registering for a room for one or two days, Simon was told that meals were served family style in the dining room at 7 to 8 A.M. for breakfast and 6 to 7 P.M. for dinner; with that settled, Simon was shown his room. That evening during dinner Simon met the other guests of the boarding house. There were seven in all including Simon. Some of the guests seemed to know each other, so Simon introduced himself to the group and sat down. The guests in turn introduced themselves, some offering a lot more information about themselves than just their names. Then the friendly chatter began as the guests helped themselves to the mutton, potatoes, gravy, and vegetables. As Simon sat there taking mental notes of everyone's demeanor, dress, and manner, he tried to determine their business which was a little game he was playing with himself. The first person to attract his attention was a middle aged man, clean shaven with a bald head and tufts of gray hair over his ears, he was well dressed in a gray suit and a blue tie and appeared to be well fed. Then there was a young married couple who appeared to be in their late teens or early twenties, so engrossed with each other they hardly realized that other people were at the table. Sitting farthest from Simon was a Confederate veteran missing a left arm up to his elbow and still wearing part of his uniform, a good looking boy with sandy brown hair; he was quit reticent. Last were two elderly spinsters with graying hair, average height and lean in stature; one wore a white dress and a pink shawl, the other a blue dress. They displayed little jewelry, plain earrings and a wrist watch; and were staying at the boarding house before departing for Garden City, Kansas, to visit with old friends from their youth.

A variety of subjects were discussed during dinner and the war was sure to claim a portion of the conversation. Everyone was pretty much convinced that the war was in its last stage with a Union victory in sight. Alice, one of the spinsters, initiated the conversation that evening with a complaint that food was so expensive in Springdale, Arkansas, and in such short supply that she longed for the good old days before the war. Most people like to talk about themselves or are curious about others and this group was no exception. The other spinster turned to the married couple and asked,

"Are you two love birds staying in Wichita long?"

"No," replied John, "We were just married two days ago and we're on our honeymoon. We're from Tulsa, Oklahoma and are on our way to Topeka, Kansas, to see what the town has to offer before returning home."

He was interrupted by the disabled Confederate veteran, who asked,

"Did you serve in the army?"

"No!" replied John, "I don't believe in cession and I didn't want to join the Union army for fear that I might have to fight my friends and neighbors back home."

"So you played it safe and stayed home; how convenient."

"Yeah, if there were more men like me, there would be no war."

The Confederate soldier didn't look pleased with John's answer but dropped the subject. Dan Shaw, the well dressed man sat quietly, not saying a word till Simon asked him,

"And you Sir, you look quite prosperous, what did you do during the war?"

"Yes, I was well off until this war came along and changed everything. I was an overseer on a plantation in Kentucky and I can tell you first hand all this talk about niggers being mistreated on plantations is a lot of nonsense. Fighting a war to free the slaves is ridiculous; they were treated humanely, given medical care, food, shelter, and taught Christianity to save their souls. They were happy and content at their work till Northern abolitionists began stirring up trouble between the peoples of the North and the South, by instigating this war. When the war reached Kentucky the Union troops ravished the plantations, destroying homes and property. When they reached our plantation the Federal troops destroyed everything, burning our plantation to the ground. Our niggers ran off, leaving behind nothing but scorched earth. There was nothing left for me but to move on; to what? I know not. If the niggers are free they will still have to work and without the benefits of plantation life. Before you know it they'll be chasing our white women and miscegenation will repopulate our country with a race of mulattos."Simon just shook his head in disbelief, and said,

"You mean to tell me you really believe what you're saying; or is all that talk just for public consumption?"

"Oh, no, every word I said is the gospel truth."

"Well, if you truly believe in what you're saying, then I must tell you that you are grossly misinformed. I've listened patiently to what you had to say and concluded that you are a warehouse of erroneous and misinformation. Allow me to correct those misconceptions of yours with some facts: This Civil War was not fought to free the slaves, it was fought to preserve the Union, freeing the slaves was a by-product of this war. The slave owners still could have had their slaves and their plantations if they were willing to confine their peculiar institution to the Southern states where it already existed. But no, that wasn't good enough, because of their greed and lust for power, they demanded additional slave territory all the way to the Pacific Ocean. This my friend, was immoral and unacceptable and precipitated a war that has already cost the death of hundreds of thousands of yong men in the South as well as in the North.

And as for your humane treatment of Negroes, let me remind you Sir, that animals are treated humanely, human beings are treated with respect and dignity. The welts on the backs of your Negro slaves bear testimony to the kindness and understanding that you so pompously proclaim.

You say that your Negroes are 'Happy and Content', yet you have conveniently neglected to recall the many slave revolts of the past, notably the Nat Turner revolt in Southampton, Virginia, in 1831. When Nat Turner, a slave, recruited other slaves from nearby plantations and in a two day rampage hacked to death men, women, and children, sixty in all, in an attempt to break their chains of bondage. Their frustrated attempt for freedom naturally failed and they were hanged. Let me add, that I do believe there are slave owners who treated their slaves 'Humanly', but that is a poor substitute for freedom. As for your fear of the mixing of the races, why that is the most fallacious and hypocritical statement of all. The slave owners and overseers were the most promiscuous fornicators on the plantations. It was they who were the proponents of miscegenation, taking unwanted liberties with defenseless Negro women to satisfy their sexual lust. Take a walk through any plantation and observe the many mulatto children who bear a striking resemblance to the overseer or the owner of the plantation. It's amazing to me how many people find their own faults in others. "When Simon concluded his diatribe the overseer was speechless and a little flushed in the face, one of the spinsters murmured in a low voice, "oh, how awful." The Confederate veteran didn't say a word but knew that Simon was much closer to the truth than was the overseer. Simon then asked,

"How about you soldier, would you like to share your thoughts with us? However, if you prefer to remain silent I'm sure we'll all understand."

"There's really not much I could tell you, I come from a small town in Alabama, thirty miles north of Mobile. I joined the army for the glory and excitement of battle; but as it turned out I didn't get much glory, only pain, suffering and the loss of my left arm. I served in the Confederate army for less than a year before being wounded at Gettysburg; there were fifteen thousand of us in Gen. Pickett's charge up Cemetery Ridge. It was a disaster, the field of battle was littered with the dead and wounded before we were forced to retreat. I was one of the lucky ones to survive. Now that I'm out of the war, I'm looking for employment, trying to find someone who would hire a man with one arm. That's about it. How about you Mr. Ganz? I've heard your name mentioned several times by some of the soldiers from Texas. They said you are the best shooter in the West with six shooters or rifle and the last they heard, you had enlisted in the Union army."

"You heard right soldier about my joining the Union army, as for my being the best shot in the West, I'll leave that for others to judge. Like you soldier, I too was wounded but I was fortunate in not having to lose a limb; although I came damned close to departing with my left leg. After the doctors examined my leg they decided on amputation. When I heard the word 'amputation' a heated debate ensued between me and the doctors; I was unalterably opposed to the amputation of my leg. They finally agreed not to cut off my leg with a dire warning of gangrene and its fatal consequences. You may have noticed that I walk with a slight limp as a result of my leg wound.

I was wounded during the battle of Shiloh, in Tennessee and taken prisoner along with hundreds of other soldiers. They lined us up and started to march us to the rear of the Confederate lines. I was determined not to rot in a prison camp, and began to think of ways to avoid that fate; while I was thinking of how to escape, I finally saw an opportunity to make my move; although it wasn't a good one, I had to take that chance. We were approaching a bend in the road that came close to a wooded area and at that point I would made a dash for the woods. If successful in reaching the woods I stood a fifty-fifty chance of escape. It all depended on how accurate a shot the guards were. As we reached the bend in the road I bolted from the line of march and ran as fast as I could toward the woods; one guard fired at me and missed, but the second guard hit me in the leg about five feet from the wooded area. I lay on the ground motionless and bleeding profusely. They could not be bothered with wounded soldiers and left me there to die as the rest of the column moved on. I lay there in a pool of blood expecting to die before sundown. I don't know how long I had been lying there in a state of half consciousness when I heard a bugle sound and the thunder of Union troops in a counter attack. They discovered me, placed me in an ambulance wagon and drove me to a field hospital. After talking the doctors out of amputation, they bandaged me up and sent me on to the recovery quarters. The first couple of weeks were critical, with no sign of gangrene, I knew then that I would live and retain my leg as part of my body. As the weeks passed, my leg was healing nicely; so the doctors decided to send me to a rehabilitation center in Quincy, Illinois, where I subsequently stayed a good part of a year in an attempt to regain full use of my leg. They did what they could for me with daily exercise and messages; when my progress seemed to stagnate the doctors knew they could do no more and decided to discharge me from the rehab. center and the Army, thereby releasing me to society as a civilian and here I be. I guess we're all casualties of this war one way or another, which has affected our lives. Would you ladies mind if I smoked a cigar?"

"Not at all," replied one of the spinsters.

Another half hour of frivolous chatter ensued before all excused themselves and went their separate ways. Simon stayed another two days at the boarding house before departing.

It was a sunny but chilly morning when Simon left Wichita and continued his journey in a southwesterly direction. It was now ten days since he had left Wichita, and the landscape had changed considerably, becoming dry and sandy. During his travels he passed numerous small towns where he would secure lodgings for the night. As the days rolled by, Simon observed an increased scarcity of human settlements. Each hamlet separated by longer and longer distances that necessitated Simon to sleep outdoors under a constellation of stars. The fall season was rapidly approaching, with shorter days accompanied by chilly mornings and evenings. After traveling a day and a half without seeing another human being he set eyes upon a small quaint settlement that seemed to be an oasis in the desert. This tiny settlement was established under the auspices of German immigrants. As he slowly rode through the settlement he was struck by their shibboleth of dress, so unlike anything worn in the West. The citizens of this community wished to preserve their customs and culture of the old world. As Simon rode through the settlement he stopped an elderly man and asked him if there was anyone in town who could provide him with room and board for the night. They were a friendly lot who would never turn anyone away, so he offered his home to Simon for the night and introduced himself as Otto Semper. Simon was much gratified and when he offered to pay for his lodging Otto smiled and said there would be no charge for his hospitality. That evening Simon dined on old European cuisine: white bread, potatoes, (German style), and a variety of different meats, topped off with German pastry. Simon couldn't remember the last time he had enjoyed such a delicious and satisfying meal.

After dinner, Simon lit up a cigar then placed a few more on the table for Otto to partake and saver. They talked a while under a cloud of cigar smoke. When the subject of the war came up, Simon learned from Otto that Gen. Sherman and his army had reached Savannah, Georgia, on Dec.10, and sent a telegram to the President which read,

"I beg to present you, as a Christmas gift, the city of Savannah, with one hundred and fifty heavy guns and.....about twenty five thousand bales of cotton."

They both realized that the war would soon be over. Otto was pleased that the country would remain as one and that slavery would not be a part of it and to that end Otto brought out a bottle of schnapps and drank a toast to the end of the war. They sat there talking a while longer, then Simon decided to retire for the night. That night Simon had a well furnished room and slept with clean sheets on his bed. Before leaving the next morning, Simon left a ten dollar bill on the dresser, went downstairs and thanked Mr. and Mrs. Semper for their hospitality and rode off.

Vengeance

A day later as Simon road through breathtaking scenery observing the abundance of mountain laurel, mesquite, and pecan trees, he came upon another small quaint European hamlet. He was looking forward to the same pleasant experience he had the previous day and he was not disappointed. Simon remained there for two days before moving on to buffalo country.

CHAPTER FIFTEEN
BUFFALO COUNTRY

Simon was fast approaching the Comanche compound which he had not seen for over three years. His thoughts were only of Sun Flower and the joyous times and love they shared together before his departure. Would everything be the same? Most assuredly conditions would not be the same, with all that had transpired during his absence. His thoughts of the past lingered on till he was brought back to reality by the sight of black smoke rising in the distance. As he advanced closer to the source of the smoke it was palpable it was the remains of a burned out homestead. The house was burned to the ground, along with the charred bodies of three individuals, two adults and one juvenile. From what Simon could make out, all indications pointed to an Indian raiding party responsible for the massacre. As his eyes surveyed the carnage some of the questions he had asked himself were answered; relations between the whites and Indians had degenerated during his absence to the point where hostility and violence replaced tolerance and coexistence. He left saddened and disheartened and continued on his way for another twenty five miles.

Simon saw from a distance another trail of smoke rising up to the clouds. His curiosity edged him closer; he discerned it was a small ranch with livestock and two men working close by. As they saw Simon approaching, they stopped what they were doing and looked in his direction. Simon rode up and asked the older of the two men,

"Howdy, would you mind if I watered my horse and filled my canteen?"

"Not at all stranger, where are you headed?"

"I'm on my way to Carlsbad, New Mexico, and would be much obliged if you would provide me with room and board for the night, that is if you don't charge more than $100 for the night." They all smiled and laughed, then the older man said,

"Sure we'll provide you with quarters for the night and don't worry about the cost, it won't make you any poorer and it surely won't make me any richer; my name is Rex Simpson and this is my son Todd, I have three other boys, ranging in age from fourteen to nineteen. We've been working this spread for over five years and are doing quite well so why don't you come in and meet the Misses."

As the three men walked indoors Simon said,

"By the way, my name is Simon Ganz."

"Simon Ganz, so you're Simon Ganz, I heard a lot of tall tales about you and often wondered if they were all true."

"Well, that all depends on what you've heard."

"Yeah, I suppose so," replied Rex.

As they entered the living quarters, Rex introduced Simon,

"Sally, I'd like you to met Simon Ganz he'll be boarding with us for the night."

Sally looked at Simon in amazement, and said,

"Really, are you really Simon Ganz? The last we heard you were in the Union army."

"Yes, I was Mam."

Sally showed an interest in Simon's military career, so he satisfied her curiosity by regurgitating his army service as concisely as possible as she continued to prepare dinner. He mentioned the battle at Shiloh, leaving out the gruesome details of being wounded and his time at the rehab. center. Simon concluded his narrative just as Sally finish preparing dinner.

During dinner there was a free exchange of opinions; it was there that Simon learned that the war between the states had come to an end. Rex made it known that his sympathy was for the South but he didn't think that dissolving the Union was the answer to its problem. As the conversation rotated around and across the table Simon mentioned that he had passed a burned out homestead about twenty-five miles from Rex and Sally's place and thought it was the handiwork of renegade Indians.

"Yeah," said Rex. "There has been a lot of hostility and tension between the white settlers and Indians and it has gotten worse during the past year. A few whites have killed some Indians and they in turn burned down a homestead, the whites retaliated by killing more Indians and so it goes. I don't know who's responsible for starting this cycle of slaughter, but it sure has gotten out of hand. Haven't we had enough killing during the past four years? Do we have to start another war with the Indians?"

Simon agreed with Rex and told the Simpson family of his experience with the Indians. How he unintentionally came to reside with the Comanches for almost a year and went on to stay.

"I was drawn into an impending confrontation between the white settlers and the Indians in general and if the situation was left to its own devices it would have resulted in a blood bath, leaving in its wake a deep rooted hatred by both sides making it that much more difficult for peaceful coexistence. But reason and cooperation between the white settlers and the Comanches quenched a disastrous confrontation to the satisfaction of both parties. Indians want to live in peace as much as the white folks do, but there are always a few Indians and whites who harbor hatred and hostility toward each other and express their emotions through acts of violence. I'm certain that you could trace this crisis to those individuals."

The discussion continued for the balance of the evening, touching on other topics before everyone retired for the night. The following morning, Simon was awakened by the aroma of coffee and freshly baked bread which terminated his slumber and hastened his appearance at the breakfast table. He ate a hardy breakfast with the entire Simpson family, as they conversed while consuming everything that Mrs. Simpson had prepared. When the time came for Simon's departure he thanked the Simpsons for their gracious hospitality, then stuffed a ten dollar bill in Rex's pocket and went on his way.

Simon had another day and a half of travel before reaching the Comanche compound. As he passed through open country the beauty of the scenery was just as he remembered it before he left. Nature doesn't change much, but its human inhabitants do. His only focus and concern now was for Sun Flower, everything else was of little interest to him. As the curtain of darkness began to descend Simon bedded down beneath a ruck of pine trees and was lulled to sleep by the sounds of the forest and its creatures.

Come morning, Simon was awakened by a symphony of song birds rather than the aroma of freshly baked bread and instead of hot coffee he settled for cold water. As he prepared his breakfast of smoked bacon and dried biscuits, the lingering memory of the breakfast he shared with the Simpson family the previous morning was fresh on his mind. His breakfast was just enough to satisfy his hunger before starting out on the final leg of his journey.

After several hours in the saddle riding through the familiar sun baked soil of New Mexico he came in sight of the Comanche compound. Some of the Indian women working around the reservation recognized Simon's approach from afar and alerted the rest of the tribe to his return. The entire tribe rushed out to greet Simon. One person in particular was out in front running to meet him; Sun Flower. As Sun Flower ran up beside him, Simon extended his arm and hoisted her up on to the back of his horse as he slowly rode through the compound. The crowd that rushed out to greet him expressed genuine pleasure in his return but he detected a diminution in enthusiasm as compared to previous occasions when returning from an extended absence. He also noticed a decrease in the general population of the compound especially amongst the young braves. Simon proceeded to the far end of the compound where Flying Eagle was waiting to greet him. Simon dismounted and walked up to Flying Eagle; both men smiled and embraced each other warmly. When you make a friend of an Indian you make a friend for life. All that evening was spent in feasting and celebrating Simon's return while reestablishing his friendship with Flying Eagle and the rest of the tribe, especially with Sun Flower. No mention was made of the problems plaguing the Comanches and the Indians in general; that could wait till morning. Simon directed his attention almost exclusively to Sun Flower who had become more beautiful and womanly during his absence. Simon didn't get much sleep that night neither did Sun Flower, nor did they want to.

The next morning, Flying Eagle called a pow-wow with all the elders, young braves and Simon in attendance to discuss their current problems. Simon learned that the relationship between the whites and the Indians had degenerated to confrontational violence and hostility. The Indians were being restricted to their reservations, limiting their ability to roam freely and hunt at will. These restrictions so antagonized the young braves that some of them left the reservation to live their chosen way of life, to roam and hunt as their ancestors did. They would resist and fight those who interfered with their way of life. These hardened attitudes and differences in culture were incompatible for coexistence. Sooner or later their paths would cross, resulting in violence and bloodshed and each hostile encounter fueled the seeds of hatred and mistrust.

After listening to all that was said, Simon emerged from the pow-wow disheartened and apprehensive for the future of all Indians. Simon realized that this problem had become so monumental, wide spread and uncontrollable that it was beyond his ability to ameliorate or bring peace to the American Southwest. The solution to this problem lay in Washington

Vengeance

D.C. The Indian compound that Simon returned to, was not the same as the one he had left behind three years ago. Simon was pretty much convinced that his stay with the Comanches was coming to an end. There wasn't much he could do for them by remaining; he knew that eventually he would have to leave and sooner, rather than later, was the preferred option. His plan was to leave with Sun Flower and put together a small spread in Southwestern Texas. Simon would rest awhile before breaking the news to Sun Flower. In the meantime, Sun Flower was busy planning Simon's schedule for the next few months.

Sun Flower was determined to restore to full function the use of Simon's left leg, to a degree of past normalcy. When Simon heard of Sun Flower's intention he was skeptical of any positive result, but agreed to let her try. When the medicine man heard of Sun Flower's rehabilitation plan for Simon, he too decided that they needed his help and volunteered his service. So every morning for the next four months, Sun Flower would go through the same procedure. She would massage Simon's leg while the medicine man hovered over it, muttering unintelligible sounds of fetish import while holding and rattling strange objects over his leg. Later in the day Sun Flower and Simon would venture out alone to engage in strenuous exercises. She would have Simon walk up and down small hills on the periphery of the compound. After the first two months, Simon was encouraged by the progress he was making and after four months, he was surprised, amazed, and delighted with the dramatic improved of function of his left leg. It had returned to normalcy, along with a massive increase of muscles of the calf and thigh. Simon contemplated in silence that maybe Sun Flower knew something that the medics at the rehab. center in Quincy, Illinois, did not know and just smiled. The medicine man was convinced that he was responsible for Simon's recovery, but Simon and Sun Flower knew better and that's all that mattered.

Now that Simon was empowered with the full use of his left leg, he deemed it time to explain to Sun Flower of his intention to leave the Indian compound and build a home for themselves in Southwest Texas, with her at his side. It didn't take Sun Flower long to reply,

"You and I are one; where you go I go."

That was music to Simon's ears, then Sun Flower continued.

"I have something to tell you Simon, I am with child and expect to give birth in five months."

Simon was pleasantly surprised and retorted,

Vengeance

"Well, that's wonderful news Sun Flower, now it will be my turn to take care of you for the next five months! Now that you're pregnant I'm looking forward to welcoming our child into the world. But because of your present condition we'll have to make some minor adjustments for our plan of departure from this reservation. I think it would be best and certainly safer for you to remain here after the birth of our child; rather than subject you and the baby to the hazards and uncertainties of a long and unpleasant trip through the wilds of Texas. You might survive Sun Flower, but the life of our child might be in jeopardy. After you give birth I think it best for me to travel alone and survey the land for a suitable spread to build our homestead. After achieving that which I had set out to accomplish and all was ready to welcome you and our child, I will return to take you to our new home. I don't think it would take more than a year to complete this task. How does that sound to you Sun Flower?"

"It would make me very unhappy to be separated from you again for such a long time; but I know you're right so do what you have to do and come back soon."

With their future plans settled Simon gave Sun Flower his undivided attention, watching over her and tending to her every need for the next five months. As her expected time grew near the women of the tribe readied her quarters for the delivery. It was late September with the autumn breeze whistling through the large conifers causing the leaves on the pecan trees to dance in the wind, signaling Sun Flower's time was fast approaching. Along about two o'clock in the afternoon, the mid-wife and her assistant were summoned from their work in the field to assist in the deliverance of Sun Flower's child. Simon was present to witness the miracle of creation. The medicine man was at Sun Flowers's side to administer a peyote cocktail to alleviate some of the pain and discomfort that accompanies child birth. As the mid-wife examined Sun Flower she discovered that the baby was not in the normal position for delivery; it was a breech pregnancy (feet first) that could present problems in delivery. Breech births are not that common and in the hands of a skilled practitioner the procedure is usually consummated without much difficulty. Sun Flower was trying to force the baby from her body but only the feet appeared outside the womb and not much more was forthcoming. The mid-wife decided to manipulate the child in order to extricate it from Sun Flower's womb. It became a very bloody affair until the child was brought into the world. The baby did not let loose a loud cry to announce his arrival into the world as in a normal delivery. The assistant grabbed the baby by its feet and gave it a slap on its buttocks which seemed to revive the child. But for whatever reason the male child did not live for more than a few minutes. Sun Flower was not told of this tragedy since her condition was precarious, bleeding profusely from her inside due to the damage of a difficult birth. Simon had little time to mourn the death of his son since his concern now was for Sun Flower's debilitated physical condition and for her to regain full strength. The woman assistant gave Sun Flower another peyote cocktail to ease her pain and induce sleep.

Twenty four anxious hours had passed, with Simon never far from Sun Flower's side. She was now resting peacefully which had a calming effect on Simon's nerves and disposition. During Sun Flower's waking hours she would ask to see her baby. Simon realized he could no longer avoid telling Sun Flower the tragic truth of their son's death. There is no satisfactory way to explain the death of a child or to mitigate the sorrow by attributing the death to divine providence. That might suffice for some, but for Simon it was irrelevant and lacked credence. After learning of the death of her child, her eyes filled with tears and she turned her head and bore her sorrow in silence. The women of the tribe tried to comfort her, bringing her food and drink of which she partook sparingly or not at all. Her vivacious spirit was gone, showing signs of depression and despondency. That evening as Simon and Sun Flower lay side by side Simon felt an increased warmth radiating from Sun Flower's body and he turned to feel her forehead; she was burning with fever. Not knowing what to do he called on the woman who attended Sun Flower's delivery. When she arrived she prepared a solution and applied it to Sun Flower's body hoping to cool the surface of her skin. Then she prepared an Indian herbal drink for Sun Flower, followed by plenty of cool water. Infection had set in ravishing her body. The next few days showed no improvement in her condition. At times she became delirious and the following day she slipped into a coma. Everyone was preparing for the worst outcome, but Simon was still hopeful and constantly at her side. He could be heard at times whispering please Sun Flower don't die, don't die. But death did come on the seventh day as Sun Flower breathed her last breath.

The complication of a difficult child birth, the loss of her baby, the excessive loss of blood and an infection (probably due to unsanitary conditions) together with her depressive state of mind, were contributing factors in her untimely demise. Simon was devastated by the loss of Sun Flower, there was nothing of interest or pleasure remaining at the Indian compound that could induce him to stay, and his desire to leave was stronger than ever. As far as Simon was concerned, tomorrow was not soon enough for his departure.

A ritualistic burial ceremony was performed for Sun Flower and her son the following day, then both were buried side by side at the Indian cemetery. Soon after the burial ceremony Simon sought out the company of Flying Eagle. They chatted for some time, reminiscing the past and the happy days they shared together. Finally Simon informed Flying Eagle that he could no longer stay here without Sun Flower and that he was leaving in the morning, not to return again. He wanted to say good-by to Flying Eagle in private before bidding farewell to the rest of the Indians on the reservation. Simon's departure was a sad and solemn occasion, a celebration or feast would not be in the Indian tradition. Just before leaving the next day he expressed his respect and admiration he had for the Indians and their culture and was on his way.

While Simon was bidding farewell to his Indian friends, Flying Eagle had a plan of his own for Simon's departure. He summoned a young twenty year old brave named Single Feather, who was a great admirer of Simon and was always at his side during their hunting forays. He was a good looking young man, tall, with braided hair running down below his neck and a single feather placed in the back of his head. Flying Eagle asked Single Feather if he would follow Simon at a safe distance to assure that nothing bad happens to Simon. Flying Eagle knew that Simon would never approve of such an arrangement and repeated his advice to Single Feather to remain at a good distance behind Simon. He then equipped Single Feather with a tomahawk and a six shooter. Single Feather was skilled in handling the tomahawk and could split an apple at twenty paces; as for the six shooter, he knew where the trigger was and how to squeeze it to discharge the bullet, but the final destination of the bullet was anybody's guess. So the stage was set with Simon's tail not far behind.

CHAPTER SIXTEEN
THE SHADOW

As Simon traveled through the western planes, he traversed through mountains and peneplain, wooded areas and grassy flat lands, his thoughts centered on his nomadic life style which didn't seem to have the same appeal as it did in the past. He was now pushing forty two years of age and seriously considering settling down somewhere on a pleasant spread of land, bordering a lake or running stream, to live out the remaining years of his life in blissful serenity. The more he thought of this change of life style, the more convinced he became of making it a reality, with or without a wife. He had been on the road for two days and had passed through some of nature's most beautiful and mesmerizing landscapes. At the end of the day when he closed his eyes in sweet slumber, scenic images danced through his mind.

The following day, he continued his travels in search of his dream location. At the end of the day while preparing his campsite, he suspected that someone was following him; he had the same feeling the night before. There were subtle telltale signs that reinforced his suspicion and the knowledge he obtained by living with the Indians taught him well. Every evening after settling down at his campsite he would see smoke rising from the trail he left behind and almost always at the same distance from his campsite. One evening after igniting his campfire as a decoy he decided to backtrack to determine who was following him. He backtracked about a mile and a half toward the source of the rising smoke. As he approached, he could smell the aroma of wild game being roasted. Simon then pushed the shrubbery aside to make his presence known and see who was following him. He was shocked and surprised to see Single Feather.

"Single Feather, I must say that I'm glad to see you, but why in the world are you following me?"

Single Feather wasn't as surprised as Simon was; he knew that Simon would discover his presence sooner or later, and replied,

"Flying Eagle told me follow you, to make sure no harm come to you when you travel."

"Well, that's very thoughtful of Flying Eagle and I certainly appreciate his concern for me, but you'll have to return to the reservation and tell Flying Eagle that I can take care of myself. In the meantime, why don't we dine on that rabbit you have roasting over the fire?"

They both sat down and enjoyed each others company, while feasting on the rabbit. After an hour or so, Simon said good-by to Single Feather and set out for his campsite. On his way back, Simon was puzzled and bemused by Single Feather's apparent willingness to return to the reservation; not offering one word in opposition to Simon's request that he return. This was so unlike Single Feather and Simon knew him well, so he concluded that Single Feather had no intention of returning to the Indian compound; if so, there was nothing Simon could do but accept his shadow.

The next morning, Simon was up bright and early and on the road looking for his private spread of paradise. He was traveling south parallel to a tributary of a larger river surrounded by cottonwood trees in various stages of maturity that decorated his path of travel. Unaware of the danger that was about to unfold, he would unknowingly come face to face with a bandit who had robbed a merchant in a small town ten miles farther south, a few hours earlier. In the bandit's attempt to flee, his horse received a gun shot wound in his romp, not serious enough to impede his escape, but a source of later concern. As he continued north his horse grew weaker from the loss of blood and the irritation caused by the flesh wound, would cause the horse to be incapable of continuing further. This realization was on Pete the bandit's mind as he traveled north. Suddenly, salvation seemed to be at hand when he spotted an old run down farm house; surely there must be a horse on the premises. As he got closer, he saw an old man puttering about in his garden. There wasn't much livestock in sight other than a mule and some chickens roaming about. He approached the old man in a polite manner to put him at ease and not to arouse suspicion as to his plight, and said,

"Good afternoon, Sir, my horse has a flesh wound and can go no farther. I was wondering if you had a horse I could buy."

"Nope, I only have a mule which I need for the heavy work around here."

"Well then, would you consider selling me your mule, I'll pay you cash for him and throw in my wounded horse. He should recover with some rest, then you'll have a strong horse to work with."

Vengeance

The old man thought for a while, then walked over to examine the horse and figured that he could nurse the horse back to health which would be an upgrade for working the farm. Then said,

"O.K. It's a deal."

With the transaction settled Pete threw his saddle over the mule and was on his way. Pete displayed a rare quality of humanity by paying for the mule rather than just taking it. Who can say what inspired this act of fairness to pay for a mule. Maybe he felt sorry for the old man living alone; maybe he had enough excitement for one day; maybe the old man reminded Pete of his father; maybe there were a half dozen different reasons, who can say. I suppose there is a little good in the worst of us; and a little bad in the best of us.

Pete the bandit, was in is early twenties, tall and lean, standing at 6'2" and looking sort of comical on the mule with his lanky legs almost touching the ground. His facial appearance wasn't much better than his physical appearance, with a short red beard covering his face, a flattened nose separating a pair of dull blue eyes, his hair slightly darker than his beard and protruding from all sides of his hat. He had only one thing on his mind and that was to rid himself of this slow moving mule and find a horse that could put miles behind him. After five tortuous miles, he decided to stop and fill his canteen with water and rest beneath a cottonwood tree. In his repose, his only thought was to get a horse; when suddenly he spotted a lone rider in the distance, it was Simon. He began to think of ways to get the stranger to stop so he could wrest the horse from him without risking a deadly confrontation. He decided to place himself in a position to be seen from the road, then feign a sprained ankle to attract the stranger's attention. If the stranger stopped to offer assistance, he would look for an opportunity to pull his gun on him or lay him flat with a blow to the head. Simon did indeed see Pete lying beneath the cottonwood tree, with an expression of pain written all over his face. Simon always ready to help someone in distress, dismounted his horse and walked over to him, and said,

"What seems to be the trouble, young man?"

"Oh, on my way back from the river, after filling my canteen with water I slipped on a wet rock and sprained my ankle. It hurts like the devil; I'll be alright I guess, I'll just rest here for a while."

"Is there anything I could do for you?"

"Yeah, If you would remove my boot from my leg, I would appreciate it."

"Sure thing."

Simon walked over to him, grabbed his boot with his back facing Pete, and said,

"Now place your foot against my ass, and push forward."

This was the opportunity that Pete was waiting for; he pulled out his gun and pointed it at Simon's back, and said,

"Stranger I have a gun pointed at your back; one slight move in the wrong direction and you're a dead man. Now let go of my leg and move forward."

Simon had no choice but to comply with his demand.

"Now turn around and unbuckle your gun belt; and do it real, real, slow."

Again, Simon obeyed instructions.

"Those are nice looking shooting irons you have mister. I'm sure going to need them, along with that magnificent horse of yours. Now turn around."

Pete then hit Simon on the head with the butt of his gun, laying him unconscious.

To complete his nefarious act, he shot the mule to insure that Simon would not followed him; then rode off.

Single Feather a half mile away, heard the shot and hurried to investigate. On his way, Pete passed Single Feather, riding in the opposite direction. Single Feather noticed that the stranger was riding Simon's horse, and realized that Simon was in trouble; he feared the worst. He was riding fast and it wasn't long before Single Feather found Simon prostrate on the ground. He rushed over to Simon and placed a wet bandana across his forehead. Within minutes, Simon was restored to consciousness and able to sit up. He was angry, his pride was hurt more than his physical injuries, to think that he was taken in by riffraff such as that. He had no time to feel sorry for himself, he had to get that son of a bitch before he got too far away. Single Feather told Simon that he saw him riding north on his horse. Simon replied in a deliberate manner,

"O.K. let's go after him; your horse will have to carry both of us."

They galloped off through valleys, wooded areas, and plains for eight miles arriving at a Mexican cantina; and to their surprise stood Simon's horse, tied to a hitching rail. Simon's face lit up with a smile of retribution, then told Single Feather,

"Let me have your gun, Single Feather, and I'll show you how to use it."

Simon sent Single Feather into the cantina to look around and report back; he wanted to know how many people were inside and if he had any accomplices, and most important where he was sitting. Single Feather didn't have to go inside, he just looked over the swinging doors and glanced around, then reported back. He told Simon that there was only one person drinking at the bar; and our "friend" was sitting at a table to the right eating with gusto and having a beer. Simon then said,

"You walk in ahead of me and keep an eye on the guy at the bar, while I take care of our 'friend.'"

When Simon walked through the swinging doors, he looked right at Pete and said with a half smile on his face,

"Well, if it isn't my sprained ankle 'friend', so we meet again."

Pete's jaw fell open, exposing part of his meal; he paused for a second, then went for his gun. But Simon had him covered before his hand reached his holster. Then Simon said,

"I'll repeat a phase you know well, unbuckle your gun belt and drop it to the floor, and do it real, real slow like."

As Simon retrieved his guns from the floor, he strapped them around his waist, and said,

"I'm returning your gun, Single Feather; would you mind fetching our 'friend's' gun from the back of my horse."

After complying with Simon's request, Simon threw Pete's gun and holster on the table and said,

"Strap your gun to your waist and when you're ready you can draw"

Pete strapped his gun around his waist, and said,

"No, I'm not going to draw, if you want to kill me in cold blood, go ahead, but I'm not going to draw."

Pete was gambling that Simon wasn't the type to shoot someone in cold blood, and of course, he was right. Besides he knew that he stood a better chance of living, by gambling on Simon's character than by drawing.

"Oh, that's a shame; you mean I have to walk out of here leaving you alive and free to assault someone else? Well if that's what you prefer, so be it."

Simon knew full well that the minute he turned his back on him, he would go for his gun, and decided to play his game. Simon turned around as if to walk out the door, but instead of making a 180 degree turn to face the door; he made a 360 degree turn to face Pete. While Simon was turning, he drew his gun; if Pete did not draw, he would not fire, but if he went for his gun, Simon would fill him full of lead. Fateful to his character, Pete did draw when Simon's back was turned and received his just reward, falling to the floor dead, from two well place shots. Simon then asked the Mexican proprietor if he would bury this stiff and gave him five dollars for his trouble, before walking out of the cantina with Single Feather, saying,

"You know Single Feather, as long as you insist on following me, you might as well ride side by side with me."

"That's good," replied Single Feather with a smile on his face."

Simon now had a loyal friend and a traveling companion.

"And since we'll be traveling and living together from now on, I'll just call you Chief instead of Single Feather. I'm giving you an upgrade and promoting you to an Indian chief."

"Me, Chief? O.K. me Chief, Tribe of One, ha, ha, ha."

They now set out in pursuit of a parcel of land to build their ranch.

They had been traveling for five days now and had seen some mighty attractive landscapes. Then on the afternoon of the sixth day, they encountered a beautiful and enchanting view of nature's creation. All of the individual wonders of nature came together to form a unique setting as if designed by the hand of God. The land mass was partially wooded and partially grassland, situated alongside a cataract with water cascading down into a large lake which in turn flowed into a river that snaked its way through diverse landmasses to the Gulf of Mexico. And to complete this heavenly scene were snow capped mountains off in the distance. Simon had found his place of habitation for the remainder of his life.

The nearest town was Pecos, Texas, 15 miles to the West with a population of seven hundred people. That night as Simon dozed off, his thoughts were of a suitable spot to build his ranch. Early next morning, Simon and Chief set out for Pecos to register their claim for five hundred acres of land along the lake. After consummating the legal formality, he wired the Territorial Bank of Kansas City to transfer all of his funds to the Pecos National Bank. Simon was well fixed for cash, having accumulated large sums of money from shooting contests, capturing bandits with lucrative price tags on their heads, and other sources.

Vengeance

While in town, he wasted no time acquiring all that was needed for the construction of his ranch. He purchased a truck horse and wagon, then filled it with implements for constructing his dream ranch: axes, shovels, saws, picks, and all sorts of farming equipment, plus a host of other tools necessary for life on the frontier. And to make his life a little easier and to expedite the construction of his ranch, he hired four Mexican laborers to help in the building his future home.

The next morning, everyone was hard at work: felling trees, clearing the brush, laying the foundation for the ranch, and after a day's work all went for a cool dip in the lake before settling down to a hearty meal. After dinner, Simon would hand out cigars and everyone sat around the camp fire drinking coffee, smoking cigars and chatting till dark before retiring for the night.

Simon had chosen well; not only was the land and its surroundings picture perfect, but the land and waterways supplied them with almost all their needs. The crystal clear water of the lake was teaming with fish, large trout could be seen swimming in the shallows in pursuit of small fry. It didn't take Chief long to fashion spears made from the branches of hardy oak trees or supple pines, then roam along the periphery of the lake spearing trout for the evening meal. He possessed knowledge of hunting, fishing, and foraging that none of the others had. He knew how to forage in the woods for eatable vegetation, gathering wild onions, asparagus shoots, tubas, and an assortment of mushrooms, that only he could differentiate between the eatable variety and the poisonous kind. Bushes everywhere were laden with colorful berries; and where there were berries, you could find wild life feeding on them, which made hunting easy and convenient. Occasionally, a trip into town was necessary to replenish their provisions of flour, coffee, sugar, salt, and eggs. The land provided the balance of their culinary delights.

The following morning they were back at work. The Mexicans were hard workers which did not go unnoticed by Simon, who was fast developing a close friendship with them. The work continued day after day for a couple of months as the ranch took shape revealing its character. The outline of six bedrooms was taking shape upstairs with a semi-circular stairway leading downstairs to a reception area and entrance hall. A kitchen and dining area were located to the right; with a study and entertainment area, which included a large fireplace to the left. A door from the study area lead to Simon's office. That completed the picture of Simon's ranch which would be finished in another couple of months with a few minor adjustments.

As the ranch was edging toward completion, including a forty foot veranda; Simon realized that his ranch was going to be much too large for just him and Chief to maintain in good order. He would need help to run his household: a cook was needed; and a person to maintain and attend to all the household chores inside the ranch; plus someone to help with outdoor maintenance. Of course, the obvious choice were the four Mexican workers he had on hand: Jesus, Poncho, Ramos and Pedro who were skilled at everything, from cooking to gardening, and were reliable workers and completely trustworthy. One evening while gathered around the campfire, Simon decided to put the question to them and asked if they would be interested in staying on after the ranch was completed to maintain and operate day to day activities. He would paid them thirty dollars a month, plus room and board. They smiled, and without any hesitation, they were eager to accept Simon's offer to stay on. They would build their own living quarters adjacent to the ranch. Poncho had a wife, and it was decided that she would do the cooking, while Poncho maintained the inside of the ranch; he and his wife would occupy one of the bedrooms upstairs. That meant that Jesus, Ramos, and Pedro would work outdoors. Simon was also thinking of Chief's future and one day during a casual conversation, he said to Chief,

"Chief, it doesn't seem right for a young man like yourself to live here alone without female companionship. Why don't you return to the reservation and find yourself a young squaw for a wife, then you both could return to the ranch and live here. I think you would be much happier under those conditions."

That seemed to strike the right note, as Chief replied.

"Yes, I think so; I leave as soon we finish ranch."

Within the required time slot, the ranch was completed and Chief was off to the reservation to find a wife. Simon was now able to relax a bit, although he did not consider himself a gentleman rancher, for he would be on hand to supervise outdoor operations as well as the indoor management of the ranch. Simon was formulating plans to go into the cattle business. He had made quite a few friends in Pecos and made it known that his location should not be revealed to anyone. While Chief was away securing a wife for himself, and Simon attending to the ranch, Billy Reed was trying to track down Simon's whereabouts; while back in El Paso not much had changed, save the popularity of Rose's fun house.

CHAPTER SEVENTEEN

BACK IN EL PASO

At this point in time, the activities of Billy Reed and Joe Young took center stage. The Ganz ranch was quiet, and a calm business like atmosphere prevailed; while Billy was in hot pursuit of the whereabouts of Simon Ganz. He was now riding east of El Paso and had asked everyone he came in contact with if they had information as to where Simon Ganz could be found. No one provided any useful information, everyone he spoke to thought that this young gun slinger was trying to acquire a national reputation for himself, as the man who gun down Simon Ganz. Billy continued on his quest to locate Simon, not only to obtain knowledge that could aid him in tracking down the three derelicts who murdered his family, but he was eager to meet and shake the hand of this legendary man whom he respected and admired and heard so much about ever since his boyhood days, working in Mr. Adam's dry goods store. He was searching for Simon Ganz for over a week now and was no closer to finding him than he was when he started his quest.

In the meantime, not much had changed in the social structure of El Paso. Joe Young still visited Rose's cathouse once a week, and the mention of Rose's place was far removed from the lips of Parson Bigelow. What did change, was the size and popularity of Rose's fun house. There was little that could impede the growth of an establishment that catered to providing sexual fulfilment, liquid refreshment, and a seat at the card table for the men of El Paso. The popularity of Rose's place spread wide and far, well beyond the town of El Paso, all the way into Mexico, winding its way around the ears of the Romaro Brothers.

In a small Mexican town not far from the border and only five miles from El Paso, sat the Romaro Brothers eating lunch in Maria's cantina, enjoying her famous Mexican stew, and washing it down with cold beer. Their eating habits were anything but refined, as not much had changed in eight years. Halfway through their meal, the subject of Rose's bordello surfaced. Jose said,

"I hear that there are a lot of pretty girls in that place. Maybe we should visit them."

"I don't know, Jose. It's very risky, since we have a big price on our heads across the border."

"Yes , but if we're careful, we could have a good time in an hour or two. While I'm upstairs with one of the girls, you could stay downstairs and take care of things and let no one leave the place. Then when I'm finished, you go upstairs with one of the girls and I'll take care of things downstairs."

"That sounds pretty good, Jose; maybe we try it."

Scarcely a day would pass that the brothers didn't discuss Rose's place. Their talks elevated to enthusiasm for a visit. Eventually they decided to put their plan into action and visit Ros's establishment.

Just about sundown on a Tuesday evening, the brothers rode across the border and entered Rose's bordello. Jose took a seat at a table near the door and asked for a bottle of whiskey, then laid his gun on the table. Pedro walked over to Rose and said,

"I think I know you."

Rose looked at him in amazement and shock. She certainly knew him. How could she not recognize or forget their past encounter and said,

"You should recognize me; you robbed our stagecoach eight years ago not very far from here."

"Oh yeah, I remember now." said Pedro.

"Did you come here to rob me?" asked Rose.

"No, Rosie I just want to borrow one of your girls for a little while."

" As long as you have the money to pay for your pleasure; you'll find the girls in the parlor, you can pick one that suites your fancy."

Pedro walked into the parlor and glanced around the room, eyeing each girl with delight. The girls were draped across the couches and armchairs with a substantial portion of their bodies exposed. Pedro was in no hurry, admiring each girl as he walked past before choosing a plump blonde, grabbing her by the wrist and dragging her upstairs. There were a half dozen men downstairs watching Pedro's antics, while being observed under Jose's watchful eyes. Rose didn't like their manners, nor the way Pedro treated her girls, but had the good sense not to protest, and to keep her emotions under control. With these two ruffians in the house, the whole atmosphere changed. It was a happy and congenial environment before they arrived; now it took on a tense and somber tone. They would gladly leave the premises if they could, but no one would risk walking past Jose.

After a while Pedro came down, and now it was Jose's turn while

Pedro stood guard. Jose went through the same routine as his brother did and picked a big busted brunette and disappeared with her upstairs. All things come to an end eventually, and so it was with the brothers; after two and a half hours they decided they had enough and would return to Mexico. Before they left Rose approached Pedro and said,

"You boys had your fun, now here's your bill of forty dollars for the girls and the whiskey you consumed."

"Rosie, I pay you next time I come."

"I need the money now, I can't run this place on credit."

"Rosie, I said I pay you next time! Don't make me angry, that's not good." Rose realized she was not going to get her money and decided to hold her peace. Rose reported the incident to Sheriff Rooney, but he could do little, since they were well into Mexico by now. Saying to Rose,

"You can't lock the door after the horse had been stolen."

Rose returned to her establishment, frightened and worried, knowing full well that this past episode was bound to be repeated in the future. She not only wasn't paid for her services, but their presence in her establishment would ruin her business. She did not know what to do or where to turn.

Two days later in the late afternoon, Joe Young dropped by Rose's place in his routine visit. As soon as he walked through the door, Rose pulled him aside and sat him down at a table and ordered two whiskeys.

"Joe," she said, "I have a big problem; two days ago the Romaro Brothers came here, took advantage of my girls, drank my liquor and made it uncomfortable for everyone here. And to add insult to injury they wouldn't pay for anything. I reported their activities to Sheriff Rooney, but his hands were tied since they reside across the border in Mexico. I just don't know what to do, I'm sure they will return again in the future." Joe thought for a while, then said,

"I'm sure you're right Rose; they will return, but when, that's the question. Let me think about it for a while and maybe I'll come up with a solution to your problem." Just before Joe was ready to leave Rose's place, he pulled her aside, and said,

"Rose since we don't know what day they'll return or whether it will be during the day or evening hours, this is what I propose. Take that statuette of a nude woman that adorns your parlor and place it on the window sill in the reception room. If they should come during the daylight hours, remove the statuette from the window sill and place it back in the parlor. On the other hand, if they should be present during the evening hours, place a candelabra with lit candles on a table near the window, then I'll know they are busy in side. I'll ride by once or twice a day to check. It won't be an imposition for me since your place is only a half mile out of town. One more thing Rose, make sure that the side door is left unlocked, O.K."

"Good enough Joe, I really appreciate your helping me out like this."

"Well, Rose, I'm also doing it for myself; you know there is a bounty of $7,500 for each of them, dead or alive. That's a mighty tidy sum."

"If you get those scoundrels Joe, you deserve the reward."

Rose was confident that Joe knew how to handle this situation and hoped that he would be on hand when the time came. Many weeks had gone by, without a return visit by the Romaro Brothers. They were far off in Mexico, relaxing in their hacienda reminiscing on their last visit to Rose's place, and contemplating a return visit. Boredom and restlessness had taken a toll, increasing their desire for some diversion and pleasure while visions of Rose's cathouse danced through their minds, inspiring Pedro to say,

"You know, Jose, I think we visit with Rosie pretty soon; I'm tired of this place and need a little excitement."

"Si, me too; I like those girls in that place. Maybe I take one home with me." "That's a good idea, Jose; then we don't have to visit with Rosie anymore. I'm ready to go."

And so they were. Five weeks after their last visit, the brothers mounted their horses and rode across the border to Rose's bordello. They walked through the door of Rose's establishment at about 3 o'clock in the afternoon. All eyes centered on the brothers as a dead silence enveloped the room. Rose was surprised, but not shocked to see the brothers, after all she was expecting them sooner or later and hoped that this would be their last visit and casually said to them,

"Well boys you're back, I guess you must have had a good time during your last visit; are you going to pay me this time?"

"Sure, Rosie, we pay you; but first you get Jose a bottle of whiskey while I look over the girls."

"Before you go Pedro, would you do me a favor and take that statuette of a nude woman off the window sill and place it in the parlor where it belongs."

"Sure Rosie, I do that for you." Now Rose was hoping that Joe Young would ride by and see the statuette gone from the window sill, indicating the presence of the Romaro Brothers. As fortune would have it, a half hour after the arrival of the brothers, Joe did ride by that afternoon and saw the statuette missing from the window sill and went into action. He cautiously approached the side door and silently opened it. When inside, he could see Jose sitting at a table by the door drinking whiskey; his gun on the table a few inches from his hand. He slowly walked toward Jose, who in turn saw Joe approaching. Intuitively, Jose knew that this meant trouble. And as both men keenly eyed each other, Jose's hand slowly edged toward his gun. When Jose's hand touched the handle of his gun; Joe drew and shot the gun from under his hand. He then walked over to Jose, and said,

"You're a wanted man."

At that instant, Pedro, who had heard the gun shot from upstairs came rushing out of his room, wearing only the bottom half of his long John underwear with gun in hand. He looked down at Joe's back preparing to shot when Rose yelled.

"WATCH OUT, JOE"

Joe made a quick turn and planted two slugs in Pedro's chest. He fell forward, breaking the wooden rails that lined the walkway of the rooms upstairs falling down to the floor below, staining Rose's floor in a pool of blood. Jose used this distraction to grab Joe's wrist that was holding his gun. Joe dropped the gun as Jose wrestled him to the floor. Both men were in a desperate struggle, punching, kicking, and rolling all over the floor for quite some time. It seemed that no one had a clear advantage, when suddenly Jose ended their tussle and made a dash for his gun lying five feet away. Rose, seeing Jose go for his gun, kicked Joe's gun toward him. With both men now armed Joe sought refuge behind the bar while Jose used the table top as a shield, rolling it in a direction of his choice. There was no point in Joe trying to shoot through the thick oak table top; he would have to wait for a clear shot at Jose. Jose knew that he was at a disadvantage and began rolling the table top toward the door hoping for a quick getaway. When in front of the door, he reached out for the door knob, turned it, and the door swung open. He quickly jumped out and ran for his horse, mounted it and road off. But Joe was right behind him and had to catch him before he reached the border. Joe's horse Thunder was a magnificent animal and could outrun any horse and proved it by gaining steadily on Jose. Within minutes, Joe was close enough to get a clear shot at Jose. Joe dew and with only one shot, Jose came tumbling to the ground. This was a fitting climax for the Romaro Brothers who were no more. Joe rode back to Rose's place with Jose securely tied over the saddle of his horse. At Rose's place, Joe dragged out the dead body of Pedro and tied him neatly across the saddle of his horse. Before leaving Rose's place for Sheriff Rooney's office with the two dead bandits he said,

"So long Rose, I'll see you next week." Rose replied.

"So long Joe, next time you come everything will be on the house."

After collecting his reward of $15,000 for delivering the bodies of the Romaro Brothers to Sheriff Rooney, Joe Young settled down to bask in the glory of terminating the activities of the Romaro Brothers and await the return of Billy to El Paso.

CHAPTER EIGHTEEN
THE ENCOUNTER

Billy was still traveling east, in pursuit of Simon Ganz and so far had little to show for his effort. He knew from stories he had heard in the past that Ganz had to be somewhere in this part of Texas. Billy was becoming quite frustrated by the lack of information. As he approached the town of Pecos, he entered with no great expectation of acquiring any more useful information on the whereabouts of Ganz than he had in the past, not realizing how very close he was to the person of Simon Ganz. As he trotted through town he stopped a few leading citizens and merchants to ask if they had knowledge of the whereabouts of Simon Ganz, and in every case he received the same negative reply. Billy's inquiries about Mr. Ganz attracted the attention of Sheriff Lockwood, who decided to have a chat with this young man. Billy wasn't hard to find; he was a stranger riding through the middle of town when Sheriff Lockwood caught up with him, and said,

"Young man, I'm Sheriff Lockwood, and I understand that you're looking for Simon Ganz, is that right?"

"Yes Sir, I am," replied Billy

"May I ask why you're interested in locating Mr. Ganz?"

"Well sheriff, I have an important personal problem that I would like to discuss with Mr. Ganz, I've been trying to locate him for weeks now with little success and would very much appreciate it if I could speak with him for a few minutes."

It seemed like a reasonable request to Sheriff Lockwood and Billy looked like a clean cut young man. The sheriff had enough experience in evaluating the demeanor of individuals to know that Billy did not pose any threat or trouble to Mr. Ganz, and said,

"Well son, hang around town for a while and I'll get word out to Simon of your presence and desire to speak with him. Maybe he'll see you and maybe he won't; we'll just have to wait and see."

Sheriff Lockwood summoned his deputy and told him,

"Smithy, ride out to the Ganz ranch and tell Mr. Ganz that there is a young man in town who wishes to speak with him on a matter of great importance. Ask him if he wants to see the young man."

The deputy rode out to the Ganz ranch and conveyed the message to Simon and returned to town a few hours latter with Simon's reply. The deputy told Sheriff Lockwood that Simon would see the young man, but first he had to remove his guns before I escorted him to the Ganz ranch. When Billy heard the news he was overjoyed and gladly removed his guns and handed them over to deputy Smith; then both men rode out to the Ganz ranch. Upon their arrival at the Ganz ranch, they found Simon sitting on the veranda smoking a cigar with his legs crossed on a nearby stool with a drink in hand. Both men walked up to Simon; deputy Smith handed Simon Billy's guns and said,

"Here is the young man who wishes to speak with you, Sir."

"Thank you Deputy Smith; you can leave now while I talk to our young friend."

After Deputy Smith left, Billy said,

"My name is Billy Reed and I'm from El Paso, Texas. Mr. Ganz, I can't tell you how glad I am to meet and talk to you; ever since I was a boy, I heard stories about your exploits and never dreamed that some day I would have the pleasure of meeting you in person."

"Well that's fine Billy, I'm glad your pleased but what's on your mind."

"Well Sir, I'm hunting down three individuals and I need your help to refine my tracking technique and to recognize any traps that I may not be aware of. Since there is no person more knowledgeable than you, I thought I would go right to the master."

"Tell me Billy, do you intend to kill these individuals?"

"Yes Sir, I sure do."

"Well Billy, I'm not in the business of advising people how to kill other human beings; I'm afraid I can't help you."

"But Mr. Ganz, I can assure you that there are no three individuals on the face of this earth who deserve killing more than these three scoundrels."

"Is that so! Well, suppose you explain to me why you think that these individuals deserve to be killed."

Billy paused for a while and realized that if he ever expected to get any help from Simon, he would have to reveal the whole story from beginning to end, and said,

"Mr. Ganz; it's a long story."

Vengeance

"That's O.K. Billy; I have plenty of time; I'm not going anyplace; so why don't you sit down here and tell me all about it."

Billy walked on to the veranda and sat down next to Simon and began to tell his story in full for the first time since that tragic event.

"About twelve years ago, my father immigrated from Southern Indiana, traveling westward in search of cheap land and an opportunity to grow and prosper along with the rest of the country. After traveling for a number of weeks we arrived within two miles of the town of Astec, New Mexico, when my father noticed a small hovel. It wasn't much to look at, but it was surrounded by open grass land with a large brook and trees nearby. My father fell in love with the landscape and decided then and there that this was the place he would settle down to build his future. After negotiating for the sale of this small house and the surrounding property, we moved in. At the time, I was eight years old and my little sister was four. With my father's hard work and what little assistance I could give, we built and converted that small hovel into a large and comfortable home. During the subsequent four years my father worked at various odd jobs around town to accumulate enough money to fulfill his dream of becoming a cattle rancher. He reasoned that with all the grass land surrounding his property, he stood a good chance of successfully achieving his goal. Eventually, he had accumulated the tidy sum of $4,000, which he had stashed away somewhere in the house to be used for the purchase of cattle. The time had come for him to make that investment and for the next week or two, he traveled all around the town of Astec and beyond looking at and examining cattle to purchase and start his own herd. Everyone in town was aware that Mr. Reed was in the market to purchase cattle and had $4,000 set aside for that purpose. Unfortunately, the news of my father's intention to purchase cattle reached the ears of three of the worst criminal elements of our society in the persons of Ben Beck, the ring leader and his two associates, Fred Freeman and Luke Butterfield. All three were in their thirties and had a list of criminal offenses as long as your arm.

Ben Beck, the ring leader is the most sophisticated and insidious of individuals; he stands at 5'10" in height, with dirty blonde crudely cut hair, gray eyes, clean shaven and a full face displaying a pug nose. He is stocky in appearance but not muscular. He is always neatly dressed during his leisure hours with a black jacket and colorful shirt, black bow tie and topped off with a black felt hat. When not well dressed, he is up to no good. He gives the appearance of a harmless citizen of the town, but beneath his benign exterior lurks the soul of a devil. There is no crime he would not eagerly commit to satisfy his lust for money or sex. He escaped the hangman's noose on several occasions for the murder of three people, one of whom was a woman, whose body was found in the woods naked and brutalized. Unfortunately, all of these crimes he was accused of could not be proven in a court of law due to a lack of credible evidence. It is the opinion of many people in town that the witnesses were either bribed or too scared to testify against him. And so, he roams free to this day, unpunished for his crimes, including those despicable acts against my family. The other two scoundrels look their part and do whatever they're told by Beck, void of any feelings of remorse or guilt. In fact, they would celebrate each crime as if it was some great achievement."

"Excuse me for a minute, Billy, while I get myself another drink. Would you like one?"

"Yes Sir, I could use one." replied Billy and continued his story when Simon returned.

"Fred Freeman is a tall, thin man about six feet in height and unlike Beck is never neatly dressed. He parades around town wearing a plaid shirt and tattered dungarees looking as if he had slept in them overnight which he probably had. His face is thin with a large thin nose and a large crop of black hair that extends down to the nape of his neck and deeply set black eyes, giving him a menacing look. On his left check is a two inch scar which he tries to conceal with a short beard. The third member of this infamous trio is Luke Butterfield, a short chubby man, all of five feet, five inches tall when standing in his high heeled leather boots. Most of his brown hair has receded to the back of his head where it hangs down concealing the back of his neck. He is sensitive of his baldness and seldom is seen without a hat on his head. His face is roundish with brown eyes and a dark brown mustache that circles the outer corners of his mouth and goes down to within an inch above his jaw bone. He is chubby and overweight for his size, with loose pants held up with suspenders. Well, Mr. Ganz, that's the description of the men I'm in pursuit of. Normally, if they did not perpetrate these horrendous crimes against my family, I would leave their faith in the hands of the law; but since my father, mother and sister were the victims of their bloody and cruel crimes, I know that justice would never be served by putting them on trial in a court of law because of a lack of evidence, so I appointed myself as the law to track them down and decide their punishment."

"Well Billy, from what you toll me, it certainly sounds like they are despicable individuals and should be held accountable for their crimes; but you haven't explained to me their roll in the crimes against your family." "I know, Mr. Ganz, I know, that's the most difficult part of my story to recall. Every time I think of it, it fills my heart with anger, hatred and vengeance and I try not to recall those terrible memories but I said I would tell you the whole story, from beginning to end, and I will. These three rascals decided to steal the $4,000 from my parents. One night, while my father was sitting in his chair reading a four day old newspaper while smoking his pipe and my mother was knitting something for us kids to wear, my sister and I were upstairs getting ready for bed. All of a sudden, we heard a noise downstairs; the door flew open and there they stood, the unholy threesome with flashing guns. As Beck spoke, 'Mr. Reed, we're here for that $4,000 of your's,' my sister and I were upstairs listening to every word that was said, when my father replied, 'What do you mean by breaking into my home like this? Get out of here immediately, I'm not afraid of your kind.' Then Beck retorted, 'We're not leaving till you fork over the money; you'll make it a lot easier on yourself and your family by doing what you're told.' My dad said, 'I'm not giving you a red cent of my money; I've worked too hard for it to hand it over to scoundrels like you.' Beck then walked over to my mother, looked at my father, and said, 'Maybe your pretty wife can loosen up your tongue.' He then put his hand on my mother's shoulder and ripped off the top of her blouse exposing part of my mother's breast, saying, 'My, but you have a beautiful bosom; how about giving us boys a little loving.' With that remark, my father came to my mother's assistance, saying, 'Leave your dirty hands off of my wife.' Then Fred punched my father in the face, sending him reeling back into his chair, bleeding from the mouth. At this point, my heart was pounding furiously; I didn't know what to do or what I could do. The three of them were hovering over my mother, tearing still more clothes from her body while she was screaming and trying to fight them off. Finally, my father could take no more and yelled, 'O.K. I'll give you the money, just leave my wife alone and go away.' All three were smiling as Beck said, 'Now you're using your head.' My father got up from the chair, and stumbled to the back of the room, lifted up one of the planks in the floor and pulled up a bag containing the money which was his life's savings and handed it over to Beck, saying, 'Here it is, now go! and leave us alone.' Beck handed the bag of money over to Fred, saying, 'Now where was I; oh yes, I was trying to offer my love to Mrs. Reed' and he continued to molest my mother. His actions so infuriated my father, who rushed over to help my mother; then Beck pulled out his gun and shot my father through the heart."

At this point, Billy had to pause to gain his composure, and with tears in his eyes he looked up at Simon and saw a tear rolling down his check. Simon was a stolid man, not given to frivolous emotions, but Billy must have touched a sensitive nerve in Simon recalling a similar episode in his past. Then he continued,

"The instant my father fell to the floor my sister lost complete control over her emotions and rushed downstairs shouting, 'leave my father alone.' But before she could reach the bottom of the stairs, she too was shot dead. Seeing my little sister tumble to the ground, I muttered, 'Oh no,' alerting Beck to my presence. He shouted, 'There's someone else up there; get him, we can't have any witnesses.' Fred ran upstairs after me, but I ran to the back of the room and jumped out of the window landing on the ground below and ran as fast as I could toward the woods. I could hear Fred not far behind me as I entered the thickest part of the woods; the sun had long disappeared behind the horizon which afforded me ample opportunity to avoid being caught. I jumped into a large bush and stood there motionless and as quiet as possible while Fred was roaming through the woods looking for any sign of my presence. He walked right in front of where I was hiding, and my heart was beating so hard that I could hear it reverberate in my ears. He paused to look around, then gave up the chase and went back to our house. From a safe distance I watched my house, waiting for them to depart so I could return and help my mother. I could still hear my mother's screams echoing through the woods; after a while I heard no more sounds. Then suddenly I saw my house go up in flames. They were standing close by watching it burn to the ground, cremating my father, mother and sister. As I sat there for hours watching the glowing embers that was once our home and contemplating the terrible fate of my father, mother and sister, it was the lowest point of my life; I had never felt so sad, angry, and alone. I was physically and emotionally spent and could not muster another tear to shed. Then and there, I took an oath before God that I would never rest till those degenerates face me and my vengeance."

"That is certainly a horrible and devastating episode in your life Billy, and I could readily understand why it is so painful for you to talk about it.

But how did you escape and survive to manhood.""As I sat there thinking, I knew I could not return to town because they would be waiting for me to eliminate the only witness to their nefarious acts of murder. Then I remembered, there is a stagecoach that leaves Astec, New Mexico, for El Paso, Texas, every Saturday morning. I had to get a ride on that stage coach some how. Since I could not show my face in town I decided to wait for the stagecoach to approach an incline in the road about a mile out of town; there I could jump onto the back of the stage coach and wait until the coach was far enough out of town to make my presence known."

Billy went on to explain the run in they had with the Romaro Brothers and their subsequent arrival in El Paso, where he was fortunate enough to find employment at Mr. Adam's dry goods store. Then continued,

"Molly and John Adam became my surrogate parents, took me in, gave me room and board and treated me like their own son since they had no off- spring of their own. I worked at the dry goods store all through my formative years growing up and into manhood. While working at the Adam's store, I made the acquaintance of two of the most admired, respected and beloved individuals of my life. The first person I befriended while assisting customers was Joe Young, a man eight years my senior. Within a short period of time a close bond developed between us and as the years rolled by he became more like a big brother to me, as well as a close friend. He would come into the store twice a week to buy bullets for his six shooters, constantly practicing his shooting skills. He handled his guns with proficiency and mastery, and there are no better shooters in the West, other that yourself. He taught me everything I know about handling fire arms and marksmanship. When he learned the reasons why I was so dedicated to becoming a crack shot with my six shooters, he made me promise to take him along when ever I was ready to pursue those three infamous murderers. The other person who ignited the flames of love in my heart was a young girl named Rachel Richardson; we were the same age, and I used every excuse I could think of just to talk to her while her widowed mother was shopping. We grew up together and saw each other frequently, which eventually blossomed into a loving relationship. I intend to marry that young lady as soon as my mission is completed. And to round out the picture at the Adam's store; it was there that I first heard the name Simon Ganz and the tantalizing stories that so fascinated me. People from all over the Southwest who visited our store had a story to tell about you."

Vengeance

"I hope those stories you've heard were more favorable than notorious."

"I can assure you, Mr. Ganz, they were most complimentary. Those tales of your exploits are legendary and inspired me to seek you out some day for advice. Well Sir, that's about it, I've told you my life story from beginning to end. Can you share with me any of your advice and wisdom?"

"Yes, I think I can help you Billy, and I'll go one step farther by going along with you to track those rogues down."

"No, Mr. Ganz, I appreciate your wanting to come along and help, but this is my problem and I have to deal with it in my own way."

"I know that Billy, I just want to tag along to protect your rear in case that's necessary. You're going to need all the help you can get; I know the type of scoundrels you'll be up against. They would just as soon shoot you in the back or shoot you while you're sleeping, than face you head on. I'll leave their fate in your hands to decide any way you see fit. I just want to make sure that you live long enough to marry that young lady of yours."

"Well, since you put it that way, how could I refuse your help. As a matter of fact I would be most honored to ride side by side with you."

"Good, now that that's settled, there is a room upstairs you can have and we'll go through the paces in the morning; in the meantime get yourself something to eat. I have a wonderful Mexican cook working for me, she'll fix you some dinner."

The next morning, Billy was up bright and early as was Simon; after breakfast they headed out to the open fields to test Billy's shooting skills. Simon was pleasantly surprised at the proficiency with which Billy handled his six shooters.

"Well Billy, Mr. Young has taught you well and you're an excellent shot. You'll only have to be taught how not to be caught at a disadvantage or by surprise and to look out for possible traps."

Billy used this occasion to ask Simon a question that was on his mind for some time, but was hesitant to ask; finally he said,

"Mr Ganz, I have a question I would like to ask you, but I'm not sure if it is a proper question for me to ask."

"Go ahead and ask Billy, I'll let you know if it is a proper question or not."

"Well sir, I was just wondering, why it was necessary for you to kill all those men who challenged you to a shoot out. Why didn't you just wound them and let it go at that."

"That's a fair question Billy and I'll give you a straight answer. Let me start by saying that I take no pride or satisfaction in killing anyone; I go to great lengths to avoid a confrontation. But there is always someone who is seeking fame by claiming to have killed Simon Ganz. If I just wounded them as you suggested, the word would spread like wild fire; that if you challenge Simon Ganz to a shoot out you needn't worry about losing your life, you'll only wind up with a flesh wound. This news would encourage gun slingers from all over the country to challenge me to a shoot out and I would be doing nothing else but defending myself against would be fame seekers. That would never do Billy, they have to realize that there is a price to pay for their misadventure. Does that answer your question?"

"It sure does, and it makes a lot of sense."

"Only once did I deliberately spare a man's life. It happened about three years ago, in a small town in Oklahoma. I was standing at the bar having a cold beer, when a young man approached me. He was a good looking chap, tall, blonde with blue eyes and could not have been older than 18. He walked up to me and said, 'Are you Simon Ganz?' I said yes I am! He then said, 'Mr. Ganz, I'm here to challenge you to a shoot out; whenever you're ready you can draw.' I was flabbergasted to think that this young man standing before me was willing to risk his life to prove that he was a faster drew than I. I certainly didn't want to kill him and said, tell me son why in the world do you want to kill me; have I offended you in any way? 'No Sir, you haven't, I just think that I'm faster and a better shot than you and I'm here to prove it.' O.K. then I'll admit it, you're a better shot than I am; will that satisfy you?'I'm afraid that won't do Sir, I'll have to prove it.' I couldn't believe what I just heard and said, well I just won't draw, so if you want to kill me go ahead. I didn't think he had the nerve to kill me in cold blood and I turned away from him. He then said, 'Sir I'm going to count to three; if you don't draw you're a dead man.' I continued to ignore him, then he said, ' One' I watched him from the corner of my eye, as he said, 'Two.' I would not draw until he went for his side arm. At the count of three, he drew. The minute his hand touched the handle of his gun, I drew and put a bullet in his shoulder. He dropped his gun and I had to invent an excuse for not killing him and said, you're a lucky man; if something hadn't got into my eye to spoil my shot, you would be carried out of here feet first."

"You're right, Mr. Ganz, it was foolish of me to challenge you. I learned my lesson."

"There you have it Billy. There are people in this world who are willing to risk everything for fame and notoriety. My popularity was never predicated on those principals. I became a good shooter out of necessity for survival on the frontier. If you couldn't shoot straight, you didn't eat. I never thought I would need my shooting skills to defend myself against people."

The next few days and the weeks that followed, a close bond developed between Simon and Billy. Simon was old enough to be Billy's father, and their relationship reflected that bond. They talked frequently about a host of different subjects: hunting, shooting, women, and of course tracking techniques, especially that which Simon had learned from living with the Indians. Simon had many friends scattered throughout the Southwest and sent word that he was interested in locating the whereabouts of Ben Beck, Fred Freeman, and Luke Butterfield.

That evening while Simon and Billy were having dinner in the spacious dining room of his ranch, Chief came walking through the door with his squaw. Simon rose from the table, walked over to Chief and gave him a hearty embrace, and said,

"Chief, it's good to see you; I'm glad your back." then turned to Billy and said.

"Billy I would like you to meet Chief and his new bride. Chief what's your squaw's name?"

"This is Smiling Face, my squaw."

"Glad to make your acquaintance," Billy replied.

Simon invited Chief and his squaw to sit down and have something to eat; then said to Billy, with a broad smile on his face,

"It's a strange story how Chief and I happened to hook up together. You see Billy, when I left the Indian compound, Chief Flying Eagle summoned Single Feather, which was his name till I changed it to Chief, and told Chief to follow me at a safe distance and to come to my aid if need be. My guiding angel didn't do a very good job in concealing his presence, so after a few days, I told Chief that instead of following me, why don't you join me which he did and now he and his squaw are part of my family."

During the days that followed, members of Simon's household maintained a well organized indoor operation, while Chief was directing activities outdoors. Simon and Billy were together most of the day cementing their relationship in conversations of themselves and their future plans.

Vengeance

Simon knew almost everything about Billy's life; but Billy was still learning things about Simon that he had not known before and he continued to be enthralled by his tales of adventure. One evening while relaxing on the veranda, Simon was in the middle of one of those secessions, when a sheriff's deputy rode up to the ranch carrying a fat portfolio. The folder contained information on the whereabouts and activities of the three blackguards in question. Simon invited the deputy to come up and quench his thirst with a tall cool drink. After satisfying his thirst, the deputy explained that he was from Sheriff Davis's office in Lubbock, Texas, and he handed Simon the portfolio containing information gathered from many different sources about the three desperados he was seeking. Sheriff Davis was an old friend of Simon's and was most happy to provide Simon with the information he sought. The sheriff had been trying to put those three scoundrels behind bars for years, but never was able to present sufficient evidence to a judge to bring them to trial. For the next hour or so Simon, Billy, and the deputy sat around drinking, smoking cigars, and discussing different ideas on how to bring law and order to the newly acquired lands of the frontier. It was now quite late and Simon invited the deputy to stay overnight and leave in the morning for Lubbock. Simon then retired to his study to analyze the contents of the portfolio. In the morning, after breakfast when the deputy was ready to leave, Simon said,

"Give Sheriff Davis my regards and tell him how very much I appreciate the information he provided."

The sheriff's deputy waved his hand in a farewell gesture, and was off.

Early next morning Simon met with Chief and told him that he would be gone for a while on business and that he was leaving him in charge of the ranch during his absence. Chief didn't like what he had heard, since he knew that Simon was off on a dangerous mission and wanted to go along. Simon used all his persuasive power to convince Chief that there was no one else he could trust to operate the ranch in his absence. Finally Chief realized the logic of Simon's argument and reluctantly agreed to stay behind to look after things.

Simon bid farewell to his employees; then he and Billy mounted their horses and rode off, as Chief stood there watching their silhouettes fade away in the distance.

CHAPTER NINETEEN
THE RETURN

As Simon and Billy rode through the dusty trails of Texas on their way back to El Paso, Billy was deep in thought, trying to decide whom he should see first; Rachel or his adopted parents. He silently reminisced the bygone days when first he arrived in El Paso roaming through town in a state of desperation and loneliness, then seeing the Adam's Dry Goods Store. It was there that John and Molly Adam took him in, gave him a job, and their love and affection, and raised him as their own son. He remained eternally grateful and returned their love in equal measure. His first stop would be John and Molly Adam.

As Billy and Simon rode through town, some of the town's people recognized Billy and waved to him not knowing who the stranger was with him. Few people knew what Simon looked like, except those who were pursued by Simon and they never lived to reveal his identity. As they rode up to the Adam's store, Billy dismounted and went inside to embrace his parents while Simon waited outside. After Billy's joyous reunion with his parents had consummated, he called Simon in and introduced him to his parents, saying,

"Mom and Dad, I would like you to meet Simon Ganz."

"Oh my lord !" shouted Molly. "Are you really Simon Ganz? We've heard stories about your exploits for years, and to think you're here in our store with our little Billy who's now a grown man."

"I'm sure those stories you've heard are grossly exaggerated." replied Simon.

"You're being too modest Mr. Ganz. If only half those stories were true you would still have led a most active and interesting life. Of course, you'll stay for dinner! I'll prepare Billy's favorite meal, lamb stew."

"No Mom, not today, I still have to see Rachel and Joe; we'll get together tomorrow, O.K."

They chattered a while longer with Molly and John; before Billy departed with Simon, saying,

"I'll bring Rachel along with me tomorrow and we'll spend the entire day together."

Then they departed for the Richardson's homestead, but before leaving town Billy decided to pay a short visit at Joe's home just to let him know that he was back in town. When Joe opened the door and saw Billy; it was apparent from the expression on his face that he was pleasantly surprised to see Billy; so much so that he was hardly aware of the stranger standing beside him. They greeted each other warmly, then Billy said,

"Joe, I'd like you to meet Simon Ganz."

Joe was flabbergasted to see Simon Ganz standing next to Billy, and said.

"Well I'll be; come in, come in, it sure is a pleasure to meet you Mr. Ganz, you're a legend in the Southwest. I underestimated Billy's power of persuasion in bringing you along."

Billy quickly interrupted,

"No Joe, you've got it wrong, I didn't persuade Simon! In order for me to solicit his advice and help in my mission, I had to reveal my entire life story. When he heard of the tragedy befallen my family, he, like yourself Joe, insisted on tagging along in pursuit of those three miscreants. We can discuss our relationship later Joe, but right now I really have to leave; I can't wait to see Rachel. We'll be in touch."

"O. K. I'll be waiting to hear from you," replied Joe.

Before leaving, Simon addressed Billy and Joe, saying;

"In a day or two before we leave in pursuit of these guys, the three of us will get together in your house Joe and I'll go over all the information I have on the whereabouts and activities of these three scoundrels. In the meantime Joe, you and I will sit tight while Billy romances Rachel."

"Oh no, Simon, you're not getting off that easy; you're coming along with me, I'm sure the ladies would love to meet you especially Mrs. Richardson." And off they galloped to meet Billy's fiancee.

Mrs. Richardson was seated on the porch when she saw two riders approaching. She kept straining her eyes to identify the riders, then realized that one of them was Billy and shouted,

"Rachel, Rachel, come quick, Billy is coming!"

Rachel ran outside and realized it was really Billy. Billy rode up to the house, jumped off of his horse and both ran toward each other and embraced with tears of joy streaming down Rachel's face. They stayed glued to each other; Rachel refusing to relinquish her grip on Billy, who didn't mind it one bit. All to the amusement of the two on lookers standing there with smiles of delight on their faces. Finally, after slowly releasing her grip on Billy, he said,

"Rachel, Mrs. Richardson, I'd like you to meet Simon Ganz. Simon and Joe will be riding along with me in search of those three infamous villains."

Janette looked up at Simon and liked what she saw, saying,

"Mr. Ganz, Billy has told us so much about you that I feel that we're old friends."

"Well in that case Mrs. Richardson, let's not be so formal you can call me Simon, and I'll call you Janette."

"Now that we're all old friends why don't we all go inside and relax, while I prepare dinner," Janette replied.

Janette was in her late 30's, and strikingly attractive, having a pulchritudinous shape that could turn the eye of any man passing by. With her brownish blonde hair framing her face with a pompadour and the rest of her hair streaming down the sides of her face. The most striking of all was her large sky blue eyes and full bust. These qualities did not go unnoticed by Simon who stood about six inches taller than Janette.

After retiring indoors, Janette went right to work preparing dinner. Simon didn't waste any time sitting around waiting for dinner to be served; he decided to do the "Flirtation Waltz" by offering to help Janette prepare dinner. She accepted his offer and gave Simon a knife then sat him down beside a bowl of potatoes. While Simon was peeling the spuds, he remarked,

"It's obvious to me where Rachel inherited her beauty; she's almost as attractive as you."

"Oh Simon, you're too kind; you're making me blush."

Billy and Rachel were keenly aware of Simon's dalliance. They looked at each other with an impish smile on their faces, in acknowledgment that a fledgling romance was starting to take root and discreetly retired to the veranda, leaving Simon and Janette alone to get acquainted.

At dinner that evening, the two couples acted as if they were in separate worlds, occasionally talking to each other but mostly Billy and Rachel were isolated from all but themselves. Simon and Janette were less oblivious to their surroundings having time to eat and converse with one and all. All things considered, they shared a pleasant evening together before retiring for the night.

Vengeance

The next morning after everyone had finished breakfast, Billy said,

"Rachel and I will be spending the day with Molly and John, would you like to come along Simon?"

"No Billy, you and Rachel run along; I'll stay here and keep Janette company."

After Billy and Rachel departed for the Adam household, Simon and Janette lingered over a second cup of coffee. It was a warm and sunny day too nice to remain indoors; Simon suggested they go for a buggy ride and enjoy the wonders of nature. The suggestion induced a positive reaction from Janette.

"That's a splendid idea; I'll drive the horse and buggy since I'm familiar with the area and you can sit back and enjoy the scenery while telling me all about yourself and how you became so famous."

"That's a tall order Janette and a high price to pay for a buggy ride, but I'll consider your request," and off they went.

Simon was reluctant to talk about his past, but it soon became apparent that Janette was too eager and too persistent to learn of Simon's past, so he complied with her request, deleting the most gory and distasteful episodes of his life.

He told her of his boyhood living in the wilds of Southwestern Pennsylvania and the death of his mother from peritonitis; and his subsequent migration westward with his father to the town of Lawrence, Kansas, including the details of the murder of his father and his pursuit of his father's killers. He went on to explain his subsequent travels westward into Indian lands and the circumstances leading up to his sojourn with the Comanches.

"I was a guest of the Comanches and had no intentions of staying longer than a day or two. However, during my stay I caught the eye of a young Indian maiden named Sun Flower. She was in her late teens and very beautiful. We became friends and spent a good deal of time together, eventually leading to our cohabitation. Our relationship was probably the reason why I stayed as long as I did with the Comanches. During my stay at the Indian compound the Civil War had erupted and in time I enlisted in the Union army."

Simon detailed the battle of Shiloh in which he fought, leaving out the horrendous descriptions of death, destruction, and dismemberment of human bodies. He described his close call with death after being shot in the leg trying to escape Southern imprisonment; after being left to die and eventually rescued by Union forces and taken to an army hospital. His wounded leg resulted in partial disability, facilitating his discharge from the army. He then explained,

"After my discharge from the army, I returned to the Indian compound to renew my relationship with Sun Flower. The Comanches welcomed me back, but Sun Flower in particular was ecstatic over my return. When she discovered my limp, she was unwilling to accept my partial disability and worked feverishly to restore my leg to full function. She subjected me to a series of vigorous physical exercises along with leg messages using warm buffalo fat. This treatment went on for months, and finally to my surprise I was restored to full mobility without any trace of impairment. During that time, we shared many happy months together, and to my great joy Sun Flower became pregnant. When the time came for her delivery, everything went terribly wrong. The baby wasn't situated in a normal position in her womb and her delivery was going to be a difficult one. There was a massive loss of blood during the delivery and our child died a few minutes after birth. Shortly thereafter, Sun Flower developed an infection, which eventually was responsible for her death. Having lost my common law wife and child, I became despondent and saw no reason for me to remain at the compound any longer and wanted to depart as soon as possible. I informed Flying Eagle of my decision; he wished me well, and I was gone the next morning."

"That is such a sad and tragic story Simon; where did you go after leaving the compound?"

"My plans for the future were to find a pleasant and serene location for me to build a ranch and settle down and retire. After traveling for a few days in search of my dream spot, I became aware that I was being followed. It didn't take me long to discover the identity of the person; It was Single Feather, an Indian from the reservation with whom I went on many hunting forays with. He was a good friend and loyal companion to me, so when I departed Flying Eagle dispatched him to follow me and look after my best interests. I suggested to Single Feather that instead of following me why don't you join me, and so he did. I changed his name to Chief, and we searched the land together for several months, till I finally found a parcel of land to my liking, situated a little east of Pecos, Texas. It is there that I built my ranch with his help and that of four Mexican laborers, who are still in my employ. That is where Billy found me. When first I set eyes on Billy, he impressed me as a solid and upright young man. After hearing his story of his tragic boyhood, I empathized with him and we became fast friends; in time he became more like a son to me than a friend. That's the reason why I insisted on going with him in pursuit of those villains."

"Oh I'm so glad you'll be going with Billy, he really is a wonderful young man."

"Yes, he sure is and I'll make sure he returns to you and Rachel safely. Now that you've heard almost everything about my life, I know nothing about yours; so how about filling me in on your little secrets."

"Compared to your exciting and dangerous life, my life has been mostly boring and uneventful, and there isn't much to tell."

"Maybe so Janette, but I sure would like to hear some of it; like where you met your husband, and how long have you been a widow?"

"Sure Simon, of course; I'll start from the beginning. I was born and raised in Little Rock, Arkansas. While growing up, my best friend was a school mate of mine, Sally Randolf. Sally lived close by and after school we would do things together. Later in life we double dated. It was on one of those double dates that Sally met her future husband. They fell in love and married. After her marriage, her husband who worked for the government, was transferred to Salt Lake City, Utah, as a surveyor. We corresponded with each other for a number of months till one day I decided I needed a change of scenery and accepted her invitation to visit her. It was there that I met Sam, my future husband at one of the few non-Mormon church functions. Sam was of medium height, thin, with black hair and brown eyes; he wasn't particularly good looking, but had an engaging personality and a pleasant disposition. We had a world-wind courtship, and after three months, we were married."

"How did you wind up in El Paso?"

"We really didn't fit in with Salt Lake City society. We were too different in culture, background and upbringing. I couldn't understand why their men folks needed so many wives. Why would any woman want to share her husband with another woman and have a household full of half brothers and sisters? So we decided to move on. We traveled south with no particular destination in mind. When we reached the town of El Paso, Texas, it appealed to us and we decided to settle down and make our home there. Sam was a good man and a hard worker; he built our home on the outskirts of town and supported his family by working odd jobs for the neighbors in town. Rachel was born and raised in that house. As I said before, Sam was

Vengeance

a hard worker and on occasions he went into town to unwind by having a few drinks with his friends. His only problem was he didn't know when to stop drinking and would return home in a state of inebriation barely able to climb the porch steps. It was one such occasion that ended in disaster. As he left the saloon one evening, three of the town's worst troublemakers were waiting to rob him of his money. He was much too drunk to be rational and a fight ensued. I don't know the details of the confrontation, but Sam was shot dead. The killers were never identified and therefore never prosecuted for that murder. Many in town, including myself, suspected Rodney and his cronies of perpetrating the crime; since he was a notorious molester of women and men alike. He was the only person capable of committing such a horrendous crime. Rachel was only six years old at the time; and many years later he attempted to molest my Rachel, and almost succeeded. She was so frightened and hysterical from that attack that when Billy found her in that condition, he become enraged with anger and decided to hunt Rodney down. We pleaded with Billy to let the law handle it. Billy was still only a teenager at the time and we feared for his life. But Billy would not listen and went in search of Rodney. Thank God that Billy survived and Rodney did not."

"Yes I know, Billy told me all about it at the ranch."

"In a way, I guess justice was done; the man who killed my husband was himself killed by my future son-in-law. And finally, I've been a widow over twelve years. That's it Simon, now you know everything there is to know about me."

"Well, that explains a lot of your past history, but there is one aspect of your life that remains a puzzle to me."

"Oh, what's that Simon?"

"How is it possible for a beautiful woman like yourself, to remain a widow for all those years. Are the men in El Paso blind?"

Janette then stopped the one horse carriage alongside the lake, looked at Simon and said.

"It isn't that the men in El Paso hadn't tried to make advances toward me or engage me in flirtatious conversations; many had tried, but none of them appealed to me. I decided a long time ago, that if I ever marry again, it would have to be to a man I truly loved and respected. Otherwise I would remain a widow for the rest of my life."

"Well Janette, I admire your principals and ideals, but I'm putting you on notice that I intend to vie for your love and affection."

Vengeance

Janette didn't say a word she just looked at Simon and smiled in a most encouraging manner. After a few moments of silent glances, Simon put his arm around Janette's shoulder and nudged her closer to him, then planted a kiss on her lips. She didn't resist but responded in a most favorable way, by hugging Simon in return. At that moment in time, they both realized that they were in love and meant for each other. They lingered a while longer in each others arms before they decided to drive the buggy home. On their return trip home they acted like two giddy teenagers discovering love for the first time. Janette realized the time was fast approaching for their departure and invited all three men for dinner at her place. She went all out for these gallant men and prepared an old fashion Western spread, primarily consisting of barbecued steaks, beans and corn. They shared pleasantries all evening as the hours passed rapidly; before departing for the night Simon suggested to Billy and Joe that they meet tomorrow afternoon at one o'clock at Joe's place to review the information he has on the three desperados, before setting out in pursuit.

Simon and Billy arrived at Joe's home at the scheduled time. They sat at a round table with Simon holding the portfolio in his hands as Billy and Joe anxiously awaited his findings. He opened the portfolio containing the information on the trio and began with the characterization of Ben Beck, the leader of the three scoundrels, and said,

"Ben Beck is a very wealthy man who resides in a mansion located about sixty miles to the north of El Paso and four miles from the nearest town. He has a cadre of twenty men working for him who maintain the mansion and the surrounding grounds and provide him with protection if needed. His mansion has fifteen rooms and is made of stone and wood on twenty acres of land surrounded by a six foot fence. He grows his own crops for sustenance and raises a few heads of cattle, which his hired hands slaughter periodically for meat. He could live there indefinitely if he wishes without purchasing any provisions from town. A stable of prize horses are meticulously attended to, of which he is very fond of. He derives his wealth from two casinos that he owns; one located about fifteen miles northeast of his mansion and is operated by Fred Freeman; the other is ten miles southwest of the mansion and managed by his other crony Luke Butterfield. Once a week, a courier arrives from each of the casinos with one half the cash proceeds and delivers it to Beck. The other half is used to maintain and operate the casino; the remaining cash is gobbled up by Fred and Luck. The two casinos are located in the middle of nowhere. The casinos stand alone in the desert and are self contained with booze, women, and music as well as accommodations for overnight guests, with rooms upstairs and a restaurant for them to dine in."

"It sure sounds like a lucrative operation," said Joe.

"It sure is; the customer doesn't stand a chance. He walks out with empty pockets every time. Everything in the casino is rigged; it's the biggest scam job west of the Mississippi. If a customer is interested in cards, he is escorted to a round table and seated with his back to the wall while Fred faces him at the opposite side of the table. What the player doesn't knew, is that the wall behind him is covered with small holes cleverly concealed within inlayed sculptured figurines and oil paintings. An accomplis sitting behind the wall can look through those holes and read the cards held by the player. He then relays this information by hand signals to an associate seated outside the room who is isolated from the general public. He in turn, transmits the information to Fred. This is done by subtle hand movements, such as touching his hat for two pairs, picking up his beer for a straight, puffing on his cigar twice for a full house; if it's a high straight or flush, it might be an eye movement up or down, and so on. So you see it's impossible for anyone to win."

"Doesn't the player realize that every hand he's dealt is a losing hand?" asked Billy.

"Oh they're pretty clever in the way they conduct their scam. They allow the player to win a series of small pots, just enough to encourage him to bet heavily at the opportune time. When the player is sufficiently boozed up with free liquor; his rational betting behavior is compromised. Fred waits for a winning hand then he springs his trap. He entices the player to bet heavily on his losing hand, which he does and eventually loses everything. This is the mode of operation in both casinos. Well, there you have it Billy; how do you want to handle it?"

"My first stop will be Fred's casino, I've been waiting for this moment for a very long time. I can't wait to confront that son of a bitch across the poker table with my back to the wall. You two can come in and watch the fun."

Now that their plan had been finalized, Billy and Simon decided to take their leave from Rachel and Janette in the morning; then set out in pursuit of their nemesis.

Vengeance

The next morning, Billy had breakfast with Molly and John, then told them he would be leaving for the second time and went on to say,

"When I return this time, it will be for good."

Molly and John knew he had to go; Molly spoke first,

"Billy, we'll be praying for you and anxiously waiting for your safe return." Then John interjected,

"Molly and I would like to retire as soon as you return Billy, since the store will be yours when we pass on. In the meantime, you'll be in charge to operate the store as you see fit; it should provide you and Rachel with a good income and a secure future. All we require is a little money for our retirement years; the rest is yours Billy. I'm going to have additional living quarters built on the side of the house for Molly and me; so you and Rachel could occupy the rooms upstairs to raise your own family. So go and do what you have to do and hurry back to us."

"Molly, John, you've been so kind and considerate to me ever since I arrived in town as a scrawny little boy; you've taken me in and shown me all the love and affection that a boy could want and I'll never forget that. I couldn't love you more if you were my own blood parents. I'll always be grateful for everything you've done for me."

He then hugged them both, kissed Molly, and went on his way.

As he rode out to the Richardson's place he realized saying goodbye to Rachel wouldn't be that easy. Simon too would have to think of something affectionate to say to Janette. Billy then joined Simon and Joe as they all rode out together to the Richardson homestead to say good by to Rachel and Janette. It will be an emotional farewell for the young lovers; while Simon and Janette would conduct themselves in a more mature and controlled manner, although their feelings for each other were equally as strong. Rachel and Janette were sitting on the veranda awaiting their arrival. They knew they would be coming shortly to say goodby. Rachel was trying to hold back her tears so as not to make it any more difficult for Billy.

As they rode up Rachel ran out to greet Billy, while Simon joined Janette on the veranda. Joe stood back at a distance leaning on a tree allowing them partial privacy for their emotional farewells. Rachel's voice broke the silence,

"Do you really have to go, Billy?"

"You know I do Rachel; I can't bear being away from you and I'll return soon and when I do I'll never leave your side again."

Vengeance

With that exchange Rachel shed a few tears and hugged Billy, remaining in his arms while Simon was saying his goodbyes to Janette.

"Janette," he said, "I've known you for a very short time, but I feel that I've known you all my life. If I courted you for the next six months I wouldn't feel any different than I feel now. What I'm trying to say Janette, is that I love you. While I'm gone would you consider spending the rest of your life with me as my wife?"

"Oh Simon, I was hoping you would say something like that. Of course I'll marry you the minute you get back. So hurry back because I'll be waiting for you and thinking of you constantly."

They kissed and embraced for a few moments, then Simon tore himself from Janette's arms and joined Billy and Joe. Before leaving, Joe too, said his goodbyes to Rachel and Janette, saying,

"Don't you ladies worry about these two guys, I'll take good care of them."

Rachel couldn't help but think of the possibility of something happening to Billy and not returning. Such thoughts were too terrible to contemplate and she quickly banished them from her mind.

The three paladins then road off, as the morning sun rose high in the firmament. Twenty year old Billy in the middle, twenty nine year old Joe on his right and the forty three year old legend Simon Ganz on his left. As they rode off Billy was silently thinking,

"The day has finally come, for me to ferrite out the murderers of my mother, father and little sister. They'll have to face the sole survivor of the Reed family; the one that got away; I cannot say God have mercy on their souls."

CHAPTER TWENTY
RETRIBUTION

It was a hot, dry summer day, as they traveled through the arid lands of New Mexico. The human body under normal conditions would be awash in sweat in this intemperate environment, but their bodies were as dry as the land itself. The hot dry desert air sucked up every drop of surface moisture from man and beast. For a thirsty man water would be worth its weight in gold. And in this land, watering holes were few and far between for anyone to feel completely safe and comfortable in this unforgiving land. When a watering hole was sighted, it would be like seeing the resurrection of the Lord. Billy and company were beginning to feel the discomfort of thirst, when they sighted such an oasis that rejuvenated their spirit. They relaxed themselves and their horses while hydrating both and replenishing their containers with cool, clean, water; before heading for their final destination to the town of No Where. The town was barely large enough to deserve demarcation on the local maps of the area. It had a hotel, saloon, restaurant and supply store: that sold food, clothing, and prospecting equipment to the transit public, and it catered to visitors from Fred's casino. It had a population of fifty people, excluding those who passed through town on a daily basis augmenting its population to one hundred and twenty five. It was only twenty miles from Fred's casino. The most popular character in town was a person named Scotty who had been prospecting this area of the desert for the past ten years. The locals in town knew Scotty as a congenial old man, constantly searching for mineral sources in the desert that were illusive and probably not there. He was considered to be eccentric in many ways, talking to his mule and never removing his hat. It was said by the locals that he even slept with his hat on and it showed; it was a mangled piece of cloth a top his head. Scotty was a tall lean man, standing at 5'10," with deep set blue eyes and a beard that was mostly gray. At age 65, he was still spry and energetic and would ride out into the desert with his mule and not return for weeks. He knew the desert like the back of his hand, and while in the desert he lived on wild game, including rattlesnakes, and slept under the desert moon. Scotty always looked as if he needed a good meal but he

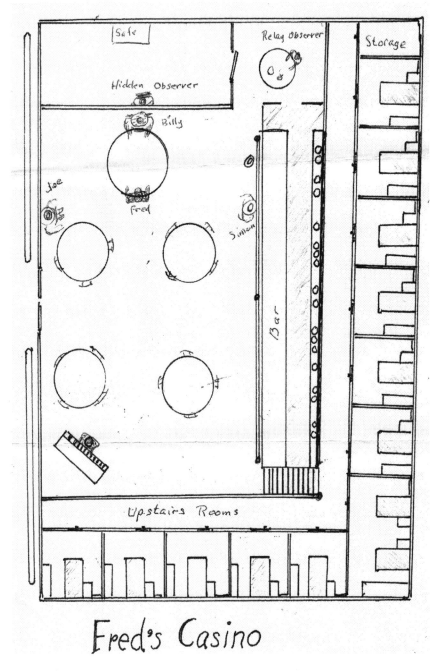

Fred's Casino

preferred a liquid diet. When not prospecting, he was a permanent fixture in the saloon. He had a magnetic personality and was able to solicit drinks from the patrons on the basis of his tall tales of the desert. Before starting out into the desert he would shave his face clean, then pack a shovel, pick, rifle, Bowie knife, and of course plenty of water, then disappear into the desert with his mule.

It was in the town of No Where that Billy, Joe and Simon decided to establish their base of operation, before dealing with Fred. They rode into town the following evening and booked rooms at the Frontier Hotel where they could freshen up with a bath, shave and a hot meal. After having dinner, there was still plenty of daylight left; Simon suggested that they have a drink or two before retiring for the night; they would deal with Fred in the morning. His suggestion was well received, and they went downstairs to the bar and sat down at a table and ordered a round of drinks.

As usual, Scotty surveyed the bar room trying to pick out an easy mark for a drink, when he spotted Billy, Joe, and Simon. He recognized them as newly arrived strangers in town and walked over to their table and said,

"Howdy folks, my name is Scotty, and I'm a one man Chamber of Commerce and could provide you with any information you need to know about this town or the desert. Could I be of service to you gentleman?"

"I don't think so Scotty; we won't be staying in town long,"replied Simon.

"Around these parts, I'm known as a desert rat because I spend so much of my time in the desert. Most people think of the desert as a forbidding and hostile land that isn't worth a damn. But I can tell you that you needn't fear the desert once you get to know it; it's a Garden of Eden and can provide you with all your needs."

Simon thought, maybe they could use a little entertainment and diversion from their mission and said,

"Well, why don't you sit down and tell us all about it."

"I don't mind if I do, but you'll have to bear with me, my throat is as dry as the desert sand and that makes the words a little jumbled at times."

Simon just smiled and yelled out,

"Bartender, bring us a bottle of whiskey!"

When Scotty heard that, his eyes lit up like Roman candles and he started to talk non stop.

"Well folks, the first thing you have to know is where the watering holes are located in the desert. There are two oases within a thirty five mile radius of this town. One is located to the northwest about twenty miles from here; the other is fifteen miles to the southeast of town. Should you become disoriented in the desert, which is common for neophytes, you can always quench your thirst by tapping into a catus plant and for solid nourishment you can scavenge almost any animal that moves. On many occasions I didn't have to hunt for my breakfast, it comes to me. I can remember on one occasion, before retiring for the night I flip my boots over on the ground. In the morning before putting my boots back on, I shook them out to make sure there was nothing inside; generally I would find a scorpion or two fall to the ground providing me with a tasty breakfast. On this particular morning to my surprise, when I flipped my boot over, a rattle snake dropped out. I snipped off its head and had it for breakfast."

Scotty let loose a belly laugh, joined by his hosts, then Billy asked, "Isn't it kind of dangerous to handle rattlesnakes so casually?"

"Not if you know rattlers, they're cold blooded and the chilly morning air makes them sluggish and lethargic and easy to handle. They don't become active and dangerous till late morning when their bodies are warmed sufficiently by the sun."

"You sure are a warehouse of information, Scotty," replied Billy.

"Yeah, people in town think of me as being a little peculiar and odd because of my lifestyle. But they have to work for a living; I don't and they buy me the drinks. So who's the nutty one?"

Hardy laughter circled the table. Scotty was having a good time and Billy, Joe and Simon were being pleasantly entertained. Scotty noticed that Billy was glancing at his crooked left arm, and said,

"Yes, it's crooked all right, instead of being straight it has a thirty degree bend in it due to an accident I had as a child. I smashed up my elbow and the doctor did a piss poor job in putting it back together and it healed up like that, but it doesn't cause me any pain or difficulty in movement."

"Well Scotty, its been a pleasure meeting you and listening to your tall tales of the desert, but the time has come for us to break up this little gathering; we have a big day ahead of us tomorrow," said Simon.

"Where are you folks headed?" asked Scotty.

"We're going to visit Fred's casino in the morning," replied Billy.

"Oh my, you should stay away from that place, you couldn't win a Confederate dollar bill in that joint. You'll just be throwing your money away. I've never meet anyone who walked away a winner from that casino. One other thing, watch out for the fire ants. The entire area is infested with them."

"Thanks for the tip, Scotty, I'll kept that in mind. Good night and good luck to you; I hope you find what you're looking for in the desert," replied Simon.

Scotty in a rare instant, tipped his hat revealing a lily white bald head and said good-bye, then Simon, Joe and Billy retired for the night.

The next morning, Billy was the first to rise at 8:30. At the breakfast table they were unanimous in their complaint: they had difficulty in falling asleep due to the loud and continuous noise reverberating through town from the unruly and drunken populous. Simon and Joe decided that if they had to spend another night in No Where, they would sleep outdoors on the outskirts of town in nature's bedroom, rather than spend another night in the noisy environment of the hotel.

"That's where you'll find us Billy, should it take more than a day for you to settle the score with Fred," said Simon.

After a leisurely breakfast, they lit up cigars and focused their attention on Fred, the manager and caretaker of one of two lucrative casinos of Ben Beck's.

"Billy, this is your call, how do you want to deal with Fred?" asked Simon.

"Well," said Billy, "after we enter the casino I'll face down Fred, while you and Joe protect my rear to make sure that his bodyguards don't interfere while I explain to Fred that I'm the little boy he chased into the woods eight years ago, who got away during that infamous night of robbery, rape, murder and arson. And now here I am all grown up, face to face with you."

"That should shock the shit out of him," Joe said.

"Maybe he'll just die of shock Billy, and depriving you of the pleasure of killing him," Simon chimed in.

When they concluded their discussion they had another cup of coffee and went on their way. Scotty was right; on the way to the casino they could see the fire ants enmasse on the side of the road. They weren't gone more than an hour before reaching Fred's casino. It was about 11 A.M. when they arrived and tied their horses to the hitching post, then walked in.

After entering the casino they paused to look around and observe their surroundings. The first thing they noticed was a twenty five foot long bar with a mirror as a backdrop, giving the casino the impression of being larger than it actually was. At one end of the room sat Fred dealing cards to an unsuspecting card player, while one of Fred's boys sat at a round table to his right, periodically relaying subtle body signals to Fred as to the cards held by his opponent. At the opposite end of the casino sat a piano player, banging out the latest tunes of the day while the lavishly dressed and sexually enticing floor girls circulated amongst the patrons, encouraging them to buy them watered down dinks or spend their money on other activities. Opposite the piano player was a flight of stairs leading to a series of rooms arranged at right angles for patrons who would like to stay overnight, alone or with a companion. It was all neatly arranged to make the visitors feel comfortable while departing with their money. And to a large extent quite successful.

After casing the casino and giving it a good once over, Simon walked over to the bar and ordered a drink, while Joe took a position near the wall opposite Simon and waited for Billy to take care of business. In the meantime, one of the seductive women walked over to Simon and said,

"Hello handsome, would you buy a drink for a thirsty lady?"

"No Ma'am, you can buy your own drinks; I'm not here for entertainment or companionship."

After digesting Simon's remark, she frowned and walked away. During Simon's terse conversation with one of the floor girls, Billy walked over to Fred's card table to observe the action. Billy wanted to face Fred across the card table but that position was occupied, so he waited patiently for twenty minutes till the card player had exhausted his resources and left. Then Billy stepped up and said,

"Do you mind if I sit down?"

"Not at all stranger, your money is as good as anybody's."

Billy pulled out the chair, sat down, and just stared at Fred, till Fred finally said,

"I don't see your money on the table stranger!"

Billy still staring straight at Fred, said,

"I really didn't sit down to play cards."

"Well, what the hell did you sit down for? If you don't want to play cards, remove your ass from the chair and let someone else sit down who does want to play."

This verbal exchange attracted the attention of some of the bystanders who were listening with interest.

"I came here to see you, Fred."

"Well, now that you saw me, why don't you get the fuck out of here."

"Tell me Fred, does the name Tom Reed mean anything to you?"

"Not a goddamn thing!"

"Well, let me refresh your memory Fred. About eight years ago, three scoundrels broke into my parent's home and robbed them of four thousand dollars, not satisfied with the money, they murdered my father and little sister, then raped my mother before burning our home to the ground, cremating my family. Their young son whom you chased into the woods that night of horror got away and now he sits before you, all grown up."

Fred's unlit cigar dropped from his mouth. His expression, once defiant and arrogant, was now pale and sober, with a genuine look of fear on his face. While staring at Billy in disbelief, he raised his right hand over his head and thrust it forward on to the table. A signal for his goons to come to his assistance. Four of his gun slinger bodyguards advanced and stood behind him. Now with his four goons in place, an expression of confidence and defiance returned to his face, as he said,

"Coming here was a big mistake, young man; now I can't allow you to leave this casino alive. You should have stayed where you were and accepted the hand that fate dealt you."

"I think you're misreading fate's hand. I see the fate of three blackguards dying a painful death and you Fred have been chosen to be the first of the three to depart this world."

Fred let out a loud laugh, and said,

"O.K. boys, let him have it."

All four went for their guns at the same time; but before they could withdraw their rods from their holsters, Simon and Joe let loose a barrage of gun fire, dropping all four of them like so many bags of rotten apples. Fred hearing the explosion of gun fire in back of him, turned around, and saw four dead bodies. Turning toward Billy, he realized he was in a precarious situation.

"Well Fred, it appears that your protection has evaporated; it's now just you and me, and only one of us will have a life span measured in minutes."

Then Billy yelled out to Simon and Joe,

"Would you boys do me a favor and clear the casino of all living creatures: men, women, everybody, I want to be alone with Fred before this casino goes up in flames."

After hearing Billy say that the casino was going up in flames, the patrons didn't wait to be escorted out; they all made a mad dash for the exit.

Fred was now visibly shaken, breathing heavily with beads of sweat forming on his forehead. As soon as the casino was cleared of all its occupants and with Simon and Joe waiting outside, Fred began to plead for his life.

"It wasn't my idea, it was Ben Beck who thought of breaking in and stealing the money. I didn't know he was going to murder anybody. I'll give you back all the money and then some and even help you catch Ben and Luke since I know all their little secrets; how about it?"

"Tell me Fred, can you give me back the lives of my mother, father and little sister?"

"No, but I'll do anything you want, just tell me what you want."

"I want you Fred, I want you dead and I'll give you better odds than you gave my parents. I'll give you a chance to defend yourself, so whenever you're ready, you can draw."

"No, no, let's talk this over."

"We already talked too much; I'll count to three and if you don't draw you're dead."

At the count of three, Fred drew. Billy waited for him to withdraw his gun from his holster then shot the gun out of his hand, and said,

"I suppose you realize that I could have killed you if I wanted to?"

Fred interpreted Billy's action as a sign that he would spare his life and negotiate a settlement, saying,

"Then you'll take the money and I'll help you get Ben and Luke?"

"No, you're wrong again Fred, the only reason why I didn't kill you outright was that it would have been too merciful a death for you. I want you to leave here with the knowledge that I'll be right behind you thinking of some dreadful way for you to die."

Billy then took one of the kerosene lamps and tossed it at the bar setting the casino aflame; Fred backed away staring at Billy and holding his bloodied hand, then turned and ran out. Simon and Joe witnessed a very frightened man ride off. There was only one road out from the flaming casino and Billy knew exactly where Fred was heading; on his way to Ben Beck's mansion to warn him of the impending danger. Before leaving, Billy told

Vengeance

Simon and Joe that he was going after Fred to finish him off, and they should wait for his return at their camp site on the edge of town. As Billy road off after Fred, he took a short cut through a narrow ravine to await Fred's arrival at a secluded area a few miles from the torched casino. As Fred approached the designated area, he saw Billy facing him in the middle of the road with both guns drawn. Fred came to an abrupt halt, but there was no way he could escape without having his body filled with lead. That would have been the best option for Fred, rather than yield to what Billy had in store for him. The desert temperature was well over 100 degrees and rising steadily. Billy told Fred to ride off trail into the scorching desert sand. As soon as they were deep into the desert, Billy told Fred to dismount and start walking, while Billy rode close behind. They continued in this manner for an hour or so, till Fred was dehydrated, exhausted, and so weakened he could go no farther. Fred didn't know exactly what was in store for him, but he realized he wasn't going to leave the desert alive. It was useless for him to try and talk his way out of this calamity, his fate was sealed. His only chance of survival was to try to escape, but he knew that was impossible. Billy stopped periodically for a drink of water, while Fred looked on. Finally, Billy said,

"Fred, this is where you'll spend your last day on earth; dying of thirst in the desert. And when you close your eyes for the last time, those vultures circling overhead will scoop down and pick every last ounce of flesh from your body till there is nothing left of you but a skeleton that was once Fred Freeman. After I leave, I'll return in 24 hours to verify your death by the remains of your bones. If there are no bones to be found for verification of your demise, I'll assume you have survived your ordeal some how and I'll continue my search for you and hunt you down like a wild animal, wherever you are."

With that said, Billy road off, leaving Fred to desiccate in the hot and burning desert sun. Fred just sat there baking in the desert oven, too weak to move a muscle, occasionally glancing up at the circling vultures. Hours had passed in the hot sun as blisters formed on his face and his eye lids were hanging heavy with death not far off. Just about that time, he saw a lone rider in the distance. Thinking it just a mirage, he displayed no emotion but continued to lie in abeyance. But as the rider got closer and closer, his eyes widened and a renewed burst of energy revived his spirit. It was indeed a lone rider and thoughts of survival danced in his head. It was Scotty, on one of his

desert jaunts. As Scotty rode up, Fred stretched out his arms, and said,
"Water, water."

Scotty dismounted from his mule and gave Fred the water he craved. The water revived Fred both mentally and physically, and after a long pause, Fred said,
"Thank you; you saved my life."

Scotty assumed that Fred was one of those unfortunate victims who got lost in the desert and was destined to die there. He told Fred that he would give him some water and a ride back to town where he could rest and recuperate from his ordeal.

Fred slowly regained his composure; then realized that when Billy returned the following day and did not find his bones, he would know that he had escaped and would be back on his trail hunting him down like a predatory varmint. He decided to satisfy Billy's thirst for vengeance; he would kill Scotty and have the vultures devour his body. This way when Billy returned the following day and found the remaining bones, he would conclude that Fred was dead. Then Fred could flee the area as a free man and live out his life elsewhere in some other part of the country. Yes, that's what he would do; but he was far too weak to attack Scotty physically and he would have to wait for an opportune time. Fred thanked Scotty for his kindness while eyeing Scotty's rifle on the side of his mule. Then edging toward the rifle, he asked Scotty for another drink of water. When Scotty went for the canteen of water, Fred went for Scotty's rifle withdrawing it from the side of the mule; then Fred pointed the rifle at Scotty, and said,
"I'm sorry old timer, but I have to kill you."

Before Scotty could say a word Fred pulled the trigger, killing Scotty instantly. He stripped Scotty of his clothes and replaced them with his, then laid Scotty on his back facing the sun. Those hungry vultures could strip a body of its flesh in an hour. Fred then mounted Scotty's mule and took off for town. It was extra-ordinarily hot when he arrived in town, which kept most of the people indoors. He rode up to the hotel and hitched Scotty's mule to the rail, then went inside to register for a room where he would hide out for a day or two; long enough for him to regain his strength and rest his right hand till it was manageable enough for him to ride a horse. His intention was to leave this part of the country and settle in California to start a new life and assume a new identity. The following day while Fred was resting in his hotel room, Billy rode out to the spot where he had left Fred. He wanted to confirm

Fred's death by viewing the remains of his bones. When Billy approached the spot, he did indeed see the bones of a human skeleton and muttered to himself,

"Well I guess Fred is dead."

As he stood there staring at the skeleton he was a little perplexed, it just didn't look right; for one thing the skull was stripped clean of flesh, Fred had a large crop of hair yet not a trace of hair was in the vicinity of the skull, could the vultures have eaten hair and all? Then looking at the right hand of the skeleton, he saw no sign of a broken or injured hand, resulting from his encounter with Fred at the casino. Billy then dismounted his horse and walked over to the skeleton to remove its shirt for closer inspection. Billy immediately noticed a crocked left arm, quite deformed at the elbow, and shouted,

"By God, these are Scotty's bones!"

Billy tried to reconstruct in his mind what had happened, piecing together the bits of evidence he came up with a likely scenario of events.

"Scotty must have found Fred near death and came to his assistance with water and whatever else he needed and in return for Scotty's kindness, Fred killed him; leaving his body here in the desert to be consumed by vultures thinking he could fool me into thinking that these bones were his. And that son of a bitch almost got away with it too. Now poor Scotty is dead and Fred is still alive." As Billy looked down at the bones he displayed strong emotions, visibly shaken and angry over Scotty's death and Fred's deception. On the one hand he was saddened that Scotty had to meet his end that way; on the other hand he had an unrelenting anger toward Fred for such ingratitude after Scotty had saved his life. It was hard to imagine any human being having a more evil soul than Fred. Billy displayed a rare quality of vengeance not apparent since Beck and his cronies murdered his family on that night of infamy. "Well, he won't be alive for long; he's going to pay dearly for his unconscionable crimes. I'll make him curse his mother for giving birth to him."

Billy turned his horse around and roared toward town at break neck speed. Riding through town he noticed a few citizens around Scotty's mule tied up in front of the hotel, but no Scotty. They were confused as to why Scotty had returned from the desert a day after he had left town, most unusual they thought. But not to Billy because he knew now exactly where Fred was.

Vengeance

He then road out to the campsite on the edge of town where Simon and Joe were waiting. Billy explained to Simon and Joe exactly what had happened from the time he brought Fred into the desert to the murder of Scotty by Fred. And now Fred is in the hotel gloating over his deception and escape, thinking he's a free man; then Billy told Simon and Joe,

"I'll wait till Fred is ready to leave town, then I'll nail that bastard; but this time I'll make sure he doesn't escape."

All three relaxed and waited for Fred to make his move. Billy didn't have to wait long; the following day Fred was preparing to move on, but first he needed a horse and was prepared to steal or buy one. As he walked over to the only stable in town he noticed his horse standing there and approached the owner of the stable and said,

"That's my horse! Where did you get him?"

"A young man gave me the horse and told me he found the horse in the desert, and if no one claimed him, I should keep him."

"Well, I'm claiming him!"

"Can you prove it's your horse?"

"I sure can."

Fred then provided some intimate details about the horse, including an abnormal tooth structure in the horse's mouth and other minor details convincing the stable owner that he was indeed the rightful owner of the horse; then handed the horse over to Fred. Fred was elated since he had his horse back; and now that Billy thought he was dead, he was on his way to California. As Fred rode confidently out of town, passing Billy's campsite, Billy nudged Simon and said,

"Simon look who's coming out from underneath the rock; it's Fred, leaving town thinking he's undetected and assumed dead. I'll wait till he's a good way out of town, then I'll take a short cut and greet him as he emerges from that shallow ravine. I'm sure he'll be glad to see me."

Simon and Joe laughed, and Simon said,

"I'm sure he will be, that is if he doesn't die of fright."

Billy then rode off and waited for Fred from behind a cluster of shrubbery. A while later, he saw Fred at a distance and as he approached, Billy emerged from behind the shrubbery and greeted him, saying,

"Well, we meet again Fred. You thought you were pretty clever killing Scotty and leaving his bones in the desert to deceive me. You almost got away with it to, but you're going to wish you hadn't."

Vengeance

Fred was so mad and frightened he was lost for words and remained silent. Billy then lassoed Fred around the chest and told him to pull his hands through the rope so he could handle his horse.

"Now Fred, we're headed in the direction of your burned out casino, so let's get a move on; any attempt to escape on your part and you'll be yanked from your horse and I'll be forced to drag you on the ground, so behave yourself."

When they arrived, Billy stopped alongside a swarm of fire ants on the side of the road. There were millions of them, so numerous that you couldn't see the ground beneath them. It was just one large carpet of brown ants, four feet in length and two feet wide. Then Billy said,

"O.K. Fred, here is where you get off; you're going to bed with the fire ants."

"Oh no I'm not, you'll have to kill me first; I'm not going into that blanket of fire."

Billy yanked him off his horse, pulled out his gun and shattered both of his knee caps. Fred fell to the ground in the midst of the ants, incapable of extricating himself from the swarming ants. They were crawling all over his body, in his ears, eyes, mouth and under his clothes. It was much too gruesome for Billy to watch and he turned away in disgust and rode off.

As Billy rode back to Simon's campsite, he reflected on the manner in which Fred died and wasn't proud of himself. Visions of Fred squirming amongst the fire ants were ever present in his mind. After arriving at the campsite he explained to Simon and Joe that Fred was no more and went on to explain how he meet his death.

The next morning they were on their way in search of their next victim, Luke Butterfield. They were riding for over an hour and in all that time Billy was reticent not saying a word and looking depressed and despondent, as if he had lost a loved one rather than expressing joy for accomplishing part of his mission. Billy's appearance and demeanor did not go unnoticed by Simon or Joe. There was something bothering Billy and Simon intended to find out what it was. He rode up alongside Billy and said,

"Billy, what's bothering you, come on out with it, get it off your chest; confession is good for the soul. You might as well tell me; I'm not going to let up till you tell me what's wrong."

"It's just that I don't feel like celebrating over the way that Fred died. God knows he deserved to die, since there was no greater villain than Fred.

He was capable of committing the foulest of crimes, and did. But I didn't have to inflict such barbaric tactics on him, the very qualities that I so detested in Beck and his cronies I find myself guilty of. My actions put me on the same moral level as they. An eye for an eye and a tooth for a tooth doesn't mean that I should commit acts of cruelty and torture on my victim. If I had killed Fred outright when I had the chance, Scotty would be alive today and I would feel much better about myself."

"Well Billy, if it's any consolation for you I have had the same guilt complex in the past over revengeful acts that I committed. Acknowledgment of repugnant behavior is the first step in regaining your peace of mind. No Billy, your method in dealing with Fred does not put you on the same level with Fred; only if you had no regret, remorse, or guilt complex would you be on his level. You Billy, have a conscience, which allows you to acknowledge and correct your misdeeds by changing your attitude and behavior in the future. People like Fred have no conscience or remorse and will never change, but continue in their nefarious ways till someone like yourself puts an end to their mischief. Now you must decide Billy, if you want to continue your pursuit of Luke and Ben Beck, or would you rather return to El Paso?"

"No, I must continue my search for Luke and Ben Beck till their presence on earth is no more; only then can I rest and return to Rachel as a normal person, free of nagging vengeance. But my approach in their pursuit has changed, it will be strictly academic in bringing them to justice. I can't derive any pleasure from their demise; nor belabor their deaths. I will just do the job that has to be done."

"Good enough Billy, let's go get them," replied Simon.

And off they galloped in the direction of Luke's casino.

CHAPTER TWENTY ONE
EVIL ENCOUNTER

Luke Butterfield was not the brightest representative of the human race, harboring many idiosyncrasies; one of which was an inordinate fear of death. Although he realized the certitude of death, he avoided the mere mention of the word when it pertained to him but had no qualms about applying the term to others, in word or deed.

When word reached Ben and Luke of the terrible and painful death of Fred by fire ants and the total destruction by fire of one of Ben Beck's casinos, a veil of fear descended over their faces the likes of which had never been seen before. Their fears were augmented when learning that Billy was the surviving son from their heinous crime against the Reed household eight years ago. Learning that Billy was accompanied by the famous Simon Ganz and Joe Young the bounty hunter, struck terror in their hearts. Each of them is a formidable adversary in their own right, taken together it meant a coup de grace, Luke in particular was terrified, not only of dying but how he would die. He had daytime visions and nightmares of Fred being devoured by fire ants. Those thoughts caused Luke to have heart palpitations and tremors in his hands and fingers. He had no way of knowing that Billy had a change of heart and abandoned all thoughts of inflicting horrific and cruel punishment on him or Beck. The thought of such a painful death was torture in its self. However, they would die in a more conventional fashion.

Their survival was now in question so drastic and immediate action was necessary. Ben Beck had no illusions of safety hiding behind the walls surrounding his mansion. Trying to head off disaster he dispatched eight of his notorious gun slingers to assist Luke in the defense of his casino, then awaited the arrival of the awesome trio. Beck was fully aware that Billy had the cross hairs of his rifle pointed in the direction of Luke's casino as his next target for destruction. Rather than hide out in the casino and wait for them to execute their plan of attack, he decided to go on the offensive and take the fight to them before they reached the casino. He called a strategy meeting with Luke and eight of his boys to explain his plan of offense to them, before departing for Luke's casino.

Vengeance

"I have an intimate knowledge of the landscape in and around the casino and have been planning our defense ever since I learned of Fred's death and I have no intention of meeting his fate. So this is what I propose; there is a rock formation about a half mile south of the casino; the rocks aren't very high, but they are numerous and can provide sufficient concealment for an ambush. Bordering the rock formation, between it and the casino, is a thicket of trees and evergreen bushes due to an underground aquifer, this spot makes an even better ambush than the rock formation. They'll have to pass through this rock formation to reach the casino; so five of you boys will hide out in the rock formation with your rifles, three of you on the right and two on the left. The other three will occupy positions in the evergreen thicket. Have your horses tied to trees on the periphery of the thicket concealed, but not entirely, expose just enough horse flesh to give away your position. Now Simon is no fool and he'll detect an ambush immediately and when he does, he'll pause to evaluate his surroundings. That will be the signal for the men in the thicket to open fire, forcing them to flee or seek shelter within the rock formation, if you should hit one of them so much the better. Simon also may suspect some men within the rock formation and might avoid that option. Now that they know where we're at, they may try to circumvent the ambushes altogether and ride around the rock formation and thicket. If so, they'll expose themselves in the open flat lands without any concealment and they'll be like sitting ducks to be picked off one at a time. Even if we get only one of them, it will reduce the odds in our favor."

Luke interrupted, asking,

"What if they decide to circumvent our ambush at night?"

"In that case, they will be successful but they will also put themselves between two firing squads; one in front by the men in the casino and the other from the rear by us. Anyway you look at it there will be a gun fight and the odds are in our favor. We'll see how that wise ass Simon gets out of this jam. Then we can all get back to business as usual."

Beck's plan brought a smile to Luke's face and his confidence was restored, by saying,

"Beck, I have to hand it to you, you're a genius."

Now that the trap was set, Luke retired to the casino and Beck sought safety in his mansion and waited for the good news to arrive. Ben Beck had a superiority complex of his mental abilities which fostered a seminal degradation of others, especially when compared to Simon Ganz. His scheme would require far more strategic planning than he was capable of to fool Simon Ganz. Simon did not reach the wholesome age of forty-five by imprudence or reckless behavior. He had an analytical approach to problems and an innate and intuitive ability to gage his fellow man which served him well throughout his life.

While Beck was explaining his plan of entrapment to his men, Simon, Billy and Joe were camping out that evening about twenty miles from Luke's casino. They were gathered around the campfire relaxing, drinking coffee, and smoking cigars, after polishing off the remains of a roasted jackrabbit that Simon had bagged earlier. Their conversation centered on their approach to Luke's casino. Simon initiated the chit-chat by explaining,

"We won't be fortunate enough to walk into Luke's casino as we did Fred's, since by now the news of Fred's death and the destruction of his casino has reached the ears of Beck and they'll be expecting us. Therefore, we'll have to be exceptionally cautious in our approach. Ideally I would like to observe the casino for a day or so, at a distance of course, to determine the layout of the place and the number of desperados we'll have to deal with. We may even decide to occupy strategic locations around the casino and pick them off one by one if the landscape is favorable. This is all ideal speculation of course and we could continue along these lines all night and accomplish little, so let's get some sleep; our actions will be dictated by the conditions on the ground.

Early next morning, they set out for their showdown with Luke and his boys. As they rode along they took notice of the semi-arid terrain, quite barren, with an occasional boulder protruding from the sandy soil and scattered shrubbery here and there, but most abundant were the gigantic Saguaro cactuses, standing like centennials guarding that which belongs to nature.

With the passage of time and distance, they came within sight of the rocky formation; Ben's foolproof trap. As they got closer, Simon stopped to observe and evaluate the rock formation as predicted by Ben, Simon proclaimed,

"Gentlemen, we can't go any farther. It would be foolish and dangerous for us to go anywhere near that rock formation, because it looks to me like a perfect spot for someone to conceal themself for an ambush, and there's no telling how many could be hiding out there."

Vengeance

At that instance as planned, a few shots rang out from within the evergreen thicket, one of which whizzed past Simon's head. They immediately retreated out of the range of fire to contemplate their next move. So far everything was going according to Beck's plan, but he hadn't planned on Simon's next move.

Simon thought for a while, then said,

"Well gentlemen, we can't ride through that ambush and we can't go around it without exposing ourselves to their concealed firing position. Of course, if we really wanted to get around that ambush it wouldn't present much of a problem, but I wouldn't feel comfortable having those scoundrels in my rear.

Our only alternative is to dispose of those naughty fellows where they are, in their rocky fortress and thicket."

Billy asked Simon,

"I'm sure you must have come across similar situations in your past Simon. Have you any suggestions for this one?"

"Yes I have Billy. We'll wait till dark then you and Joe can walk the half mile to the base of the rock formation and settle down for the night on the right side of the rocks and remain perfectly quiet during the night. I'll do the same, but occupy the left side of the rocks. Come morning, those fellows within the rocks will be curious about our whereabouts and I'm hoping they'll make enough noise or communicate with each other to give away their location; but you must continue to maintain your silence long enough to determine the number of men you'll be up against and their location. Then you and Joe can move out one at a time, covering for each other as you go. I'll occupy the other side of the road and if I should get a beat on one of them, I'll hold my fire till you start shooting. When I hear that first shot ring out that will be the signal for the gun fight to begin and I'll commence firing. That will assure us of at least two less fellows to contend with. One other thing, once you are in position, we'll move at first light since it's best to attack them while they're still groggy from a night's sleep."

"I'm ready to go, it should be dark in an hour or so," said Billy.

"Yes, but we'll wait till early morning to move out, we want to give those fellows a chance to get to sleep and that will improve our chances of not being detected," said Simon.

At the appointed time, about one o'clock in the morning they walked the half mile to the rock formation and proceeded to advance inward to find a suitable hiding place for the night, then settled down and waited till day break. The only sounds that could be heard during the night were the movement of the night creatures on the hunt. It occurred to Joe that both he and the night creatures were on similar missions, stalking their prey. Then Billy and Joe slowly shut their eyes and waited for first light.

The next morning when the sun's refulgence appeared on the horizon, Billy heard stirring amongst the rocks not far from where he was situated. A few minutes later, the gunmen began to communicate with each other in a whisper. Then Billy signaled Joe as to their location they both moved in unison toward their prey. Two of the gunmen were in their immediate vicinity and a third man was about twenty five feet farther down toward the road.

In the meantime, Simon had located two of the gunmen on his side of the road, both of whom occupied secured positions behind large boulders with a clear view of the meandering road. Just about that time Billy and Joe let loose a barrage of gun fire putting the two gunmen out of action, while the third man remained glued to the ground too terrified to move.

After hearing the gunfire from the other side of the road, Simon was close enough to his prey to say

"Drop your gun, Mr."

His partner, not far away turned around in an attempt to shoot Simon, but Simon was aware of his presence and nailed him before he could lift his gun out of his holster. Then Simon shouted to Billy and Joe,

"Are you guys O.K.?" Joe yelled back,

"Yeah, we got two of them."

"Good, be on your guard; I have a little business to attend to."

Simon signaled the lone gunman, saying,

"Come over here. I want to talk to you!"

Simon hustled him to a secure location and said,

"I have a proposition for you. I need information and if you tell me what I want to know you can go free to live out your life; if not this will be your burial ground."

"Alright, I'll tell you what you want to know."

"How many of you are in these rocks and in the evergreen thicket, and if you lie to me you're as good as dead."

"I'm the only one left on this side of the road and there are three on the other side of the road and three more in the evergreen thicket."

"And how many are in the casino with Luke?"

Vengeance

"There are five more in the casino, not counting Luke."

"Now I'm going to tie you up; if you're telling me the truth, I'll be back to set you free. If not, you know how the story will end."

"I'm telling you the truth; I swear it."

"O.K., then you have nothing to worry about. Now lie on the ground face down while I tie you up."Then Simon yelled out,

"Billy, there is one more guy on your side of the road and three more in the thicket. I got all the hired guns on this side of the road."

Then Billy walked over to the lone gunman lying on the ground, and said,

"O.K., get up and drop your gun."

He did what he was told. Then Billy said,

"I want you to walk over to the evergreen thicket and bring those eight horses here."

"I can't do that; they'll kill me if I tried that."

"I'll kill you if you don't; besides we'll be out of sight but close behind you and if they should open fire we'll blast them to kingdom come. If you try any funny business, you'll be the first to get a bullet through your head. Now get moving."

As he walked nervously toward the horses, Billy and Joe followed close behind concealing themselves within the underbrush. As he approached the horses one of his buddies yelled out,

"Get away from those horses, Todd."

He was frozen in position. If he released the horses they would surely shoot him; if he didn't do what he was told he would be the recipient of Billy's bullet. He decided to take a chance and release the horses then hit the ground and hoped for the best; maybe Billy and Joe will get them before they got him. He situated himself between the horses then proceeded to release the horses; immediately shots rang out from the thicket and he fell to the ground. Billy and Joe began to blast away, killing all three hired guns. Simon heard the shooting and quickened his pace toward the thicket. A quick evaluation of the situation by Simon indicated that Billy and Joe had everything under control, prompting Simon to say,

"Well, I see you boys handled the situation very nicely; so if you'll excuse me for a few minutes, I still have some unfinished business to attend to."

Simon then turned around and walked to where his informant was tied up and cut him loose, saying,

"You didn't lie to me so I'm keeping my word and releasing you. We'll have to walk over to where the horses are together otherwise you're sure to be shot."

As they got closer to Billy and Joe, Simon yelled out,

"It's O.K. boys, he's my informant and I promised him safe passage if he gave me the information I was seeking. He did, so give him a horse and let him ride off."

Now that they had disposed of part of Luke's arsenal of men they sat down together to plan their strategy for their attack on Luke's casino. The patrons of the casino were long gone, pending the showdown at their gambling site. Simon explained that there are six men defending the casino, including Luke. Luke too was preparing for the defense of his casino. By now all were aware that they were up against Simon Ganz and two other very dangerous gun fighters. He had heard the gun fire echoing across the terrain and wondered as to the outcome of the engagement and decided to dispatch one of his boys to find out and report back. Unfortunately, the fellow who tried to release the horses received a mortal wound and died within minutes. As Simon, Billy and Joe were sitting around the edge of the evergreen formation, they saw a lone rider approaching in the distance and knew instinctively that it was one of Luke's men. Should they kill him or pump him for information? they decided on the latter. When the rider saw the three paladins sitting there, he came to an abrupt halt, and said,

"Don't shoot, don't shoot."

"O.K.," said Simon,

"Come over here and sit down beside me. I'd like to talk to you."

He realized he had no chance of survival if he didn't do what he was told and anything else that they demanded.

"Now tell me, how many men are in that casino?"

"Right now only five including Luke."

"How loyal are those men to Luke, and will they fight to their death?"

"They're hired guns and will fight for whomever pays them. They're only interested in money and in saving their own skins."

"What's the layout of the casino; is it the same as Fred's old casino?"

"It's exactly the same, inside and out, and operates in the same way."

"What color is Luke's horse."

"It's a black and white pinto."

Vengeance

"O.K. Mr., I'd like you to knew that we're not in the business of killing bad boys for the sake of killing, we kill only when necessary or for self survival. So since you were cooperative with us, we'll let you go. You could take off and go your own way, or you might try returning to the casino to die with the rest."

"No Sir, I'm getting the hell out of here. I don't want any part of this gun fight."

"Smart decision," replied Simon.

His anxiety to leave was apparent and he mounted his horse and fled in the opposite direction of the casino. Now that they had disposed of the only obstacle between them and the casino, they sat down beside the greenery and planned their strategy of attack on Luke and his gunmen. Simon suggested that they observe the casino at night, under the veil of darkness where they could evaluate their surroundings without being detected, rather than during the daylight hours.

He explained, "There is no need for us to attack their stronghold if we could achieve the same results with a little patience. We'll conduct an old fashion military siege on the building. First we'll cut off their water supply by guarding the water tank or filling it full of holes. They'll be hesitant to leave the casino knowing that we're waiting for them outside. It's amazing what thirst, hunger and fear can do to a man; it can affect their thinking and judgement and when that happens they sometimes become desperate enough to act foolishly; that's when we'll make our move, when conditions dictate."

"That sounds good to me Simon, I'm sure glad I brought you along with me. Why don't we ride out to Luke's place and look around," said Billy. They nodded in agreement; as daylight gave way to darkness; then they waited till just before dawn, got up off the ground, mounted their horses and took off for Luke's casino. In the meantime, the gunmen in the casino were discussing their fate.

As Luke and his four remaining gunmen waited in vain for the return of their surveillance buddy, it became apparent that he would not return. Either he had taken off or had been killed. They now knew that the five of them had to face the awesome trio; and the prospect of having to defend Luke against such formidable shooters made the remaining four gunmen nervous and apprehensive. All through the night the hired gunmen thought of their chances of survival, they were keenly aware of the skill demonstrated in disposing of the eight hired gunmen sent out to ambush them at the rock formation. This knowledge was pressing on their minds, as they began to discuss their plight and ultimate fate. After all, what chance would they have being bottled up in this casino if eight men couldn't stop them in an ambush shoot out. Another gunman suggested that they flee, rather than face the famous Simon Ganz and his two buddies. Luke didn't like what he was hearing and tried to dissuade his gunmen from leaving, saying,

"Now boys they'll be an extra one thousand dollars for every man who stays and fights."

The reply from one of the gunman was terse and simple.

"You can't spend the money when your six feet under ground. I for one am getting the fuck out of here before it's too late."

"Yeah, me too,"or"So am I," replied the other three.

"Boys, you can't leave me here alone; you have to stay. I'll give you as much money as you want," shouted Luke.

"Fuck you Luke; I'm not risking my ass to save your skin."

Luke was pacing up and down the floor in a cold sweat, not knowing what to do next. He was in a quandary and certainly wasn't going to face the deadly trio alone. The only thing he could do was to leave with the rest of the gunmen.

"O.K. then I'll leave with you boys too," Luke replied.

"No you won't; they want you Luke, not us! If you try to ride along with us we'll kill you and save them the trouble."

Then the four gunmen filed out the door, mounted their horses and rode off. Luke did the same, following his former hired guns a good distance behind, heading for Beck's mansion. Just as the gunmen left the casino Simon and Co. arrived just in time to witness their departure, especially the man trailing behind riding the black and white pinto horse; it was Luke. They weren't interested in the fleeing gunmen, only Luke was the object of their concern. Billy took the lead in pursuing Luke, while Simon and Joe followed Billy riding at a leisurely pace. The fleeing gunmen quickly dispersed in different directions giving Billy a clear view of Luke a half mile away, but didn't press his horse Lightning for additional speed; he wanted Luke to contemplate his fate knowing that the sole survivor of the Reed family was in hot pursuit seeking revenge; by Luke's death. After about five miles into the chase, Luke came upon a bend in the trail with a scattering of shrubs and ponderosa pine trees on both sides of the road. He couldn't continue riding through open country and not expect Billy to overtake him, so he decided that the cover within the greenery offered the best chance for his survival. It was his only chance. He therefore quickly dismounted and concealed his horse behind a large evergreen shrub, drew his gun and took a position within the shrubbery to await Billy's arrival, hoping to get a clear shot at Billy. As he heard Billy's approach he took a small step back, readying himself for that first shot which had to be accurate. If he missed, the result could be quite different. Luke was unaware that lurking within the underbrush was a Diamondback rattlesnake coiled in a striking position. His thoughts were so concentrated on getting off a clear shot at Billy that he was oblivious to his surroundings and failed to hear the familiar ominous warning of the rattlesnake's tail. Billy surmised that since the trail ended at the green shrubbery, he must be hiding out somewhere within the greenery. He dismounted, drew his guns and proceeded cautiously. When Luke saw Billy dismount he took another step back in an attempt to conceal his presence, coming within striking distance of the rattlesnake. Snakes are not aggressive animals and never strike unless they feel threatened. As Luke edged further back, the Diamondback struck injecting its lethal venom into Luke's leg. Luke felt something hit his leg, he looking down and saw the rattlesnake. Shocked and frightened from what he saw, he uttered a cacophonous sound, lost his balance and fell down alongside the Diamondback. The rattler didn't want company and struck Luke again, this time sinking his deadly fangs deep into Luke's side. Billy heard the commotion in the shrubbery and now knew where Luke was hiding. He walked over waiting for Luke to expose himself but by the time Billy reached Luke he was prostrate on the ground squirming in agony as the Diamondback sought shelter deep within the underbrush. Luke's flesh was starting to turn blue at the puncture site as the neurotoxic chemicals circulated through Luke's body. By now, Simon and Joe had arrived; seeing Billy looking down into the shrubbery, they rode over to witness Luke's painful struggle with death. As the neurotoxins continued to work its' destructive power, Luke's breathing was becoming labored as his central nervous system slowly started to shut down, causing him to die a painfully slow death within a day or two. Billy turned to Simon and Joe and said,

"It looks like I didn't have to kill Luke; the Diamondback did the job for me. I gave up the practice of torture with the death of Fred, but mother nature had her own plan for Luke's demise."

Simon then commented,

Vengeance

"Well Billy, that's two down and one to go. It will take less than a day of agonizing pain before Luke's succumbs to his final hours on earth. In the meantime let's backtrack to Luke's casino, drink his booze and plan our assault on Ben Beck mansion and his boys. In the morning we'll burn the place down, and go after the big fish, Ben Beck." They did just that; in the morning they torched the casino and watched as the flames consume the gambling establishment down to the ground in a pool of simmering ashes. As they turned away from the burned out casino, Simon remarked, "The sooner we take care of Beck the sooner you can close that chapter of your life Billy and you can return to Rachel and normalcy."

They nodded in agreement; and rode off in the direction of Ben Beck's mansion to add finality to Billy's mission of vengeance.

CHAPTER TWENTY TWO
THE FINAL SOLUTION

As Simon, Joe and Billy rode off in the direction of the small town of Semper, Texas, twenty two miles north of Beck's stronghold to plan a strategy conference for an assault on his mansion, they were in a jovial mood. To break the monotony of a long ride they sang the latest ballads of the day. Their vocalization could not be considered entertaining to anyone but themselves, which was probably the reason they chose to express themselves vocally in the middle of the desert. Along with the "singing" was a heavy dose of bantering, frivolity and risible comments, provoking a great deal of laughter.

It was initiated by Joe, who jokingly asked Simon, "Hey Simon, do you think the widow Richardson will still be waiting for you when you return? Maybe some young buck came along in your absence and won her heart."

"That could be Joe, but I'll put my money on Janette and trust that my magnetic personality will sustain her devotion. I never thought that I could love another women after the death of Sun Flower; she nursed me back to health and brought life and vitality to my very being. Her death affected me profoundly. In a state of depression and despondency, I struggled on and slowly regained my mental stability. Part of my life was still missing until I met Janette who captivated my heart the minute I laid eyes on her."

They all smiled; then Simon asked,

"How about you Billy; do you think Rachel will be glad to see you when you return?"

"I sure hope so. I see her face before me every night before I close my eyes in slumber and again the first thing in the morning before I open my eyes. If she misses me half as much as I miss her, she must be pretty lonely and miserable. I've loved her since I was a young boy and nothing has changed."

Then Billy asked Joe,

"How about you Joe? Is there any gal waiting for your return? Don't you think it's time for you to get married and settle down?"

"No Sir Billy, not me. I love too many women to be devoted to one gal. I'm a confirmed bachelor. Besides, I don't think I could be faithful to just one woman and have her around all day long. When I'm not in the arms of a woman, I like my peace and quiet."

"That's because you never really loved any woman," said Billy.

"That may be Billy, but until I do I'll maintain my bachelor status."

Simon just smiled and couldn't resist commenting,

"Joe, Billy hit the nail on the head. Some day you'll meet the right girl and realize how wrong you were. I'll tell you one thing more, you'll never meet the right woman at Rose's place."

And so it went, solving no problems but certainly self entertaining as they rode along singing their songs and joking with one another, passing the time in good order. Finally, they arrived at their destination, Semper, Texas, in the early afternoon. The only hotel in town wasn't hard too find, so they walked through the door and checked in; then sat down to have a late lunch and a few cold beers. After satisfying their hunger and thirst, Simon announced,

"Gentlemen, this is what I have in mind, come morning I'll ride out to the Beck compound and survey the area to determine exactly what we're up against; we have to know the layout of the land and the kind of natural barriers that we can use for concealment. I'll evaluate his mansion as to how it is built and if there are any weaknesses in its construction. Also, how many gunmen we'll have to face. There should be twelve of them and three Mexican maintenance personnel if what we were told by Luke's gunmen was true. I'll leave in the morning while you and Joe sit tight here."

"No Simon, I'm going along with you just in case you run into trouble."

"I can't let you come along Billy; it's too dangerous; don't worry about me I can take care of myself."

"I'm sure you can Simon, but you insisted on riding along with me on my mission, now I insist on riding with you on your surveillance. Joe can stay and look after things."

"WHAT? Are You Guys Out Of Your Minds? Do you think I'm going to sit around here twiddling my thumbs while you guys have all the fun? Not in your life. I'm going too!"

"Well, I see it's hopeless arguing with you guys so we'll all leave together in the morning. Let's have another beer,"said Simon.

They talked, drank beer and continued their bantering for the balance of the evening. Simon's last comment before the clock struck 11 P.M. was,

"Gentlemen, we've come a long way together and have been quite successful so far, we've disposed of two of Ben Beck's henchmen and burned down his two casino, but bringing Ben Beck down will be no easy task. We'll have to proceed slowly and cautiously; I'm committed to returning you two guys to El Paso in one piece." Simon then yawned, and said,

"Let's go to bed."

And so they did, fully tanked.

That evening, while Simon, Joe and Billy were relaxing at the Dirty Spoon Hotel, in Semper, Texas, Ben Beck was planing his own reception committee for his nemeses. He called a meeting, gathering his men around the fireplace in his large living room for a pep talk. After serving a round of whiskey and distributing expensive cigars, he said,

"I know you've all heard by now of the devastation of my two casinos and the fate of Fred and Luke, but I can assure you that their campaign of terror will end here with their deaths."

One of the gunmen asked.

"How can you be sure? We're up against Simon Ganz and two of his gunmen."

"I'm well aware of Simon's famous reputation. He's only human, made of flesh and blood just like you; he can't walk on water nor perform miracles and he can be stopped and killed by a bullet just like you can. Just remember I have twelve of the most ruthless and fearless gunmen in the West under my roof and if you guys are too scared to tackle this trio, then you're not worth a bucket of warm piss."

He wounded their pride by his comments; then Beck continued to try to reestablish their confidence in themselves.

"Now boys, we're in a pretty solid fortress here surrounded by a seven foot tall fence with sharp metal spikes protruding from the top of each pole. I'm also placing two sentries as lookouts twenty four hours a day for any sign of their approach. I have enough food, liquor, and ammunition to last a very long time. They have to come to us and we'll be waiting. So tell me, who should be afraid of whom?"

They all seemed to be more reassured and relaxed, as Beck continued,

"When they do come, they'll face a rain of gunfire that would deter the devil himself. In the meantime, there's no reason for us to be bored for lack of entertainment. So for your pleasure I sent a hired hand into the adjacent towns to round up some women of the demimondaine class for tomorrow night's entertainment."

That seemed to please everyone, as they shouted their approval and sucked up the whiskey. There is no better distraction from fear than whiskey and women. The more they drank and talked amongst themselves, the more brave and fearless they become. Beck convinced them that once Simon and his boys were disposed of, he would reign supreme and they would be the beneficiaries of his power. The profusion of liquor and the prospect of female entertainment put them in a receptive mood to believe Beck's propaganda.

Simon, Joe and Billy rode along three abreast or sometimes in single file, depending on the physical contours of the terrain keeping a sharp eye on natural ground formation that could spell danger. As they got ever closer about three quarters of a mile from Beck's compound, Simon noticed a rapidly flowing river about ten feet below ground level with the ground gradually declining to the river bank. Simon suggested that the river bank would be a suitable place to tie up their horses while they proceeded the rest of the way on foot. Then he said,

"We'll approach Beck's place under the veil of darkness. I brought my old army shovel with me to dig a trench for concealment in the event that there is no natural cover for us. This will enable us to observe the surroundings during our reconnaissance of the area. So while we're waiting for the sky to darken, why don't we try spearing some fish for dinner? My Indian friends taught me how to fashion a spear from tree limbs and that should keep us entertained till we're ready to move out."

They spent a good part of the afternoon and evening fishing and hunting with their man made spears. Their endeavor to hunt with spears didn't prove very productive but they had a lot of fun trying; they refrained from using their weapons for fear of alerting their foe. When their activities were consummated, they drank the crystal clear water of the river then rested in the grass at their camp site to await darkness to envelope the river bank before setting out for Beck's mansion.

That evening, as they walked closer to the compound they could see Beck's mansion from a distance, standing slightly above the surrounding ground and well illuminated by numerous kerosene lamps. As they came within a hundred feet of the fence, they observed a few trees and scattered shrubbery as part of the landscape; but Simon deemed it prudent to dig a trench for additional concealment and protection. They commenced digging their trench, taking turns with the shovel while the other two stood guard. Within forty-five minutes, enough ground had been excavated to provide them with protection and a clear view of their surroundings. After resting for a few minutes they spread out and advanced in different directions toward the seven foot fence to peer through the slender openings between the poles. A composite observation gave them a panoramic view of the interior of the compound grounds. When satisfied that they had seen enough they returned to their trench to discuss their findings. The consensus of their observations were: a rock constructed water well stood about thirty feet to the right of the entrance to the mansion; and a large shed which stood fifteen feet to the right of the well; to the left, two wagons stood in tandem close to the fence. But most important were the two sentries standing guard, one on each side of the entrance to the mansion. They were comfortably seated in chairs which were on a large platform resembling a veranda and requiring four steps to ascend. As they retreated to their bunker, they sat there stymied as to their next move. Their dilemma was to find a way to get beyond the fence without being detected. Beck certainly had his mansion well protected and fortified, convinced of its impregnability. It seemed to be an unsolvable problem which needed a solution if they were to continue in their pursuit. Sitting there in silence, Simon occasionally scratching his head in frustration while Joe and Billy were deep in thought. They sat there for over an hour pondering their plight, when suddenly they heard a faint sound in the distance that got their attention. The sound seemed to be coming from wagon wheels making contact with the ground. As their heads popped up over the embankment of their trench, they heard voices, voices of women laughing, subdued screams and finally the wagon come into view containing eight women to be exact, fully clad in fanciful garments of brilliant colors. The wagon stopped at the entrance of the fence door as the women were helped down from the wagon by a Mexican servant who escorted them into the ornate building. The attitude and demeanor of the women suggested they were favorably impressed with the mansion and its surroundings and anticipating a pleasant and profitable evening.

A few minutes ago, the trio were despondent over the existing stalemate, but now a reversal of fortune was possible as Simon turned to Billy and Joe, saying,

"It appears to me that they're getting ready for a wild party with a plethora of booze and promiscuous women for entertainment to keep them happy and hopefully distracted. I would think this shindig will last well into the night and maybe provide us with the opening we're looking for."

As the hours passed, they sat there huddled in their trench, watching and listening as the bacchanal got louder and more vocal, especially the sounds of screaming women; it didn't have the intonation of an orderly affair. Along about midnight one of the woman exited the door smoking a cigarette, looking quite exhausted in a state of disarray. One of the guards asked,

"Where are you going?"

"I need some fresh air; I can't stand it in there any longer! Why are you guys sitting out here anyway? Why aren't you inside with the rest of the sex starved men," she asked.

"Yeah, we have to stand guard to make sure no strangers appear."

"Well, why don't you boys go inside and have a drink and some fun; I'll watch out for any party crashers."

"What do you say, Jake; you want to go inside and have some whiskey and a piece of ass?"

"Yeah, that sounds good to me as I'm getting pretty tired sitting out here while those guys are having all the fun."

And in they went. Although she was outside she still could hear the screaming women and the boisterous men. Her escape and solitude were not complete so she walked further away toward the fence, opened the latch and stood outside leaning against the fence smoking her cigarette. Her actions were keenly observed by Simon and the rest, as Simon said,

"Fellows this may be the opportunity we have been waiting for. Joe do you think you could sneak up behind her and bring her here without making a sound?"

Joe went right into action sneaking up behind her and putting his hand over her mouth, saying,

"Don't be frightened lady; you won't be harmed, just come along with me."

Joe dragged her into the trench and said,

"Lady, I'm going to remove my hand from your mouth and don't make a sound." Joe then released his grip.

"Hey, what's the big idea?"

Then Simon interjected,

"Listen lady, I don't have much time; in a few minutes all hell will break lose in that place and we don't want you to get hurt. We're going to clean out that den of rats and you should be thankful that you won't be caught in the crossfire. So just stay here, be quiet, and watch the fireworks."

"If that's what you fellows are up to I'm all for it. I spent my whole life dealing with men in intimate situations, but never have I witnessed a bunch of vulgar, abusive, riffraff as those bastards. I know that I'm not the type of woman who associates with decent men; but that doesn't mean that I have to be treated like dirt. They seemed to forget that I'm human and have feelings too. I wouldn't give two cents for the lot of them and if you should come across a crude cut red head with a pug nose, shoot him between the eyes for me."

Joe then spoke,

"Lady, if you need a decent place to stay with fairly good wages and respectful treatment there's a place in El Paso called Rose's place; tell her that Joe sent you and she'll take care of you."

"Well thanks Mr., you're a real gentleman; no one has called me lady in a long time."

Simon interrupted,

"O.K., boys let's go. We can't waste any more time. You wait here Miss where you'll be safe."

Then all three advanced toward the fence and entered, taking positions of concealment but close enough to communicate with each other. They remained concealed behind their respective positions; Billy crouched behind the well; Joe standing erect along side the shed; Simon moving back and forth behind the wagons. Before long the two guards came back out, smiling and a bit tipsy from their liquid refreshments. One said to the other,

"Where's that bitch who was supposed to be our lookout."

"She probably went back inside to join in the excitement," said the other.

After a while one of the ruffians came through the door, dragging one of the woman by the wrist and hustled her around the side of the building. saying,

"O.K. bitch, lay down here, we're going to do our fucking outdoors where we can't be disturbed."

Simon thought that this would be an opportune time to bag him and the two guards and signaled Joe to take care of that "sophisticated lover." If he or she made any noise to alert the guards, Simon and Billy would go into action and fill them full of lead. While lover boy was busy enjoying sex, Joe silently approached and plunged a knife deep into his back severing the aortic artery. The woman perplexed and in a state of shock, let out a scream, alerting the two guards who jumped to their feet and just as fast fell to the ground as Simon and Billy discharged their weapons. The revelers within heard the gunfire and came rushing to the door trying to determine what was going on without stepping outside into possible danger. They tried to remain concealed, but Simon and Billy didn't need much of a target and fired away at any human flesh that was visible. When the firing ceased, four more desperados lay dead. The hysterical women in a state of panic rushed outside oblivious to the possible danger; fortunately Simon recognized them immediately as the demimondaine and gave them free passage to safety. All eight women were now safely huddled together in Simon's bunker, watching the action unfold with wide open eyes.

The remaining gunmen were shocked and alarmed to see their numbers dwindle down to five in the span of a few minutes. Beck in particular was visibly shaken by the sudden turn of events, realizing for the first time that his compound was not impregnable and his fate very much in doubt. The only alternative Beck now had was for him and his men to shoot it out with his nemeses. Beck quenched the lights from all the kerosene lamps, save one at the far end of the room that shed light on the side of his mansion that would reveal the presence of anyone trying to sneak around the side of the building. He then stationed one or two gunmen at each window, instructing them to listen and watch for any sign of movement or noise that may give away their position. One of the gunman exited the back door of the room and quietly walked alongside the building when he spotted Joe fifteen feet away with his back facing him. With his gun drawn, he advanced toward Joe and stuck his gun in Joe's back, and said,

"Drop your gun cowboy, and don't try anything foolish."

As soon as Joe dropped his gun, he continued,

"Now turn around and walk ahead of me."

He then directed Joe into the rear door of the mansion and yelled,

"Hey Ben, look who I found sneaking around outside. What should we do with him?"

"Kill him," shouted one of the men.

"Not so fast boys, he might be useful to us; let me think about his fate for a while. By the way, what's your name?"

One of the gunman said,

"I think he's the one they call Joe Young."

"O.K. tie his hands behind his back and have him lie down on the floor, face down." said Beck.

Simon and Billy didn't know where Joe was. They were patiently waiting for any sign of movement within the compound that would precipitate gunfire on their part. Beck gathered his gunman to one side out of ear range of Joe, and said,

"I have a plan that may work; we'll stand this fellow Joe in front of the doorway using him as a shield, while I offer Simon a proposition. I'll tell them if they want to see Joe alive they'll have to give us free passage out of here without being pursued or followed. I'll tell Simon, we're going to take Joe as a hostage and when we're sure we're not being followed we'll release him. They may or may not accept my proposition since they might not believe me. If they do agree, we'll leave and kill Joe anyway at the appropriate time. On the other hand, Joe may not agree to my plan and offer resistance to it. In that case, we'll give Joe an opportunity to escape by pushing him further out on the platform and hope he makes a dash to safety. When he gets to within fifteen feet of Simon we'll shoot him but not mortally. If I'm not mistaken they'll try to rescue him; if they do, they'll expose themselves; then we'll all fire together killing all three of them. If they don't try to rescue him we'll have at least one less gun to contend with. This plan is not perfect but it's our only chance."

"I sure hope you're right," said one of the gunmen.

Then they hustled Joe to his feet and cut him loose then pushed him in front of the open door, as Beck shouted.

"Hey Simon, we got your boy Joe here! And I have a proposition for you to consider."

Beck explained his diabolical scheme to Simon and Billy, but before they could reply, Joe shouted.

"No deal Simon it's a trap."

Joe didn't know Beck's real plan, but he knew that any plan of his had to be fraught with deceit and trickery. Simon yelled back.

"Release Joe first and I promise to let you and your boys ride out of here as free as the wind."

Vengeance

Some people seem to find their own faults in others; since Beck's character was laden with lies and ill will, he assumed Simon was too. And yelled back.

"I don't trust you Simon; you'll have to agree to my plan or Joe dies."

Beck permitted Joe to stand three feet in front of him hoping that Joe would seize the chance to make a run for it, which he did. Joe jumped down from the steps, rolled over onto his feet, and ran toward Simon and Billy. As planned, Joe was shot only 12 feet from Simon. It didn't take Billy long to react taking the first step toward Joe when Simon grabbed him and said,

"No Billy, don't go; that's what they want us to do then they'll open fire and kill all three of us."

Billy was mentally unbalanced by seeing Joe bleeding and suffering to grasp the significance of the moment and struggled to break loose from Simon's grip. Joe yelled out to Billy,

"Stay where you are Billy, otherwise we'll all be killed !"

At that moment in time no amount of logic could restrain Billy's attempt to rescue Joe as he continued to try and break loose from Simon's grip. Finally Simon realized the only way to restrain Billy was to knock him out, which he did by landed a hard blow to Billy's jaw. Billy lay there unconscious for three minutes. When he came to, Simon said.

"I'm sorry I had to do that Billy, but if I didn't restrain you, you'd be lying there beside Joe. We'll just have to get those bastards, then we can help Joe, I only hope it won't be too late."

Billy now realized the wisdom of Simon's advice as both had fire in their stomachs for the blood of those human misfits. They let loose with a rain of gun fire at the slightest movement or no movement. During an exchange of gun fire, one of Simon's bullets hit the lone kerosene lamp setting off a small fire. The gunmen were too busy exchanging gun fire to notice the small blaze. In rapid order the flames spread along the floor and ate its way up the wall. By the time the gunmen noticed the fire it was too late and within minutes it was a raging inferno. The gunmen began to cough from the toxic smoke, as one of them said,`

"We can't stay here, or we'll all be cremated; we'll have to make a run for it and shoot our way out."

All five gunman rushed out the door with guns blazing only to be riddled with lead from Simon's and Billy's red hot guns. Beck still remained in his burning mansion too scared to leave and too frightened to stay. As he walked back and forth with a wet cloth over his mouth, a burning cinder landed on his pants leg making him part of the burning building as the flames licked at his skin. He became hysterical and ran outside screaming for help as he rolled on the ground trying to extinguish the flames. He got his first taste of hell; if not in the hereafter, here on earth. He slowly expired leaving behind an unrecognizable charred body. They didn't pay much attention to Beck's cremated body since their only concern was for Joe. Rushing to his side they found him still alive, but barely conscious. Some of the women watching from the trench rushed out to render whatever assistance they could. One of them ripped off her white linen under garment to be used as a stretcher in transporting Joe to one of the wagons. They had to get Joe to the nearest doctor located in El Paso. Two of the women stayed in the wagon with Billy trying to make Joe as comfortable as possible, while Simon drove the wagon. The other six women commandeered the other wagon and followed close behind. As they road away, the women in the wagon looked back to see the charred remains of Beck's body and his five gunmen scattered about illuminated by the conflagration of his mansion. Simon announced to the ladies that they were headed for El Paso and if anyone wanted out at any time before arriving in El Paso, she should make her intentions known and could depart. The women replied individually.

"No, El Paso is good enough for me." or

"I don't have any better place to go." or

"I'm heading for Rose's place."

And so it went, all deciding on El Paso as their final destination.

Joe was in extremis, and shortly after their departure from the burning mansion, Joe expired for the last time and died as Billy looked on. Realizing that Joe, his adopted brother was gone, he stood motionless as tears welled up in his eyes. As Billy sat there staring at Joe's dead body, his thoughts went back to when he first made Joe's acquaintance and how Joe became his hero growing up. Joe was his friend, brother and mentor who taught him everything he knew and now he was gone, a part of Billy was gone too. Billy hadn't shed a tear since the time he watched his home being burned to the ground with his parents and sister within. He hoped that this would be the final man made tragedy in his life, and he would never have to shed another tear under such circumstances again. Yes, there would be other tragedies in his life, but they would be acts of nature and unavoidable (not man made). Simon glanced down at Billy and realized immediately that Joe was dead.

Vengeance

Simon too had a few tears to shed, for he had grown fond of Joe and would miss him greatly. The women rode along in silence, sensing the tragedy revealed by the expression on their faces.

After a long and somber trip, they arrived in El Paso at day break and placed Joe's body in the care of the undertaker, instructing him to make arrangements for Joe's funeral and burial at a prominent location in the only cemetery in El Paso.

The women thanked Simon and Billy for their help and expressed their sorrow over Joe's demise, then went their separate ways, a few intent on establishing a home at Rose's place while Billy and Simon rode out to the Richardson homestead to announce their return. Rachel and her mother were sitting on the veranda reading or sewing as they generally do during the morning hours. Janette heard the sounds of riders; sound travels a great distance in the silent morning air; she looked up and stared for a few seconds, then saw two riders in the distance approaching. The figures looked familiar, could they be....., as their heart's pounded with excitement and anticipation, it didn't take Janette and Rachel long to recognize the riders in question; yes it's Billy and Simon. Rachel and Janette were now standing a good distance from the veranda with smiles and tears of joy in their eyes as Billy and Simon dismounted and melted in their arms. They hugged each other passionately, although both women sensed a little strangeness in their reunion when Rachel asked,

"Billy, is anything wrong?"

"Yes Rachel, Joe is no longer with us; he was killed yesterday."

The sorrow that accompanied their joy had a dampening effect on their intended celebration. They all went inside and quietly accepted life's verdict. The atmosphere would slowly return to normal in a week or two. In the meantime, Billy had to go see his parents to announce his return and consummate burial arrangements for Joe, along with other details. Rachel was very much aware of the bond of love that existed between Billy and his parents, and said,

"Go Billy, do your duty and return at your leisure; I'll be here waiting for you."

Billy hugged Rachel, kissed her tenderly and left. As Billy rode into town he reflected on how lucky he was to have a woman as intelligent, considerate and understanding as Rachel; she was indeed a gem amongst women.

Vengeance

Billy walked into the dry goods store just about closing time and saw John behind the counter. John looked up and saw Billy. His eyes weren't as strong as they once were, and he thought he was seeing an apparition and said,

"Bill, is that you?"

"It is indeed Dad, and I've come home to stay! Where's Mom?"

"She's upstairs, wait, I'll call her," he yelled out.

"Molly, come down stairs and see who's here!"

As soon as Molly hit the bottom step, she looked up and shouted,

"Billy, it's you, thank God you're back safe and sound."

With that, they kissed and hugged each other, their hearts filled with joy and happiness. Molly prepared an elaborate dinner for Billy that evening as they talked through the night about the past and the future.

The next morning Billy was off to visit Parson Bigelow to request his presence at Joe's interment and for him to give his eulogy at the grave site. Joe's burial was to be held at 10 A.M. the next morning.

The news of Joe's death spread like wildfire through town. The town's people could not believe that they no longer would see Joe's statuette figure riding through town atop of his magnificent horse, Thunder. He was such a familiar sight in town and he always could be relied upon to extend a helping hand to those in need. When the day of Joe's burial arrived, almost the entire population of the town of El Paso trekked out to the little dirt mound where Joe's body would be laid to rest. The Reverend Michel Bigelow stood beside Joe's casket, erect in his black suit with his wife and two daughters standing beside him, and with bowed heads, he began his eulogy:

"We are gathered here on this sad day to pay tribute and bid a fond farewell to the most loved and leading citizens of our fair town. Everyone knew Joe Young, everyone liked Joe Young, and everyone respected Joe Young, and now we commit his body to the ground. He was not a perfect man, none of us is, but he had at one time or another extended a helping hand to those in need; and through his protective aegis made this a better town to live in. He was a true friend to those who knew him and a feared enemy to those who would do us harm. He help the poor and succored the weak and never turned his back on anyone in need; for within his veins flowed the blood of a nobleman, that no Roman emperor would deny. Joe was not a church going man. I have never seen him sitting in one of the pews of my church, but that did not make him a bad person. That's all the more reason for him to be admired, for his church was in his heart and he preached his sermon with good deeds. He needed no holy book to guide his actions through life or to teach him right from wrong; and although he strayed at times from moral rectitude, his foibles and peccadillos harmed no one. If you have tears to shed, prepare to shed them now, for with a heavy heart and sadness in my soul, I commit his body to its final resting place; the way of all flesh. And let God alone be his judge. Amen."

At the conclusion of Rev. Bigelow's eulogy, their wasn't a dry eye in attendance. The inner circle of Joe's family shook the hand of Rev. Bigelow and thanked him for his wonderful tribute to Joe. Billy and his loved ones departed along with the town's people, some of whom were still sobbing as they slowly departed.

The sadness of Joe's demise eventually gave way to thoughts of more pleasant events. Now that Billy's mission of retribution had been accomplished, his thoughts now were only for Rachel and their life together. Marriage to Rachel would be the fulfillment of his life long dream. He didn't have to ask Rachel for her hand in marriage, it had been mutually understood since their early teens. However, it would be nice to ask Rachel for her hand in marriage anyway, which he did, and she accepted with overwhelming joy.

Simon too, had marriage on his mind, along with a quick departure to his ranch with Janette his wife at his side. Janette had already accepted Simon's proposal of marriage before his departure with Billy and Joe. Since both couples were committed to getting married, why not make it a double wedding; mother and daughter, both getting married on the same day, standing side by side. It was a brilliant idea, emanating from the imaginative mind of Rachel. The suggestion brought smiles to everyone's face. Billy in particular was eager to ride into town and inform his parents of his decision to marry Rachel; then a visit with Rev. Bigelow, to formalize the day, time, and place for the double wedding ceremony. Billy knew that any day would be acceptable to all.

With the excitement burning in Billy's heart, he rode at great speed into town and went directly to the dry goods store to inform his parents of his plans to marry Rachel. After hearing the news from Billy, it came as no great surprise to John and Molly who had long anticipated their union and were as glad to hear the news as Billy was to announce it. John advised Billy to go on a vacation with Rachel after their marriage before taking over the full responsibility and operation of the dry goods store, for now it was his store to run as he saw fit. The suggestion appealed to Billy as they sat around the dinner table in reminiscence of the past.

The next morning Billy was off to Rev. Bigelow's domicile to request that he officiate in a double marriage ceremony of Billy to Rachel and Simon to Janette. Rev. Bigelow was delighted to hear the news of their intended marriages and was happy to administer the sacrament of matrimony to the two couples. He was glad to perform this joyous ceremony, rather than the one of sorrow and sadness which he had recently performed. The ceremonial arrangements were scheduled for the day after tomorrow at 11 A.M., in Rev. Bigelow's church.

When their wedding day arrived, they had mixed emotions of nervousness and joy, standing before Rev. Bigelow waiting for the wedding ceremony to begin. It was a beautiful and magnificent sight to behold. Rachel never looked more beautiful than on her wedding day; dressed in a gorgeous white gown, which she had purchased months ago in preparation for this day. With a floral wreath adorning her head, she looked like an angel who just flew down from heaven. The absence of wings spoiled the illusion, but did not diminish her beauty. Janette too was elegantly attired in a pink gown with a red sash around her waist and holding a bouquet of flowers, giving the impression of a bride waiting to be crowned queen of a mythical god. The bridegrooms were more conventional in their attire. Simon standing beside Janette, clad in black with gold pipping down the front of his shirt, cuffs, and pocket, black pants and polished boots. Billy was similarly clad, but with a white shirt and black pipping, navy blue trousers, and black leather boots. John and Molly looked on with pride as the ceremony commenced. Molly looked on with a tear in her eye, as she thought back to when Billy first came to her as a twelve year old boy, so very long ago. And now here he stood, a grown man getting married. It was a lovely ceremony, after which they retired to John's store to celebrate the occasion, including the Reverend Bigelow and his wife. The celebration continued into the evening, until each couple peeled off and went their separate ways. The married couples, Simon and his new bride, along with Billy and his, retired to the Richardson homestead to rest and spend the night. It would be the last night that Janette would sleep in her home. In the morning, Simon and Janette would be off to Simon's ranch with Janette as the mistress of their household; while Simon concentrated his energy on expanding his fledgling cattle ranch.

Billy too was reorganizing his life. The first thing he did was to place his guns in a safe location, hidden in his bedroom closet; hopefully never again having to strap them around his waist in anger. He and Rachel would spend the next two weeks exploring the art of relaxation before Billy returned to the dry goods store and settled down to the serious business of managing and operating this well established store. They presently occupied the Richardson home, and every morning Billy would ride into town to supervise every aspect in running the store to insure an efficient and well managed operation.

Before Simon and Billy departed, they agreed that once a month they would get together to socialize and strengthen their bond of friendship; alternating between Simon and Janette's ranch and Billy and Rachel's home.

With Simon and Billy pursuing a normal and busy life style, happy and content with their vocation, I conclude the saga of Simon Ganz, Billy Reed, and Joe Young.

Epilogue

Ten years have gone by since I put down my pen, concluding the saga of Simon Ganz, Billy Reed and Joe Young. As I sat at my desk in my Dallas office I was often distracted from my work wondering how Billy and Simon had fared during the past decade and what their present status is. I could not rid my mind of these thoughts and with the passage of time my curiosity grew more intense. Finally, I decided to travel West in search of the answer to this nagging question. I spent over a month on my investigation till my curiosity was satisfied; then I informed my readers of my findings.

My first stop was El Paso and a visit to Billy's dry goods store. Walking through town I could not see any sign of the familiar store; instead there was a large department store with a sign on the window reading El Paso's Emporium and in the lower left hand corner was printed in gold letters Mr. Billy Reed, proprietor. Billy was indeed a very enterprising young man – sagacious and industrious – possessing all the trappings of business acumen. Billy's skillful management of the store during the subsequent years had transformed it into the first large scale department store in the Southwest. The Emporium was an extremely successful and popular department store attracting customers from neighboring town miles away and across the border into Mexico.

Billy was now a very wealthy man; he had built a large luxurious home in town for his family and employed a maid and two servants to attend to their needs. His family had grown too; he and Rachel had two children, a seven year old boy named Joe Young Reed and a five year old daughter named Molly. And although both had put on a few pounds, they were still the most attractive couple in town. John and Molly were living in a four room apartment attached to Billy's home, living in splendid retirement and enjoying the antics of their grandchildren.

While in town, I thought I would look in on Rose Engel's bordello, from the outside of course, to see if anything had changed. When I arrived I was flabbergasted to see an enormous entertainment place comprised of a restaurant, hotel, and theater. I walked inside to investigate further and discovered to my surprise a first class restaurant with linen tablecloths, crystal glassware and a complement of well groomed waiters and waitresses. But the biggest cynosure of all was the adjacent theater, featuring a large stage to accommodate dancing girls, traveling comedians and acrobats, all exhibiting their talent to an appreciative audience. No longer were there women of ill repute in attendance; instead these women were dancing on stage, employed as waitresses, or engaged in other capacities that a large enterprise like the Palace required.

Opera companies on tour from Las Angeles and San Francisco would fulfill contract agreements to perform at Rose's Palace several times a year. In addition to operas by Rossini and Verdi; Rose scheduled symphony orchestras to grace her palace with works by Beethoven, Mozart, and other composers during the summer months. There was something for everybody at the Palace; authors of new plays would test the worthiness of their work at the Palace, along with traditional standards by Shakespeare. What was once a sordid place for men and women was now a cultural center that El Paso could be proud of.

My final visitation before returning to my Dallas office was to delve into the operation of the Ganz ranch. It had grown enormously since its inception which made its location a secret that could no longer be kept; and I was curious to see for myself how big it really was. To find out, I headed for the town of Pecos, Texas, one hundred and seventy miles east of El Paso, the nearest town to the Ganz ranch. When I arrived in Pecos, I was greeted by its sheriff who informed me that Mr. Ganz requested that all visitors to his ranch register with him before intruding on the Ganz household. Registration was not mandatory, but if you needed the cooperation of the town's people and legitimate access to the Ganz compound, you'd best register. The registration was designed to prevent an avalanche of unwanted sightseers who would disrupt daily activities. After I complied with the registration requirement that included my name, occupation, and business, I was given directions to the Ganz ranch. Before my departure from Pecos, the sheriff sent word to Simon of my impending visit and therefore my arrival came as no surprise.

When I got within a mile of the ranch, I was stopped by an Indian, who I surmised to be Chief, Simon's trusted Indian companion and now acting as Simon's security guard.

"What's your name! And why you want to see Simon?" he asked.

"My name is Harry Dillon, I'm from the Dallas Republic newspaper and I have followed Simon Ganz's career for years, had written about it and would like to speak to the great man," I replied.

I was surprised to learn that Chief knew who I was. He had heard all about me from Simon and agreed to take me to see him. When I arrived at the ranch, I was greeted by Mrs. Ganz, who was very gracious, asking me to come inside and partake in some refreshments while waiting for Simon's arrival. When Simon did arrive he greeted me as if I were an old friend, although we had never met before.

We exchanged pleasantries, then Simon told me he had read all my articles in the Republic for years and how very pleased he was to make my acquaintance. He told me that I could stay as his guest as long as I chose and after I had rested from my long trip he would show me around his ranch.

I took advantage of Simon's hospitality and lounged around the premises for most of the day while Simon retired to his study to attend to the paperwork that's required for the operation of an enterprise of this magnitude, while Janette proudly showed me around the interior of the ranch. She drew my attention to one of four fireplaces that was supported with Florentine marble and the Persian rugs that adorned the floors of all the rooms. The credenza was embellished with Venetian glassware and at the entrance to each room was a three foot marble statue.

That evening we sat down to dine on prime rib of beef from Simon's cattle and sipped imported Burgundy wine from France. We had a lively discussion during dinner which carried over to Simon's library and lasted well into the evening while sipping French brandy and smoking Cuban cigars. I had a most enjoyable evening. Needless to say I slept like a log that night.

Come morning, Simon took me on a tour of his ranch. He escorted me to his stable of fine Arabian horses, ten in number, known for their speed and stamina. These horses certainly looked impressive lined up in tandem in their individual stalls. I thought to myself, "what a great experience it would be to ride one of those magnificent horses," when suddenly Simon saddled up two of his horses for us to mount and tour the grounds of his ranch. We rode out to the open grasslands to view his Texas Longhorn cattle. There were hundreds of Longhorns, each with a horn spread of over six feet, feeding on the lush green grasses. The cattle looked healthier than some people I know. Simon told me that he had bought up most of the land around these parts to accommodate his growing herd.

Simon also had an acre or two set a side for pigs and chickens raised for personal consumption. This was a big operation and to manage and maintain it required a great deal of help. To accomplish this, Simon employed twelve Mexican farm hands, in addition to the four Mexicans who helped him build the ranch plus four local cowboys to tend the cattle.

I stayed with the Ganz family for two and a half days and could not have had a more pleasant and enjoyable stay. But then it was time for me to leave before I wore out my welcome. So I bid a fond farewell to Simon and his lovely wife Janette, and departed for my home in Dallas to sit at my desk and do what I do best; write stories of legendary people.